THE SMALL BACK ROOM

NIGEL BALCHIN was born in Potterne, Wiltshire in 1908, and educated at Dauntsey's and at Peterhouse, Cambridge, where he was an exhibitioner and prizeman in Natural Science. After graduating from Cambridge he took up various occupations, becoming for a time a fruit farmer, and later an industrialist. During the Second World War he worked as a psychologist in the Personnel section of the War Office, before transferring to the Army Council and becoming Deputy Scientific Advisor. By the end of the war he had risen to the rank of brigadier-general. In 1934 he wrote *How to Run a Bassoon Factory* under the pseudonym Mark Spade. Thereafter he published his remaining novels under his own name, including *Lightbody On Liberty* (1936), *Darkness Falls from the Air* (1942), and *Mine Own Executioner* (1945). He died in 1970.

THE SMALL BACK ROOM

I saw another at work to calcine Ice into Gunpowder, who likewise showed me a treatise he had written concerning the Malleability of Fire, which he intended to publish.

SWIFT

THE SMALL BACK ROOM

NIGEL BALCHIN

CASSELL

Cassell Military Paperbacks

Cassell & Co
Wellington House, 125 Strand,
London WC2R 0BB

Printed and bound in Great Britain by
Cox & Wyman Ltd., Reading, Berks.

It has been suggested that I should
point out that the characters and
incidents in this book are purely
fictional. This I gladly do. They are.

N.M.B.

I

In 1928 my foot was hurting all the time, so they took it off and gave me an aluminium one that only hurt about three-quarters of the time. It would be all right for a bit, and then any one of about fifty things would start it off and it would give me hell.

It struck a bad patch in the car coming back from Graveley with Colonel Holland. I tried kicking my shin with the heel of my other foot, which sometimes helped. But that meant wriggling about, and old Holland glared, so I stopped.

We drove for about twenty minutes after leaving Graveley without saying a word. I knew the old boy was in one of his bad moods and as I didn't feel very sweet-tempered myself I didn't start anything. People coming away from Graveley are usually a bit snappy. I suppose the bangs do it. Finally I think old Holland reached a stage where he had to be rude to somebody or burst. Anyhow he let out a loud snort and said :

" Now I suppose your people will send in a report saying that's a marvellous weapon."

I said, " That depends on the figures."

Old Holland just said, " Figures ! " and snorted again.

I knew it was no good arguing with him in that mood. Every now and again he liked to do the plain-dumb-soldier act, and then the only thing was to let it go. He said :

" If you boys would stop playing with figures and start learning a bit about soldiering, we should save a lot of time. Or you might try using your eyes. That would do."

I said, " You don't like it ? "

" I think it's a bloody useless contraption."

" Why ? "

Old Holland shook his head. " Just army conservatism," he said wearily. " Just the army's usual trick of shooting things down."

He was always pretty bitter about these development jobs. Most of the army people were. They had a good deal of reason. Nobody took enough notice of what they said, and then if the thing went wrong they had to carry the can back.

" Well, go on," he said suddenly. " You tell me. You saw the thing and you've got eyes. What's wrong with it ? "

I wasn't having any. I had my own views about the Reeves, but I knew that Waring and the Old Man had been talking to people about the thing and wasn't sure what they'd said. I just shook my head and said something about seeing the figures first.

Old Holland gave an extra loud snort and said :

" God make me patient. Have you ever *seen* a tank ? "

" Yes."

" Well, they *move* don't they ? They crawl about. They zigzag. They don't like being shot at and they try to get out of the way. They don't just drive in a straight line posing for their photographs while you shoot at them with your bloody contraptions."

I said, " You don't think the Reeves is easy enough to lay ? "

" I think the type of chap we've got to use wouldn't get a moving tank in his sights in a week."

" Reeves chap was hitting them all right."

" Of course he was. What is he ? A trained engineer who's done nothing but muck about with that thing for months ; even now he has a hell of a job with it. You people seem to think that if you can train a research chap to do something in a laboratory by six months hard practice, we can train an ex-farm hand to do it in the field in ten minutes. Your feet aren't on the ground, you scientific chaps. That's your trouble."

I didn't say so but this was just what had struck me. The thing was pretty, but darned complicated. All the same I was sorry Holland had taken against it. If Waring and the Old Man were for it, it would mean another row, and I was sick of rows. As far as I could ever see, whenever we had a row with one of the services, we were always right. Dead right, except that they had to use the stuff and trust their lives to it whereas we hadn't.

" I never quite understand about your outfit," said old Holland suddenly. " What d'you call yourselves ? "

" I don't think we call ourselves anything," I said. " We're just Professor Mair's research group."

" Who d'you come under ? "

" Nobody. Professor Mair has a lot of contacts, of course. He's an old friend of the Minister's."

" Oh, I know *that*," said old Holland. " I've got reason to. But you haven't got any establishment or any terms of reference or anything old-fashioned like that ? "

" Not as far as I know. We just tackle any job we're given."

Old Holland shook his head. " Y'know this game's spreading," he said. " The country's crawling with this and that chap's tame research outfit. They don't belong to anybody. They don't report to anybody. They've got no responsibility and a lot of power. It isn't right, y'know. It isn't *right*. You've got some Service personnel ? "

" One or two."

He shook his head. " Don't see how it's done. They must be on *somebody's* establishment. And what's-his-name— what's he ? "

" Waring ? "

" Yes. Mair's second, eh ? "

I hesitated for a moment and the old devil was on it like a knife. " Or reckons he is anyhow ? "

I said, " Well, I suppose in practice he is. Rob Waring's a very capable bloke."

" I can well believe it," said the old boy. " Don't like him myself but I should think he's capable of anything."

I thought of doing my usual act about R.B. being very charming and a grand chap to work with and so forth. But my foot was hurting and somehow it hardly seemed worth while with old Holland. He would have known anyhow.

We stopped and put him down at the bottom of White-hall. He stood up on the pavement in his British Warm, and shook himself like a big dog. He was a huge old boy and he looked pretty good.

" Well, good-bye," he said with a grin. " Remember, feet on the ground and don't look at figures too much. Make you cross-eyed. Good-day to you." He stumped off and I started in to kick my shin good and hard. It helped a lot.

It was nearly six o'clock when I got in. Till was poking away at his calculating machine with his glasses up on his forehead. I didn't say " Hallo." Till hated people to say " Hallo " or " Cheerio " however long they'd been away. It made him uncomfortable. He liked just to start as if you'd been there all the time.

Till said, " There's an extraordinary thing here, Sammy."

" What ? " I said. I knew Till's extraordinary things.

" You know those penetration figures ? "

" Mm."

7

" Well, there's a positive correlation between penetration and the height of the man firing."

" Easy," I said. " The taller the man, the more rarefied the atmosphere and the less the air resistance."

" You think that might be it ? " said Till, putting his spectacles down and blinking.

" Might be ? " I said. " It's obvious. At least it would be if they hadn't all been lying down when they fired. As it was, I suppose the longer chaps were nearer the target. How the hell did you get their heights anyhow ? "

" I thought they might be interesting," said Till vaguely. " But if they were lying down, it's very puzzling isn't it ? "

" What is the correlation ? " I said. " About 0.01 ? "

" Oh no," said Till, hurt. " It's about 0.09."

" Well, that's lower than the correlation you got between Roman Catholicism and weight lifting ability, so I wouldn't worry too much about it."

Till shook his head. He wasn't satisfied. He never was satisfied.

" It's a very odd thing anyhow," he said. " How did you get on ? "

" Middling," I said.

" Think it's any good ? "

" God knows. Holland hates it."

" The soldiers always do," said Till, like a child repeating its piece. " They make emotional decisions without reference to the facts."

I went into Waring's room but instead of Waring there was Susan. All the furniture had been moved and she just had a typing desk.

" Hallo," I said. " What's happed to R.B. ? "

" Gone into the inner room," said Susan with a grin.

" What ho ! " I said. " Impossible to pass without stating your business to his secretary, eh ? "

" That's the sort of thing. He's bagged a carpet too."

" Is he in ? "

" No. He's just gone to see the Minister with the Old Man."

" Been a busy day altogether it seems," I said.

" You bet it has," said Sue, a bit viciously. " Not a moment has been wasted from R.B.'s point of view." She looked at me pretty hard and said, " For the love of Mike sit down, Sammy, you look tired."

8

I sat down and said, " I am. Darned tired."

" Foot all right ? "

" Fairish."

" Why not push off ? "

" Want to see R.B."

" Well, I've no idea what time he'll be back," said Susan. " In fact he may not come back at all." She looked at me for a bit and then said in a low voice, " Look darling—why not go home and take some of your stuff ? I shan't be long."

I said, " Cut out the darling stuff. You know the rules."

" Yes, sorry. But why not go home ? I don't think R.B. will come back."

I said, " I think I'll hang on for a bit. I want to tell him about the trials of the Reeves."

" Is it any good ? "

" I doubt it."

" That won't suit R.B. He thinks it's marvellous."

" Why ? "

" Well, the Old Man has told the Minister it is, so it must be."

I said, " You're very bitter about him to-day. Has he been filthy to you ? "

" Filthy ? " said Susan. " He's been sweet. Like having your week's sugar ration in one cup of tea. I think the Career must be going well." She looked at me with her lovely big grey eyes very cold. " Why don't *you* start having a Career, Sammy ? I could put you in the way of it in five minutes. It's quite easy."

I was just trying to think of the answer to that one when the door opened and Waring came in. I felt myself going pretty red. Not a soul in the place knew about Susan and me, but it always felt as though it must stick out a yard.

Waring was looking very big and handsome—rather like a film star playing a successful business man. I noticed that he'd started wearing a stiff white turn-down collar, and I thought, " He'll be carrying an umbrella next."

Waring said, " Hallo, Sammy—this is fine ! I hoped you might be back. Come in." He started towards the inner room, pulling off his overcoat as he went. He pulled it off his big shoulders like a boxer taking off his wrap.

" You're in new quarters," I said, as we went in.

" Yes," he said carelessly. " I got tired of the bloody telephone ringing, so I moved in here for peace and quiet."

9

He hung the big dark coat on a hanger and picked up his despatch case. " Excuse me for just a second, Sammy. I want to settle this stuff."

He dived back into the outer office. I glanced round the room. Waring had done himself very well. He had a whacking great partner's desk about six feet square, with a leather top. There were three telephones on it, with a filter extension to Susan. One was a green Secret phone. He had a big leather swivel desk-chair and an arm-chair for visitors. The whole thing made our rabbit-hutch upstairs look pretty poverty-stricken.

I heard Waring say to Susan, " Three copies of that. Marked ' Most Secret.' One to the Minister, one to Professor Mair and one for me. There's a note to go with the Minister's. I'll give you that later. As quickly as you can, please."

Susan said, " It'll take about two hours." I looked at my watch. That would mean that she wouldn't be home till nine.

" Yes. I'm sorry, but it's a very urgent matter," said Waring in his remotest voice.

" Will Professor Mair be here to sign the note ? " said Susan. " He usually goes about now."

" Never mind about that," said Waring sharply. " I'll sign it."

There was a sharp " zip " which was Susan taking something out of the typewriter with a jerk. Waring came back and shut the door.

" Now then," he said. " Why not sit down and be comfortable ? " He grinned his boyish grin and patted the arm-chair. " Look Sammy. Chair. Beautiful, padded, comfortable arm-chair. Especially for important visitors like you. Try it. Nothing happens. It doesn't give way and tip you into a cold bath or anything, honest it doesn't."

I sat down and said, " You've gone very grand."

" Well, to tell you the truth I was getting a bit fed up with Manchester carpentry tables and chairs," said Waring lighting a cigarette. " When you think of the stuff that we turn out here it seems a bit hard if we can't have civilised furniture. Look at that bloody place you and Tilly work in. Some of the finest and most valuable stuff in the country comes out of that den. And look at the conditions you work in. It makes me wild." He opened his green eyes very wide and looked positively indignant.

I said, " Well, it was darned nice of you to get yourself this stuff just for my sake."

It was no good of course. It never was any good hitting R.B. He just roared with laughter and said :

" Go on, you bitter old devil. All I mean is that now you can kick up a fuss and say you won't stay in that dump, while I roll about in luxury."

I said, " I never notice. Besides the sales side always has to have flash offices. It impresses clients."

" Well anyhow, you certainly ought to have a room of your own, without that darned machine of Till's clicking all the time."

I said, " I might speak to the Old Man about it." I knew I shouldn't, but it was the quickest way to shut him up.

" I should," said Waring. He settled back in his chair. " Now tell me about the Reeves gun. Good show ? "

" Moderately," I said. " The whole thing was quite well laid on. The gun was there and the ammunition was there. There was a range, and only a few people went to Gravesend or Grantchester by mistake. So as these parties go, it wasn't bad."

" What did you think of it ? " said Waring eagerly.

" I'm not sure yet. I haven't seen any of the figures. It's certainly an ingenious affair."

" It's a bloody marvellous weapon," said Waring.

" Maybe," I said a bit doubtfully. " Plenty of snags at present."

" Oh, it isn't *perfect*," said Waring, waving a hand. " It needs cleaning up. But that's easy."

" I'm afraid old Holland took against it," I said.

" He would ! " said Waring. " He always takes against anything." He smiled at the end of his cigarette. " Luckily it doesn't matter what Holland thinks. The thing has been sold above his level."

" Sold ? "

" Yes. I made the Old Man take me round to see the Minister, and I put it across to him. He's all steamed up about it."

I was a bit shaken.

I said, " What did you sell it to him on ? What the Stars Foretell for this week ? Or just intuition ? "

Waring shrugged. " The idea's right," he said shortly. " Anyhow, we shall soon have the facts. When are you getting the figures ? "

" Over the next week. We should be able to get out a report in about ten days."

" Fine."

I said, " It will be if the figures say what we want."

Waring laughed. " They'll bloody well have to after what I told his nibs."

" Holland thinks the laying's too difficult."

" Oh, to hell with Holland," said Waring irritably. " If he had his way we should just be coming on to the rifled musket about now."

" He's got brains," I said.

" Ganglia," said Waring. " I wouldn't put it higher than that."

" What's more, he knows his job."

" Oh God ! " said Waring. " How sick I am of these people who know their jobs ! "

He got up and slapped me on the shoulder. " You're losing your nerve, Sammy. You're letting medal ribbons impress you. It's a bad thing to do. Nobody gets medals for having brains. I'd back the stuff you and Till turn out against an Omdurman medal any day."

I didn't say anything. I was pretty tired of being bracketed with Till anyhow.

Going out I passed Susan. She was crashing away on the typewriter, and she looked at me as though she'd never seen me before. I got back to the office and was thinking of going home when Pinker rang up.

Pinker said, " How about a drink ? " I didn't want a drink, and didn't much want to talk to Pinker. But I knew Susan wouldn't be home for hours, so I went. Till was still punching away at his calculator. When I left he was sitting back in an exhausted sort of way while the machine divided something by something else. The machine still seemed as keen as mustard but Tilly was looking a bit used up.

Pinker was in the pub looking as dapper as ever. He always looked as though he'd just had a hair-cut. I was never quite sure whether Pinker was one of my closest friends or just a bloke I knew, until we started to talk. Then it was all fixed for you in the first two minutes. He insisted on buying me a drink and said it was a long time since we'd met, so I thought this must be one of the times when we were blood brothers.

12

Pinker said, " Well how's everything going with the back-room boys ? Have we won the war yet ? "

I said, " I don't know. Nobody ever tells me anything."

" Well, I think I've made a substantial contribution to-day," said Pinker. " My spies report that Godsall is definitely going."

" Godsall ? " I said. " Who's Godsall ? "

" Godsall's a menace," said Pinker.

" Maybe, but whose staff's he on ? "

" I think he's in the Secretariat," said Pinker, a bit vaguely. " Anyhow he's a menace. Whenever you come across a bit of dirty business or obstruction and start to poke about in it, Godsall comes popping out. He's the universal nigger in the woodpile. Anyhow, he's going now, thank God."

" Did you fire him ? " I said, knowing Pinker.

" Not alone I'm afraid. I fired at him all right, but the body was riddled with bullets. There was a Godsall Must Go Society. I was a founder member of that."

Pinker drank some beer and said :

" Y'know I think we need a new Permanent Secretary. Higgins is a dear good soul, but there's a war on. Maybe we could get him a nomination for an almshouse somewhere."

" You're having him kicked out ? " I said sarcastically.

" Give me time," said Pinker calmly. " He's on the list. In fact now Godsall's gone I'm not sure he isn't at the top of it. Anyhow, action is being taken. I'm having a drink with the Minister's Principal Private Secretary's cousin to-morrow. I shall drop a little poison into his ears in the normal way, just to get things started."

I took a drink of beer and said :

" I don't see how the hell you've got the patience for this stuff."

Pinker shrugged. " What else is there to do ? What else can *I* do ? If I work for six months, one of these bastards like Godsall can undo any good I've done in five minutes. So why not spend the six months getting rid of Godsall ? " He shook his head reflectively. " I've done damn' all in this war except to arrange to get fourteen incompetent nit-wits flung out of important jobs. Nothing much. Just a drink with a man here, and a D.O. note there, and a bit of a rumour now and again. That's all. But it works. It works surprisingly well."

" Gangster stuff," I said.

" That's it," said Pinker. " Gangster stuff. Bumpings off and takings for a ride."

He finished his beer and said, " D'you think Higgins goes in for women ? We might hire him a suitable P.A."

After the second drink we got on to our outfit.

Pinker said, " That boy Waring. He's moving in very high society now."

" Yes," I said.

" Y'know I hope Mair isn't getting ambitious," said Pinker. " That was a good outfit of yours when it started."

" What's wrong with it now ? "

" Oh nothing. D'you think Mair wants a knighthood ? "

" I shouldn't think so."

" Well then, who wants what ? Come on. It's pretty obvious that somebody wants something. Who's the ambitious boy ? Waring ? "

" I don't quite understand," I said, not liking it much.

Pinker made an impatient gesture, but he didn't say any more.

I ordered another beer.

" Look," I said. " Just what is your job ? I've never really known."

Pinker grinned. " I'm a harmless Assistant Secretary in Gower's outfit," he said. " But don't let it worry you. Dion O'Banion kept a flower shop in Chicago." He looked at me and said suddenly, " Why do you stick your job ? "

" I like it."

" Hm," said Pinker. " You and Waring get on ? "

" Oh yes. We were at school together."

" Doesn't follow," said Pinker rather irritably. He looked away. His eyes were opaque and brown. When he wasn't smiling they looked queer and angry. I had a feeling that I wasn't saying the right thing.

I said, " You're right about Rob Waring going up in the world. He's got a new office and an arm-chair." I thought he'd like that. Pinker's eyes came back and he smiled.

" *Arm-chair ?* " he said raising his eyebrows. " Nice work. Tell me about it. Hey—waiter ! "

I went on wishing more and more that I hadn't come. I was never sure whether talking to Pinker made me feel very grown up or very young, but it was one or the other and anyhow it wasn't comfortable.

" And how are all your cloak and dagger developments ? " said Pinker with a grin.

14

"Developing," I said.

"Is the Reeves gun any good?"

I was a bit startled. There was no particular reason why Pinker should know there was such a thing as the Reeves gun.

"I don't know anything about the Reeves gun," I said.

"Oh, that's been Waring's job has it? I thought you might have been in on it."

"Nobody knows anything about it yet," I said.

"That's what I thought," said Pinker smoothly. "But you boys seem to be selling it pretty hard all the same." He drank some beer. "You know Mair and Waring saw the Minister about it to-day?" he said casually.

"I suppose you were under the table?" I said.

"I was there in the spirit. That's why I asked you who wanted what."

Pinker knocked out his pipe. "Look," he said. "You like old Mair, don't you?"

"Yes. I'm very fond of him."

"Quite. So am I. Grand Old Man and so forth. Well then why don't you look after him?"

"How d'you mean?"

Pinker waved an impatient hand. "Christ, it's obvious enough. Why do you let that pup Waring use him as a stalking horse? Mair may be a scientist, but anybody can sell him anything if they go about it the right way. Then he tools off and sells it in high places." He stared at me hard with the hot brown eyes. "Have you ever thought where your outfit would be if there were a change of Minister?"

"Why?" I said trying to laugh it off. "Are you going to have the Minister chucked out?"

"He'll arrange it himself sooner or later," said Pinker. "Politicians are a pretty unreliable foundation to build on, you know. They come and they go. And when they go the people who depended on them tend to take a jolt."

"But what the hell's all this got to do with me?" I said, getting fed up. "I tell you I'm not interested in the politics of the job. I'm only interested in doing it. I do my work and give the stuff to Mair. What he does with it after that's his business. I'm a scientist, not a bloody politician."

Pinker finished up his beer and said, "Well, well. It's nothing to do with me. But I don't mind telling you that Mair's getting a reputation for talking some pretty loose stuff. You know where he gets it and so do I. If you can't do anything about it, there it is."

15

He stood up. "I must go. Don't let me hurry you. Bungho." He jammed on his hat and coat and hustled out. Pinker was always hustling.

I sat back in my chair and looked round the place. It was after eight and I knew I ought to go home, but I didn't want to turn out in the cold.

I thought, "I suppose Pinker's gone off to make friends and influence people again." I liked that and grinned to myself, but I wasn't really very happy about the whole thing—particularly the bit about Mair getting a reputation for talking loose stuff. I hardly ever went to his big talks with people, but Waring did, and I knew he'd sell lead in a shipwreck.

There was a lot of conversation going on at the table behind me. Somehow it sounded queer so I looked round, and saw it was just one chap talking to himself. He looked quite all right—sane and so forth, and as he talked he leaned forward and knocked the ash of his cigarette like people do when they're arguing. He was a big, dark man about fifty, rather well dressed, with a light grey trilby hat. I don't think he was English.

He said, "But why go to Amersham? It only means more trouble."

Then he said, "You don't see the difficulty. If we hadn't gone to Amersham, how were we to keep in touch with Fred?"

Somehow it seemed rude to sit there and listen—much ruder than it would have seemed if there had been two people talking, so I drank up my beer and came away. As I came out he sat back and laughed. I suppose the chap he wasn't talking to had made a joke.

I got home about half-past eight. I knew I ought to get on and get the supper so that it would be ready when Susan got back. But I was darned tired and somehow I couldn't muster the energy to go out to the kitchen, and start. While I was just sitting there Susan rang up and said:

"Look, I shall be home in about half an hour. I'm bringing some food so don't do anything. Have you taken your dope?"

I said, "No. Not yet."

"Well, take some and sit down quietly. I won't be long."

I went and got my dope and was going to take some, but the darned stuff never did any good so I put it back, and decided just to let the thing hurt and not do anything about it.

After a few minutes I knew it wouldn't do, and I was sick of kidding myself about the whole thing, so I went and got the whisky and took a sizable drink. The trouble was that the dope didn't do anything, or if it did it made me darned depressed. Whisky didn't stop the thing from hurting either, but at least it left me not caring whether it hurt or not.

Susan came in. She was carrying some parcels. She said: " Have you taken your stuff ? "

I was going to say " Yes," then I realised that she'd know anyhow.

I said, " I've taken some of Mr. Haig's well-known remedy." Susan looked as though she was going to say something, then she changed her mind and nodded.

I didn't like this. I said, " A policy of understanding tolerance will now be adopted."

Susan took off her coat and said, " Well, why shouldn't you have a drink ? Probably the best thing for you. You're always tired after Graveley."

" I seem to have heard that argument before," I said.

Susan went off to get the supper. When she had gone I wandered out to the kitchen. She had put an overall on and was frying some sausages. She looked very sweet. The back of her neck always got me.

I said, " Problem. If I don't have another drink I shall be filthy to you all the evening. If I do, I shall be slightly drunk but affectionate. You can have it which way you like."

Susan said, " Darling, *do* stop sounding like the Turvey treatment Before Taking."

" Well—that's what it comes to."

She turned round suddenly and stood very close to me, looking at me with those huge grey eyes. She said, " You know quite well you're never filthy to me."

I kissed her and said, " You're a nice child, but some-times you're not very helpful."

I went back and shoved the whisky away. I thought, " The thing to do is to talk hard until bed-time. As long as we talk about something that doesn't matter, it will be all right."

II

ON the Wednesday, Corporal Taylor came back. He had been off on a very hush-hush job on fuses for the Old Man. Mair was always mad on fuses. I believe they were the only warlike thing that ever really interested him.

I went down to the basement to say hallo to Taylor. He was in his little den, with a watchmaker's glass in his eye, peering and poking about at some minute bit of one of his trick gadgets. As usual, there were parts of about thirty other sorts of fuse scattered about the bench.

He took the glass out of his eye and jumped to attention as I came in. Taylor was always very polite.

I said, " What ho, Taylor. How did it go ? "

Old Taylor did a queer formal little bow like a butler and said, " Very well, sir, thank you."

" Does the detector detect ? "

" Yes, sir. The detector is extremely sensitive. But it slightly lacks d-discrimination."

" You mean it doesn't know which is a target and which isn't ? "

" Yes, sir. Presented with a target it acts p-perfectly. But it is liable to be m-misled by rooks, trees, c-clouds and suchlike. Had we been using charges it would have been very d-dangerous."

" Just goes off whenever it sees anything ? "

" Not *anything*, sir," said Taylor defensively. " But quite a number of things. Particularly rooks. It seems very sensitive to rooks."

I said, " Well, it's got the right idea. I don't see how you're ever going to train it to know a rook from a plane. But if it feels strongly about clouds, that's a big snag."

" I think it can be overcome, sir. I've suggested to the Professor that we should sh-shutter the detector so that the cell is only exposed by the r-rotation of the shell after the round has left the g-gun. That would dispose of the tree difficulty and of the r-rooks unless they were flying at a g-great height. The clouds we can overcome by simply r-reducing sensitivity."

Taylor shot up to attention again suddenly. I looked round and saw that the Old Man had come in. I think he had just arrived from home, and he looked terrible. He was wearing old flannel trousers, a blue lounge-suit jacket, and a shirt with a frayed collar. He had gone back to his old pipe that was mended with copper-wire, and it smelt like a drain.

I said, " Good-morning, sir."

" 'Morning, Sammy. 'Morning, Taylor. How's the rook rifle ? "

" I think I can arrange the shutter, sir," said Taylor, picking up the nose-cap he'd been messing about with.

" Hm," said Mair. " D'you realise what strength of spring you'll need to hold it in place when the shell's spinning ? " He grabbed a bit of paper. " Look," he said, turning to me. " This is rather pretty. Worked it out last night." He started to draw. Taylor put on his glasses and peered at the paper.

I was in a bit of a quandary. I wanted to tell the Old Man what we were doing about the Reeves, but I wasn't sure whether this was the moment or not. If he once got stuck into it with Taylor, you couldn't get near him.

I decided to chance it and said, " Just before you settle down, sir—the Reeves trial came off yesterday."

Mair looked up. " Yes ? " he said a bit vaguely.

" I wondered whether we could have a talk about it."

" Of course. Of course. Whenever you like." The Old Man's head had gone down again.

I said, " When would you suggest ? "

" Oh, any time," said Mair. " Any time. Soon as you like. Have you talked to Waring about it ? "

" Only for about five minutes," I said, knowing what was coming, and not seeing what to do about it.

" Ah," said Mair, picking up Taylor's glass and putting it in his eye. " Well, you should talk to Waring about it. He's very keen on it. Very keen. Talk to him about it, Sammy."

I said, " I will. But I should like to talk to you about it as well."

" By all means," said the Old Man, looking up at me with one eye looking enormous behind the glass. " Of course, just whenever you like." He bent over the bench and added vaguely, " Waring's most enthusiastic about the whole thing. He'll tell you about it." He pushed his lovely silver hair back impatiently and settled down with a little grunt. I gave it up and came away.

When I got upstairs Joe was telephoning to his wife. He couldn't have been in the office more than half an hour, but

19

he always rang Madeleine up at least once in the morning and twice in the afternoon. Till was sitting in front of his calculator looking annoyed. Joe made him stop clicking while he telephoned and it always made Tilly furious.

Joe was saying, " No darling, I'll get it. Of course I will. It's hardly out of my way at all." Apparently Madeleine then made quite a speech. Anyhow Joe just sat and looked adoring for a bit.

I said, " When you and Madeleine can bear to part, Joe, it's Wednesday, and we ought to do the Keystone Komics."

Joe said, " I'm afraid I'll have to go now, honey. Yes. . . . Yes . . . oh yes . . . no . . . No, I won't. No. . . ."

Till looked at Joe in a sulky way and prodded his machine. It started to make a loud chattering row. Joe was furious. He said, " Oh, for Christ's sake . . . No, darling. I was talking to somebody here. . . . I must go now. Good-bye . . . yes . . . good-bye. . . . I'll ring you later. Good-bye . . ."

At last he hung up and said, " What the hell do you want to make that God-awful row for when I'm telephoning?"

Till just stared at him coldly through his glasses and didn't say anything.

" Come on," I said. " Keystone Komics. Let's get going."

They came and sat at my table and Joe produced the Keystone Komics file. The Komics were bright ideas which had been sent in to Mair. Joe and Tilly and I used to run through the week's bag every Wednesday.

Some of them were sent in by departments who'd received them and wanted Mair's view or wanted to be rid of them. But the others were from all over the place. The thing which always puzzled us was how these people got to know the address.

Joe opened the file and took out the first one.

" Poisoned barbed wire," he said. " You scratch yourself on it and die in agony two hours later. Any bidders ? "

" What's the poison ? " I said, " Curare ? "

" Oh, he doesn't go into *that*," said Joe. " He says he isn't a scientist himself. He just has ideas."

" If I had ideas like that I'd see a doctor," I said. " Out."

Joe put the letter aside and picked up the next.

" Specification of the Barnes Retractable Bayonet. The bayonet is carried in a housing on the forepiece of the rifle. When the bayonet is required, a button is depressed and the bayonet is forced forward into the ' Ready ' position by a strong spring, and locks itself rigidly. After use it can be pressed back into the housed position where it is retained by a catch."

I said, " I like ' after use.' Nice phrase."

Till said, " It's not a bad idea though. Saves carrying the bayonet separately or having it sticking out all the time."

" An experimental model, fitted to a sporting rifle, works perfectly," Joe read. " The device costs very little. He's sent a drawing of it."

We looked at it. It was quite a workmanlike drawing.

" I think it's a darned good idea," said Till. He was always a perfect customer for the Komics.

" Hardly that," I said. " If it works and doesn't jam or break or mind being buried in mud or anything like that, it might have been a good idea before the war. That's about the size of it."

" Why ? "

" Well, damn it, we can't start re-equipping the whole army with joke bayonets. Anyhow, if the poor devil but knew it, what's really wanted is a bayonet that will open a bully beef tin without cutting you. Send him a nice note though, Joe."

" Sure," said Joe, " and a free entry form for next week's competition. A bàs the Barnes Bayonet." He pulled out a big blueprint. " The next's a radio thing which Williams has sent across. Leave that to the Old Man ? "

" Yes. He wants to see all the radio. What is it ? "

" Search me," said Joe. " I'm not a radio man myself. I saw something about the Heaviside Layer and decided it was out of my class. Now *this* is much more my sort of thing.

" ' Dear Sirs, I have always been interested in birds . . . ' " He stopped and laughed a lot. " Can you beat it ? "

" Funny joke," I said. " What's he invented ? "

" It occurs to me," read Joe, " that migrating birds are one of the few agencies which can enter enemy occupied territory without arousing suspicion."

" Oh God ! " I said. · " Which does he want them to take ? Little bombs round their necks or bacteria ? "

Joe looked on down the page. " You've got it," he said, looking up. " Or nearly. Plant diseases. Out, I take it ? "

" Yes. Y'know it's amazing what *dirty* ideas people get. That using animals one is a hardy annual, and it always gets

21

me. There was the chap who trained dogs and wanted to teach them to take explosive booby traps across to the enemy."

"Another radio," said Joe, " and a fuse thing from Reynolds. That's Old Man, I suppose ? "

" Yes. I'd like to see the fuse thing first."

" Two things on rations from doctors. Pass 'em on ? "

" Yes. Nothing to do with us."

" A bird named Schrenck who wants to sell a pig in a poke."

" What sort of pig ? "

" He doesn't say. He just says that he has invented a weapon which will revolutionise war, and he'd like to give us the first chance because England is such a marvellous country."

" That's an old gag. Write back and say we're in the market for new weapons that revolutionise war all right, but we don't usually write the cheque without being told a bit more. Anything else ? "

" Yes," said Joe. " A thing about power traverses for anti-tank and A.A. guns. Darned ingenious idea. It's too long to read. Have a look at it for yourself."

" Talked to any one about it ? "

" Yes. Graves. He says they've been trying to do it for years and that it won't work. But it seems worth having a look at. The bloke seems to know what he's talking about."

" What's he after ? "

" Harnessed recoil."

" That's an old friend."

" Yes. But not done like this. You read it. Tilly says his maths are all right."

" Adequate," said Till. " Not very pretty. But he's an engineer and engineers never do satisfying stuff with figures."

I said, " Well, thank God he's an engineer for a change. I'm fed up with cheese salesmen who throw off inventions in the kitchen in spare time. I think that one's worth going into pretty carefully, Joe. Don't just hand it over to Graves. He doesn't know anything about anything. Go and see Waterlow and see what's really happened about harnessed recoil. I've never seen why it shouldn't work. It does in small arms."

" Righto. And meanwhile just send the bloke an acknowledgment ? "

" That's the idea."

The figures of the Reeves trials didn't turn up for nearly a week. They weren't very impressive at first glance—at least not to anybody who was used to trials figures. I turned them over to Till to get into shape, and he put his glasses up on his forehead, sharpened three pencils, chased Joe off the telephone and got going.

I didn't want to touch them myself, because I was busy with the report for the progress meeting. Not that anybody would read it properly. No one ever did. But it kept things straight for me.

I was a bit shaken by the number of things we were messing about with. The Old Man would take on anything, whether we knew anything about it or had the staff to tackle it or not.

I said to Joe, " This colour filter thing. It's been on the books for about six months and nothing ever happens to it."

" There are four other outfits messing about with it anyhow," said Joe.

" Who ? "

" Passingham. The doctors. Rea. The Staines Lab. and I think the R.A.F. are doing something themselves."

" Where did we get it ? "

" God knows. The Old Man came back from a meeting full of it. The whole place was chucked on to it for about half a day, and then he got bored and it's never been touched since."

" Think we might write it off ? "

Joe said, " I should think we might write off about two-thirds of the stuff you've got there."

I said, " I think I'll go through and do a grand scrap."

Till said, " That's a most extraordinary thing."

" What is ? "

" According to this," said Till, peering at his figures. " The seventh round had a *negative* muzzle velocity."

" Oh come ! " said Joe.

" *Was* there anything funny about the seventh round ? " said Tilly to me.

" Not as funny as all that," I said. " Otherwise the damn' thing would have sucked it in like a vacuum cleaner."

" Well there it is," said Tilly defiantly. " There are the figures."

" Do 'em again."

" I've done 'em three times and it always comes negative. It's a most extraordinary thing, but there are the facts."

23

"Listen, Tilly," I said gently. "I was there, and the seventh round went out of the barrel—not backwards through the breech-block. So you try again."

"Well facts are facts," said Tilly sulkily.

"So they are, and figures are figures. Stop subtracting the date and get on with it."

Tilly started to poke at his calculator in a discouraged way and I went back to my stuff. About five minutes later he gave a sharp little yip which meant he'd found, and started to mutter something about "the principles of elementary arithmetic." Then he looked up and said, "You were quite right. Slip on my part."

"Good," I said sarcastically. "I was getting quite worried. If the thing started having negative muzzle velocities we shouldn't know which end of it to stand."

By the time I'd been through the progress report properly it had shrunk from thirty-six items to about fourteen. The rest were things we hadn't done anything about and didn't look like doing anything about. I thought I'd see if the Old Man would agree to write them off, but I knew it would be a tricky business to get him to make up his mind to it.

About eleven we all went along to his room. Waring was already there, and looked as though he'd been there some time. We arranged ourselves round the table and Mair sat back and lit his pipe. It was one of his less poisonous ones, and he was looking quite respectable. He looked at me with his very nice smile and said :

"Righto. Let's hear what we've been doing."

I said, "Well, sir . . ."

"Just before you begin," the Old Man interrupted. "I think I ought to tell you that the Minister was very complimentary about us when I saw him recently. He's coming down to have a look at us one day soon." He beamed round in his paternal way. "Go ahead, Rice."

I started off and began to wade through what we'd actually done in the month. Mair asked a question or put in a word here and there. I couldn't help thinking again that he was beginning to show his age. He was still darned good in some ways, but he'd got into the habit of bringing out whacking great platitudes in the way all these old boys do, and then sitting back as though he'd said something.

When he got on to the Reeves gun both he and Waring began to sit up and be interested, but I stalled them off.

We had only just got the stuff, and we couldn't really tell them anything.

"It's a very urgent matter," Waring said, as though we ought to have been quicker.

I said, "I'm afraid it will be a week before we can say anything definite."

"Couldn't you get out an interim report?" said Waring.

"Saying what?" I said. "We don't know anything about it yet."

"I think the Minister would like to have something to strengthen his hand," said Waring, turning to Mair. "Don't you, sir?"

I said, "We can only give him our opinion for what it's worth. I understand that he'd already had plenty of opinions."

Mair said, "You can't rush these things. Scientific inquiry is always a slow business. But Waring's quite right about the urgency. Do your best to hurry it on."

When we'd been through the live stuff I said, "That's all we've really done. About the other items on the list I wondered whether we could do some scrapping. It's no use having a huge list of stuff which we never do anything about."

Mair nodded, "Quite right. It's no use taking on too much. Do a little and do it well."

I said, "Well, taking those items in turn—can we wash out the colour filter stuff?"

"Oh," said Mair in a disappointed way. "You want to give *that* up?"

Joe said, "We've never really started on it, and there are a lot of other people doing it. Passingham . . ."

"Passingham?" said Mair, going a bit red. "Passingham's quite incapable of dealing with a job of this kind. I told the Minister so. Passingham's mad on this refraction nonsense of his. The man's a menace." He shook his head vigorously, "I don't think I could agree to hand over anything to Passingham."

"We haven't got anything much to hand over, have we?" I said. "There's no one here who knows much about optics."

"Well, then, we must get somebody," said Mair. "Graves. Or Lewis from where's it, or somebody like that. I don't think we can just *drop* it. The Minister himself asked me to advise him on the whole matter."

It was like that the whole way through. Mair fought like a tiger against giving anything up ; and if we suggested that it wasn't our job or that perhaps somebody else could do it better, it just made him furious. It was odd to hear the Old Man, who was a very gentle person, who usually had a good word for everybody, saying that darned nearly every well-known scientist in the country was a fool or a knave or both. In the end we got rid of about half a dozen little things which he agreed to drop very grudgingly. But that still left us with a mass of stuff we knew nothing about and had nobody to tackle. I was thoroughly fed up with the whole thing.

Waring had been sitting through all this looking pretty bored and not saying much. Towards the end he weighed in and said. " Well, I quite agree that we want to cut down, but are we tackling it in the right way ? " He threw out a hand. " All this detailed stuff we've been talking about— it's very nice and very interesting, but does it really matter ? Will it win the war ? "

" Not by itself," I said. " But it may help."

" Oh, I dare say," said Waring. " But what good does it do us ? I think we ought to go for the *big* things—the things that really count."

Mair nodded and lit his pipe. " Agree. First things first."

" What sort of things had you in mind ? " I said, knowing quite well.

" Well, take this stuff," said Waring tapping the report. " Now the Reeves gun is important. The Minister's really interested in that. He's interested in the colour filters too. If we put forward proposals there we shall get something done. But a lot of this . . ." He waved his hand again.

I looked at Mair, but he didn't say anything.

I said, " I should have said we ought to go for the jobs that want doing and that we can do, not just for what will amuse the Minister."

Waring laughed in his boyish way. " Oh get on with you, Sammy. You're too modest by half. You talk as though our opinion was worth having on about two things and that on the rest we were stooges."

" Well, that's what I do think," I said bluntly.

" Nonsense," said Waring cheerfully. " Don't you realise that on most of these things, even if we're not absolutely expert, we're miles ahead of any one else the Minister's got to advise him ? " He glanced at Mair and added, "It's a matter of having a scientific approach as opposed to a non-scientific one."

It was very pretty. Waring knew the Old Man by heart and he knew that one never failed.

"That's right," said the old boy, brightening up. "A scientist isn't a man who understands physics, or chemistry or biology. He's a man whose training has taught him to think in a scientific way. . ."

He went on giving Selling Talk Number One for about twenty minutes. I caught Waring's eye and he gave me a quick wink and looked like a mischievous kid.

When Mair had finished the long and short of it seemed to be that we were Scientists and Scientists were God's Own People, if they weren't God Himself. It made me feel pretty sick, particularly after the way he'd been cursing every other research man we mentioned. I said :

"I should feel quite happy about this if we stuck to facts. But I don't think our opinions are worth more than anybody else's if we haven't got any facts, and on a lot of these things we haven't because we've never done any work on them."

"Nor has any one else," said Waring.

"Oh rot," I said, getting fed up. "Passingham has been working on this colour filter business for fifteen years."

"Chasing a will-o-the-wisp," said Mair. "Complete charlatanism and showmanship. I exploded the Passingham bubble in an article in the *Journal of Physical Science* in 1938."

"It's agreed then that we shall have a shorter list with priorities ? " said Waring quickly.

"Yes," said Mair. "Yes. I quite agree."

"I'll draft one," said Waring, before I could speak, "and put it up to you." He nodded to me. "You and I will talk it over, Sammy."

"That's right," said Mair, with relief. "You get out the list and we'll go ahead with that."

I saw Joe and Tilly looking at me. I felt myself going red. I said, "I think I'd like to draft one too."

"Yes," said Mair vaguely. "We'll get together and agree on it." He nodded at Waring. "You're quite right in what you say. We mustn't be too academic. Strike while the iron is hot and people are interested. We must be sure of our *ground* of course, but, after all, we're general advisers to the Minister. That was my agreement with him."

When we got back to our room Joe and Till both took deep breaths.

Joe said, " Look here . . . ," and Tilly said, " I say . . . "

" All right," I said wearily. " I know."

" If R.B. drafts that list," said Joe, " you can bet your boots it'll be pure boloney. We might as well set up as an advertising agency right away and be done with it."

" I know."

" It's like his bloody cheek anyhow. We do all the work and then R.B. sails in and does a God Almighty on us."

" I'm not surprised at Waring," said Till, wiping his spectacles. " He knows nothing about statistics. But I'm disappointed in Mair. Very disappointed. He should know better. Sometimes lately he seems positively—positively *commercial*."

" It's a bloody scandal," said Joe in his loud bray.

I said, " Pipe down, Joe, for Christ's sake. You're voice gives me a headache."

" I should go and ask him what the hell he means by it," said Joe.

I said, " I know precisely what he means by it, so don't worry."

I had to go through the hall to get to Waring's room. As I passed through, Corporal Taylor was standing by the door talking to a girl. She was very dark—black hair, black eyes, and a brown skin, almost like a gipsy. Taylor and I said, " Good morning," as I passed, and she turned her shiny black eyes on me and gave me a very on-coming smile. I thought she was an odd-looking specimen to be a friend of old Taylor. Susan was in the ante-room to Waring's office and I said : " Who's Taylor's girl friend ? "

" Girl friend ? "

" Yes. Very dark, gipsy-looking female he's talking to in the hall."

" Oh," said Susan. " *That* one. That's his wife."

" His *wife* ? "

" Yes."

I said, " I didn't know he had a wife."

" They were married about six months ago."

" Rum looking girl for old Taylor to marry," I said.

" Yes," said Susan. " I should have expected Taylor to marry something mousy with glasses."

" She must be twenty years younger than he is. Where did he get her ? "

" Lord knows. I think she's Moroccan or Gibraltese or something. Anyhow, she isn't English."

28

Waring came out of his office carrying some papers.

He said, " Hallo, Sammy. Want me ? "

I said, " No. But I've got to have you."

" Sure. Just half a mo'."

He plonked the papers down on the table and said to Susan, " Look here—this is absolutely first-rate. I've been through it and I'm not going to touch a word. If I did I should only spoil it. Type it out properly, and we'll get the Old Man to sign it and bung it straight off."

He turned to me and said, " Y'know, Sammy, this Susan of ours is a most remarkable young woman. I give her four lines of completely illegible notes on a most complicated subject and ask her to turn out a rough draft, and she turns in this." He picked up the paper. " The whole thing absolutely taped and as clear as crystal. You read it sometime. It's worth it. Lovely job." He grinned at Susan. She went very red and pursed her lips, but I could see she was as bucked as hell.

" *Now* what are you looking sulky about ? " said Waring.

" I'm waiting for the catch in it," said Susan coldly.

Waring roared with laughter. " You cynical old dame ! " he said.

" Well, come on," said Susan smiling a bit despite herself. " What is it ? Want me to stay here till ten to-night or want me to buy you some socks in lunch-time ? "

" Neither," said Waring. " There's no catch in it. I was just genuinely admiring your lovely piece, and what's more I shall buy you some chrysanthemums to put on your desk after lunch. There."

" Bronze ones ? " said Susan hopefully.

" Yes," said Waring. " *Bronze* ones. Present for a good girl." He patted her on the shoulder. " Come on in, Sammy."

We went in to his office and sat down. Waring chucked a pile of paper into his tray and said, " That was a bloody waste of time this morning wasn't it ? "

I said, " I thought it was rather important in some ways."

" Yes," said Waring. " But did five of us sitting round for an hour do any more than you and I could have done in ten minutes ? " He lit a cigarette thoughtfully and shook his head. " Y'know, Sammy, I don't see a lot of point in having Till and Joe Marchant waste their time talking about these things. They're good chaps in their own line—particularly Till. But policy isn't their job. They're pure research

29

workers, and they ought to stick to research and leave the rest to us. Don't you agree ? "

" Us being who ? " I said.

" The Old Man and you and me." Waring did his film-star smile—the one with the teeth and the dimple—" Chiefly you and me."

I said, " What I really came down to talk about was this programme . . ."

" Programme ? "

" Yes. The short list of jobs we were going to do for the Old Man. When shall we tackle it ? "

" Oh that ? " said Waring. " Whenever you feel like it. I should say the sooner you could get it out the better."

" The idea is that *I* should do it ? "

" Well, of course," said Waring, looking at me in a puzzled way with his slanting green eyes. " You're the only person who knows the stuff."

" Oh quite. But I didn't know you thought that mattered. In fact at one point *you* offered to do it."

" Did I ! Good God. Well, of course I'll help if you want me. But it's really your show, Sammy." He grinned. " I'm only the bloody vacuum cleaner salesman after all. I pretend I know a lot about it when I'm talking to other people but I don't try to tell you that. You might laugh."

I couldn't help smiling. He said it so bluntly and cheer-fully. That was the trouble with him. If you wanted to be rude to him he always said it first.

" All right," I said. " I'll do it."

" Fine," said Waring. " You say what there's going to be in the shop and give me my sales talk and I'll go and sell it." He got up. " Meanwhile you do agree about these meetings ? That they waste time ? "

" I suppose they do," I said.

" Good. Then I'll tell the Old Man we think so and that we'd better wash them out. I'll tell him that we'd both rather just see him together and leave the rest out."

" Shall I tell them ? "

" Shouldn't bother. We don't want to hurt their feelings. We'll just let the meetings lapse."

As I went upstairs I wondered whether the point was that Waring was clever or that I was dumb. It was always the same story. He'd say something in his careless way that made you darned angry. Then as soon as you tackled him he'd open his eyes very wide and explain that he'd meant something else quite innocent. The trouble was that other people only heard the first bit. They didn't hear the explanation.

III

THE OLD MAN had been wearing a cleanish collar, so I guessed he must be seeing somebody important. Half-way through the afternoon his secretary came tearing up to say that the Old Man had telephoned, and that he was on his way back with the Minister. The Minister was going to look round the place, and would I see that everything was put out for him to see ?

As they'd be back in about twenty minutes it didn't leave me a lot of time to put on a show. I cursed to myself as I went downstairs and thought that was just like the Old Man. He'd got no idea.

There wasn't really much I could do. Most of the stuff was out on the stations anyhow. Old Taylor was in his den with one of his chaps, messing about with his fuses. I told him to fix up one of his detector cells and an electric bell so that the Minister could see the idea behind the thing. In the main lab. they had the blast wave record stuff already fitted up and working, and Corporal Ellis had a lot of his micro photographs up on a board. I didn't think the Minister would get much kick out of the low temperature lubrication thing. He'd probably got a refrigerator of his own at home. But the model room had all its stuff on show and I thought that would probably get him—it always did get people— unless they started asking awkward questions about what use the things were.

I met Waring in the hall and he was furious about the whole thing. He said, " I've sent somebody out for some whisky. There isn't even a drink in the bloody place, and the Minister likes a whisky and soda. Old Mair couldn't sell life insurance to a ghost."

I told him what I'd done and we agreed that we should have to let it go at that.

When I got back to the office Joe and Tilly were pinning graphs up all over the place. Joe said, " It's a damned shame we haven't got a few paper chains and a bit of mistle-toe for the old boy."

After we'd done what we could we sat down and waited,

but they took a lot longer than we thought, so we all got bored and went on working. I had forgotten all about them when they finally turned up. Mair came in first followed by the Minister, with Waring doing an A.D.C. act in the rear. The Minister was a tall, lanky man with grey hair and rather a good face. I knew he was quite old, but his face was surprisingly fresh looking, and but for his hair he might have been about forty. We all stood up.

The Minister looked round with a very nice, rather practised-looking smile and said, " These are the backroom boys, eh ? "

" Yes," the Old Man said, beaming round at us paternally. " This is where all the work's done."

We simpered.

The Minister looked round the room. " Not very luxurious quarters are they ? "

" No," said Mair. " I'm afraid not. They were the best we could get."

" Ah well," said the Minister, " I always find the best work's done in the barest rooms." He smiled at me and I smiled back. His eye fell on Tilly's calculator and he said, " What's that thing, Mair ? Another of your inventions ? "

" No," said the Old Man. " That's an electric calculating machine, Minister. Very useful too, isn't it, Till ? "

" How does it work ? "

Tilly sidled forward and started to explain his machine. The Minister seemed to like it. He poked at the keys and added something up. Then Tilly showed him how it divided, and that thrilled him to the marrow. He must have spent about ten minutes messing about with the thing. " Marvellous, isn't it ? " he said to the Old Man. He turned to the rest of us and said, " I wish you'd turn me out something that would write speeches. Good ones. That's a long felt want if you like."

We all laughed.

Waring said mischievously, " Or answer questions in the House, Minister."

" That's right. That would be even better," said the big man, pleased.

He looked round and said, " Well, there's certainly a lot of most interesting work going on here, Mair. Most interesting." Just to show how fascinated he was he started for the door. As they got to it he turned his head and said, " Thank you very much, gentlemen," and out they went.

32

We looked at one another for a moment.

Then Joe said, " Science is a marvellous thing, isn't it ?

Tilly said, " What d'you think of that ? A Minister of the Crown, and he's never seen a calculating machine before ! " He said it as though he couldn't really believe it.

I didn't say anything, but I was very sick. I thought the Old Man might at least have introduced us to him.

Susan and I always went out on Wednesday night. This wasn't a very good night out. We were a bit late and the Bonaventure was packed out. Alfred was very apologetic but he said there wouldn't be a table for half an hour.

I was damned annoyed. I said, " I should have thought you could have kept our table. You know we're here every Wednesday."

Alfred said, " I'm sorry, sir, but you see it wasn't booked, and I can't keep tables if they're not booked."

I looked round the room and said, " What you mean is that you can charge these innocent Yanks thirty shillings a bottle for your half-crown Vin Ordinaire, and you can't do that with me."

As we came out I said to Susan, " One of the main reasons why I want this war to be over is that I want to be able to get back at some of these bloody tradesmen. Hell, you can't even bully a Soho restaurant proprietor nowadays. Alfred was the one man in London who used to let me feel important for ten bob an hour."

Susan said, " It doesn't matter. Let's go to the Hickory."

We got a table at the Hickory, but the food was pretty foul. I said, " Why the Pete do we come out, Sue ? It's uncomfortable and crowded and the food's bad and it costs a lot, and yet we keep on doing it."

" Let's have an economy campaign and stay in next week," said Susan.

I said, " All right. We will." We said that every week.

There were some chrysanthemums on the table and they reminded me.

I said, " Did R.B. produce your chrysanthemums ? "

" Oh, yes."

" What did you do with them ? "

" Put them on my desk. What else should I do with them ? "

I said, " You couldn't find it in your heart to slap his face sometime when he does that stuff, could you ? "

33

" Nothing easier," said Susan. " But can we afford it ? "

" You could get another job."

Susan said, " I suppose so. Would you rather I did ? "

I thought for a bit and said, " I'm not sure. What I'd really like would be for you to stay in the place and not have to put up with him."

Susan said, " You know what I think about that. I'll leave it if you like. But if I'm going on doing the job I must *do* it. And putting up with R.B. is part of it. After all, he's not bad really. He doesn't paw or anything."

I said, " Well, Christ, I should hope not."

" So should I. But you see, darling, he doesn't know about us. God knows I think he's bogus, and worse than that. But he isn't bad to work for as people go."

After a bit I said, " You know it would be a lot easier in some ways if we were married."

Susan didn't say anything. She just looked at me in a questioning way.

I shook my head and said, " But not in others."

Susan said, " You know I've never really understood about that, Sammy."

" I should have thought it was obvious enough."

" Yes, I know what you always say. But surely it's for me to decide ? It's damned silly if we should both like it, not to do it because you think I shouldn't like it."

I said, " Listen—I'll take things from you with both hands. I always have and I propose to go on doing it. But one of these days you're going to get tired of it. And when you do, I want you to be able to put the whole thing in the wastepaper basket and forget it in just ten seconds."

Susan said, " The trouble with you is that you're a defeatist. I believe you'd carry an umbrella in the Sahara."

" There's nothing defeatist in this," I said. " I know about you and me. When I get a bad patch I want somebody to flutter around and tell me that I have a bloody time and that it's too bad. And you like doing that, so there we are."

" Well, what's wrong with that ? "

" (*a*) That I don't really have a bloody time, or if I do it's my own fault, and we both know it. (*b*) That fluttering around isn't really your sort of job ; and we both know that too."

Susan didn't say anything. She just looked across the room rather moodily.

34

I said, " There aren't really any women. There are only people's mothers, and people's daughters. And you're not really anybody's mummy. The whole thing's an example of unstable equilibrium. I shall now have a drink." Susan's eyes came back to me with that queer worried look at the corners. I grinned and said, " I shall drink half a pint of bitter beer." This was an old game. She knew I never drank whisky except at home, but she was always wondering if I should start. I don't know why I thought it was funny to pull her leg about it.

We were just thinking about going when Susan suddenly said, " Oh, my God ! Hand me a false beard."

" Why ? "

" Gillian."

" Who's Gillian ? "

" That female who's just come in with the tall man. I used to know her. She's terrible. Engage me in earnest conversation quickly or she'll come."

We both lowered our heads and I said earnestly, " To be called upon to engage a person in earnest conversation at a moment's notice is very difficult."

" Oh quite," said Susan with a lot of gesture and a toothy smile. " Rather like being told to be funny."

" It's so difficult to choose a subject. Admittedly there is all art, all nature, all life. But . . ."

The female Gillian rushed up and said, " *Hallo*, Sue ! Fancy seeing you. How are you, darling ? "

There was nothing we could do about it and we were sitting at a table for four, so we gave up and they came and sat with us. This girl Gillian was quite pretty in a fluffy way. Her young man, one Maurice Iles, was a tall, fair, rather languid bloke with a moustache and a patronising manner. I think he was as fed-up at being brought to sit with us as we were at having him. As soon as we'd been introduced, the girl Gillian started to gabble away to Susan, and just left us to get on as best we could.

For a bit we just sat there in silence. Then Iles looked round the place and said, " I notice that a large number of our gallant fighting men have managed to snatch a few moments from the scenes of carnage. As usual."

I worked that one out and said, " Well, presumably even soldiers have to eat."

Iles nodded slowly, with his eyelids drooping slightly. " Yes," he said. " I suppose so. It's difficult to see why, but I suppose it's unavoidable. But I wish they'd do it in their messes. I see quite enough uniforms during working hours, without having them all round me during my rare periods of leisure." He paused for me to ask what he did. I kept quiet, but it was no good. I'd got to have it. He said, " I spend my time trying to provide the forces with this and that."

I said, " Oh, do you ? " Lord knows I might have guessed it.

He nodded slowly, " And you ? " he said inquiringly. " To which part of the national wheel is your shoulder applied ? "

I said, " Oh. I do a rather odd job. We do quite a lot of work for your people."

" For *our* people ? In what way ? " said Iles, looking at me as though he found it hard to believe that we could be connected in any way, however distant.

" I'm in Mair's Research Unit."

" Oh, you're in this peculiar outfit of Mair's ? I come across traces of your activities occasionally."

" What branch are you in ? " I said.

" We're Central Co-ordination."

" Oh yes, Pilkington's department ? "

" We *have* Pilkington," he said languidly. " But of course he's more or less obsolescent now."

" Are you the deputy director ? " I said, knowing he wasn't.

He hesitated and then said, " It's a little difficult to say at present. We're in our usual state of flux. Last week I worked for forty-eight hours without a break from Monday morning till breakfast on Wednesday. But that's quite normal of course." He turned to me. " It must be pleasant to do something nice and leisurely, like research."

" What were you doing for forty-eight hours ? " I said. " Writing a minute ? "

Iles shrugged his shoulders. " New requirements. They were wanted for the Cabinet on Wednesday. We didn't get the figures until Monday, so there was nothing else for it but to work right through. When the figures did come in they were complete nonsense of course." He smoothed back his hair. " Luckily we don't worry ourselves much about what these people ask for nowadays. It's a farce really to wait for them."

" Which people ? " I said.

36

"The Services," said Iles. "The Navy's demands occasionally have some relation to the facts. The R.A.F.'s and the Army's never." He closed his eyes wearily and said, "It's a thousand pities that the Services are allowed to interfere in matters they don't understand. If they would concentrate on their fighting and leave the thinking to us, we should get on a good deal quicker."

"Maurice hates the Service people," said the girl Gillian brightly.

"Still, you can hardly blame them for being *interested*," I said sarcastically. "After all, they have to use the stuff."

"Oh quite!" said Iles. "They have to press triggers and drop bombs and so on. Why can't they concentrate on that? They don't seem to be so frightfully good at it." He glanced languidly at me. "Don't you find the same in your own work? This constant interference from incompetents with uniforms and no brains, in matters which are *quite* beyond them . . . ?"

I could think of several pleasant things to do, but not of anything to say, so I kept quiet.

"Of course it's our own fault," said Iles reasonably. "We make our armed forces a profession for fools in peace-time, and then we put ourselves in their hands in war."

I said, "What strikes me as being wrong is that too many of the *really* good people stand outside the services and criticise them instead of going into them and putting them right." I said it pretty viciously, but the chap Iles took it in his stride.

"Quite. That's just the point. The good people won't join the services because there's no guarantee that they will be used. Take myself. Why should I?"

He threw out a hand. "I should be quite prepared to join one of the services if I could be given a decent job. But you can hardly expect me to join an outfit that can find no better use for me than carrying a rifle."

"Maurice has often thought of volunteering," said the girl Gillian. "But I tell him that it would be such a *waste*."

"What of?" I said.

"Of his ability, darling," said Susan solemnly. "It's everybody's duty to avoid waste in the national interest. Like having leaky water taps mended."

"That's right," said the girl Gillian a bit doubtfully.

"Or saving pieces of string," I said.

Iles didn't say anything. He had a curious knack of missing remarks of that kind. Whether it was that he didn't hear them, didn't understand them or just ignored them I was never sure.

Iles flapped ineffectually at a passing waiter. "Of course," he said magnanimously, "you mustn't take too much notice of me on the subject of the Services. I know I'm prejudiced. But we really have had a lot of trouble with them—a lot of trouble. In fact we've had to tell them in so many words that this is a serious war and that we shan't stand for any of their nonsense."

"Just how did you do that?" I said.

"Oh, we simply made it a rule only to deal with them at proper levels. I don't deal with any one below the rank of colonel now, and if Services people want to see me, they come to my office." He smiled and blinked languidly. "It shakes them you know, to have to deal with people who don't spring to attention and click their heels at them. But they come to heel in the end, medals and all."

I said suddenly, "Do you have anything to do with Colonel Holland?"

"Holland?" he said puckering his brow. "I don't think so. Why?"

"Nothing," I said. "I somehow thought you didn't."

"Is he any different from any other colonel?"

"I think he's good."

"Then he certainly is different from most colonels. Most of them are almost illiterate."

I said, "Oh, I think Holland can read and write—or make his mark anyhow. What's more, he's had quite a lot of experience of what the sharp end of a war's like."

"The what?"

"You know. The childish bit at the end of the production process when they kill people."

"Experience?" said Iles. He waved experience aside. "My dear man, that's the great illusion. Experience of the last war's worse than useless. War's been revolutionised. Who are the people who've been wrong every single time all through the war? The experienced soldiers. We see it every day—demands made for material which can't possibly be used. We carry out experiments with the greatest care. We prove beyond all doubt that what the Services need is X. Do they accept it? No. They want Y. Some stupid prejudice in their silly minds you see. In the end we have

38

to tell them flat that they'll get what we produce—and like it—without any more nonsense."

I said, " It's a great pity when you come to think of it that we can't abolish the Navy, the Army and the Air Force and just get on with winning the war without them."

" I couldn't agree with you more," said Iles perfectly seriously.

Iles had been staring at Susan a lot under his drooping eyelids. Suddenly he uncoiled himself, clambered on to his feet and said, " Would you care to dance ? "

Susan looked a bit surprised. He'd barely spoken to her before, and he'd shown no sign of dancing with Gillian. Then she smiled sweetly and said, " I don't think so, thank you."

The girl Gillian weighed in and said, " Oh, darling—but you must dance with Maurice. Dancing with Maurice is an experience. He's marvellous." She said to him, " It'll be good for you to dance with anybody as good as Susan. You won't be able to criticise her like you do me."

Susan hesitated and looked at me. She danced damned well and liked it. It was one of the things I knew she missed.

I said, " Go on, darling. One shouldn't miss experiences like that." Susan got up. I knew the Gillian girl would expect me to dance with her. She was a silly little ass, but I didn't want to hurt her feelings, so I said, " I'm afraid this is where I appear very useless. I don't dance."

She looked at me and said, " Not at *all* ? " in real amazement.

I said, " No. Not at all. But I'm a damned good sitter out."

The bloke Iles was a four-letter man of the finest vintage, but he certainly could dance. Even I could see that. The floor at the Hickory Tree is very small and crowded, but he and Susan just looked in a different class from any of the rest.

Gillian said, " Maurice is a wonderful dancer."

" He looks good."

" They make a perfect pair, don't they ? Susan's the best girl dancer I know, but she's rather tall for most men." She looked at me in a thoughtful way. I wanted to say, " Five feet nine inches, my dear. Only two and a half inches taller than she is. I know."

I looked at them dancing. She was quite right. They were a perfect pair for size—one with fair hair and one with dark. They danced as though they'd never danced with any one else in their lives. Iles had pulled his left arm in because of the crowd, and they were almost still, just standing there in one another's arms. There was a chap playing a break on a muted trumpet. It was like vinegar.

Gillian said, " Why don't you dance ? It's very easy."

I said, " Too old and too lazy."

" It would be nice for Susan though."

I said, " There are a hell of a lot of things that would be nice for Susan."

The band stopped and everybody clapped. Susan clapped. They started to play " Hasta la ruelta." Gillian let them play about six bars and then said, " Oh good ! A tango. Maurice loves tangos."

They came across to our side of the floor. I watched their feet. Iles didn't go in for fancy business—at least it didn't look fancy when they did it. As they turned I saw Susan's face.

Gillian said, " But you *ought* to dance."

I said, " Why should I ? There are plenty of other men who dance. Men and women are all the same when they dance."

IV

GRAVELEY BANK was a bare, bleak place with a tearing east wind that never stopped blowing. I must have heard as many loud bangs as most people, but they still gave me a headache if there were many of them, and an afternoon watching firing at Graveley could be guaranteed to leave me feeling like death. What with that and the fact that I had no official standing at all, and no real right to be there, Graveley wasn't much fun. Luckily, all the people who always turned up on new weapon demonstrations knew me by now. I don't suppose they knew who I was or why, but they took me for granted. As we assembled for the usual preliminary chit-chat I said " hallo " to old Holland, Piercy, Ribon from the E. & P. Lab. and several more.

" 'Nother masterpiece I expect," said old Holland with a grin.

" Do you know anything about it ? "' said Piercy.

" Sort of air-gun," said Holland. " What do they think we do ? Shoot sparrows ? "

I said, " Have you seen it, sir ? "

" No," said the old boy. " Haven't even seen the drawings. Who is this bloke Charles ? One of your protégés."

I said, " No. We've never heard of him."

" Oh, I know Charles," said Ribon. " I don't know whether his thing's any good but he's a good chap. Done a lot of first-rate stuff."

After a few minutes Charles was brought in and introduced by the commandant. He was a very ordinary looking chap who might have been sweating on the top line for promotion to cashier. I was rather impressed by him. He waded straight in and told us about his mortar and how it worked. Apparently the idea was to produce a silent close support weapon chiefly for night work, and what he'd done was to turn out a sort of airgun-cum-mortar. You cocked the thing by pulling down a long lever which gave you a very big air pressure. The bomb was dropped down the nozzle, you pulled a trigger, and the air pressure was released behind the bomb and blew it out. The thing only had a range of a few hundred yards—you ranged it by a calibrated dial which showed your air pressure. But it was silent, which was what he'd been asked for and as there was no propellant explosion the bomb could be very light and have a very high charge-weight ratio.

Charles didn't tell us how marvellous it was, which was a change, and when Holland asked what it weighed he said straight away, " That's one of the snags. The air pressure chamber is a rather heavy job for such a short range weapon. I think it would have to be carrier-borne." He smiled and added. " The other snag is that on this model the pressure chamber's begun to leak after a few rounds."

A few other people asked questions but most of us felt the next thing was to see the gadget, so we trooped out and went down to the mortar range. The thing was set up there ready. It looked like a three-inch mortar with gout—just an ordinary three-inch mortar barrel with a big round compression chamber at the base, a darned great handle about four feet long running up beside the barrel and a big dial on the side. The whole thing looked a bit Mark I. But then demonstration models always did.

Charles handed one of the bombs round. It was a very neat-looking plastic job and very light compared with an ordinary bomb. Charles told one of his chaps to set for 300 yards and told us to watch the dial. The chap yanked down the long handle two or three times, and the dial needle went up to 300. Then another chap dropped a dummy bomb down the spout.

Charles said, "All set, gentlemen. This is the firing trigger." He pressed a trigger at the base of the barrel, the thing gave a sharp "chunk!" and the bomb went kiting off. As far as I could judge from behind it was pretty well dead on the 300 mark, but it seemed to me to drift a lot in the wind. Old Holland spotted that too and said quietly to me, "I wonder what his range is against the wind?" The field telephone report gave the carry as 290 yards. Everybody began to ask questions. Charles was very good and quite frank. He said at once that he was having trouble with the tail of the bomb, partly because the thing was so light and partly because the tail had to be shaped to take the kick of the air pressure.

His scale was calibrated up to 1000 yards, but when I asked him to go right up to that he said he didn't think we'd get over 500 in those conditions, and in fact he didn't get much over 450. Then Holland made him have a go against the wind and that brought his maximum down to just under 400. Even so, the extreme ranges took a lot of pumping up. Holland shook his head and said, "The trouble is that at that range you're under enemy fire from damned nearly anything except a catapult." He shook his head again when they showed how the thing was brought into action. It was a heavy affair, and even with four of them it was rather a job.

Charles said, "You realise that the original idea was for night operations. That was the idea of the silence."

Ribon wanted to see how a live bomb functioned and so did I. Charles smiled and said, "Right. But if you don't mind, I'd rather you all got away a bit. I've never had anything go wrong with a live bomb, but I had a dummy once which just trickled out of the muzzle and landed about ten yards away, so I'd rather not risk anything."

We all got back about thirty yards and he pumped the thing up, prepared a live bomb and dropped it in. He was just pressing the trigger when suddenly the field telephone operator who had been up near the 300 mark got up and started to amble into the fairway. I suppose he thought when we went back that we were packing up.

Everybody let out a terrific yell, but Charles had pressed the trigger and the thing went off. We all yelled "Down!"

and waved our arms. The chappie looked up in a startled way, but luckily he was quick in the uptake and dived into a slit trench at the side of the fairway like a rabbit. The bomb landed about three seconds later and the big charge went up with a hell of a wallop. It was at least fifty yards from where he had been, and the lethal radius was only about thirty yards, so he would probably have been all right anyhow. But it was against every conceivable range rule for him to have come out without orders, and with the flag flying. I saw the commandant look as black as thunder and speak to his sergeant-major ; and I guessed the wretched bloke was for it later.

Of course there was the usual roar of laughter and lighting of cigarettes that you always got if something dangerous happened at a trial. Holland said to Charles, "I suppose you're quite sure your mortar's outside its own 50 per cent zone ? " Charles grinned in a good-tempered way, but I think it was pretty plain by then what we all felt about his gadget—put another five hundred yards on the range and everybody would be interested. I think that was what Charles expected, and what he thought himself.

I had meant to stay that night in the pub at Graveley and go on looking at some more stuff the next day, but just about tea time Waring rang up from town. I thought he sounded excited about something. He said, " Listen, Sammy. The Old Man wants you to go across to Ribbenham as quick as you can. It's only about thirty miles from you. Contact Captain Stuart at the police station. He knows you're coming."

I said, " What's this all about ? "

" Stuart will tell you. I can't talk about it on the telephone, but it's important and very urgent."

" All right," I said. " Is it important enough for me to ask the commandant for a car ? "

" God yes—anything you like. The main thing is to get there in an hour if you can."

" After that I use my own judgment about what I do ? "

" Yes. You'll see what's wanted all right. Cheerio, Sammy. I'll tell the Old Man you're on your way."

I rang off, chucked my stuff into my bag, paid my bill and went up to the camp to get a car, wondering what the hell it was all about.

They coughed up a car almost without a struggle, and

as they gave me a driver who apparently had something he very much wanted to do back at the camp, I was in Ribbenham police station by six. Stuart was there. He was a young sapper officer. I thought he looked a good chap. When we'd introduced ourselves I said, " Can you put me in the picture ? I've no idea what this is all about."

He looked a bit surprised. " They didn't tell you ? "

" No. I simply got a call from London telling me to come over and that you were expecting me."

He said, "That's right. I contacted Professor Mair." There was a pause. Then he said, looking a bit embarrassed, " Look here, I know it's rot, but may I check up on your identity ? You see . . . "

" Sure," I said. I brought out my pass and my identity card. He looked at them and handed them back.

" Good," he said. " Sorry to bother you, but I don't like to risk anything on this business. Let's sit down, and I'll give you the dope."

We sat down and Stuart said, " Well, what's happened is that a kid's been killed by an explosion."

I was a bit disappointed, after all the cloak-and-dagger business. " Accident, eh ? "

He shrugged his shoulders in silence.

" Found a dud and hit it with a hammer ? "

" No," said Stuart slowly. " We don't think it was like that. As far as we can make out she simply picked it up. Or maybe only touched it."

" What was it ? "

" We don't know."

I said, " I don't quite understand where I come in. Accidents aren't really in our line. . . ."

Stuart said, " We don't think this was an accident."

" Then what was it ? "

Stuart lit a cigarette. " It's the fourth this week," he said abruptly. " Always the same sort of circumstances, and always after Jerry planes have been over."

I said, " You mean they're dropping booby traps ? "

" Yes. It looks like it."

I thought for a bit.

" Always kids ? "

" No. Three kids and one man."

" No survivors, of course ? "

" The people who've touched the things have been blown to glory. Frightful mess. This time we've got a

44

survivor—the kid's little brother. By some miracle he wasn't touched. But as he's only three he isn't a lot of help."

" Have you talked to him ? "

" Only for a moment. He was still badly shaken. But the police say he's much better now. I thought we might go along together and see what we can get out of him. It's only five minutes' walk."

As we walked along I said, " Odd that it should have been kids three times out of four."

" I expect the damned things are disguised as teddy bears or something," said Stuart bitterly. " Jerry has a lovely mind."

" What makes you so sure they are Jerry booby traps and not just bits of our own stuff left about ? "

" Where they're found, chiefly. This was in the Park. God knows we leave things lying about all right, but we don't leave them in places like that. The idea that they're dropped is pure speculation. As I say, it just happens that they're found directly after planes have come over."

We walked on for a bit and then Stuart said, " The bit that I find rather shaking is that these damn' things, what-ever they are, seem to go up so easily. We have no idea what happened with the other two kids—nobody was there. But with the man, somebody about fifty yards away saw him stop, stoop down as though he were picking something up and immediately, up she went. No question of hitting the thing or dropping it or anything like that. From the story I was told it was even too quick for him to have taken the pin out of a grenade. Well, damn it—even if it were some-thing of ours left about it wouldn't go up as easily as that."

I said, " How reliable's the evidence on that ? About when the chap picked it up ? "

" Not very. That's the trouble."

Stuart turned off suddenly down a side street and knocked at the door of one of the rather slummy houses. A woman opened the door. She looked about forty, but I should think she was younger really. She was very thin and her face was ghastly—pale, with almost purple shadows under her eyes. She recognised Stuart and said, " Oh, good evening, sir."

Stuart said, " Good evening, Mrs. Davis. How's Bobby?"

" He's a lot better," she said. " Almost himself again now, sir. Won't you come in ? "

We went in. Stuart said, " Do you think he's well

45

enough to talk to us ? I hate to bother you, Mrs. Davis, but we must see if he can tell us anything that will help to . . . to . . . ''

I saw her face twitch, but she was a darned good woman.

She said, " Oh yes, sir. I think he's quite all right now." She hesitated and then said, almost apologetically, " I did ask him a bit myself, sir, but he can't tell me much. He's only just three, see. He doesn't understand."

" No, no," said Stuart. " Of course not. But he might be able to give us *some* lead about what happened."

" Yes," said Mrs. Davis. She hesitated and then said " If you'll sit down, sir, I'll go and get Bobby."

She went out. I glanced round the room. It was a sort of living-room-cum-kitchen, small and very dark."

I said, " Is there a husband ? "

" The poor devil's husband's in North Africa," said Stuart shortly. I liked him. I could see he wasn't enjoying himself any more than I was.

Mrs. Davis came back carrying a little tow-headed kid in a jersey and torn knickers. He looked quite normal, though a bit shy.

Stuart said, " Hallo, Bobby ! "

The kid looked at him for a long time and said " Hallo ! " in a whisper.

Stuart held out his arms and said, " Come to me ? " but the kid went shy and hid his face in his mother.

I suddenly had a bright idea. I said, " Don't you go to him, Bobby. You come to me. *I've* got chocolate. Look ! " I brought a bit out of my pocket and held it up. Mrs. Davis said, " Oo ! look there, Bobby ! "

Bobby looked up a bit doubtfully and looked from me to the chocolate and back and then did a half-grin. Mrs. Davis put him down and he toddled over to me and stood looking at me very solemnly.

I gave him a bit of chocolate and he slowly started to suck it, still staring at me.

" Say ' thank you,' Bobby," said his mother.

He said, " Thank you," in a whisper. Stuart leaned forward and said, " Look, Bobby, I want to ask you something. What happened when the thing went bang ? "

The kiddie turned and stared at him and repeated, " Thing went bang."

" Were you and Sheila playing ? "

Bobby nodded.

" What were you playing ? "

No reply for a moment. Then he suddenly started off, rather falling over himself in getting it out. " Sheila wouldn't Sheila wouldn't play any more and she went she went away and she called and said what I've got, Bobby, and it went bang."

Stuart said very gently, " Did you see what it was she found, Bobby ? "

He nodded.

" What was it like ? "

" In the grass. It was in the grass."

" How big was it ? " Stuart took his fountain pen out of his pocket. " As big as this ? "

Bobby was silent, staring at the pen.

" Or bigger ? "

" Don't know," said Bobby in a whisper.

I said, " What colour was it, Bobby ? "

" He doesn't know colours, sir," said Mrs. Davis. " He's only just three, see. I don't think he really saw it, did you, Bobby ? It was just in the grass and Sheila found it, didn't she ? "

" Sheila found it and she called what I've found and it went bang."

" Did Sheila pick it up ? " said Stuart.

Bobby shook his head at once.

" Sure of that ? "

" Sheila didn't pick it up, she put it down and called."

" She just left it there ? "

" Yes and called, What I've found."

I caught Stuart's eye and shook my head slightly. He gave a resigned little nod.

Mrs. Davis said apologetically, " Of course he's not very old, sir. He can't tell you, see, like an older one—can you, love ? " She sat down in front of him and said, " Bobby, tell mummy. Did She-She pick the nasty thing up ? "

Bobby went very red and a strained frown came over his face. You could see he was trying with all his might.

He said, " No, She-She wouldn't play and she called what I've found she sat down she found it."

" She sat down ? "

" Yes, on the ground." He suddenly crouched. " Like that She-She did and she called what I've found."

"Show us what she did, Bobby ? " I said quickly. " What did She-She do ? "

He looked at me with the strained little frown. " She called," he said rather pathetically, " she called what I've found . . ." He saw it wasn't the right answer and tailed off into a whisper. His face puckered and I thought he was going to cry.

" Never mind, lovey," said Mrs. Davis quickly. " It's all right." She picked him up again. He hid his face and said something to her in a whisper.

" With Blackie ? " she said.

Bobby nodded.

" He says he wants to go and play with Blackie," said Mrs. Davis with a little smile. " Blackie's his kitten."

" So he shall," said Stuart smiling. " Right away. Thank you very much, Bobby. You've been a real help."

Mrs. Davis put him down, and I gave him another bit of chocolate. He looked solemnly at both of us and then turned and scampered out. Mrs. Davis said, " I'm afraid he can't tell you much, sir. He's too young, see."

" I think he's an extremely nice and intelligent little boy," said Stuart. " He told us a lot more than I thought we should get."

I was glad he said that. She looked pleased.

" He's much better than when I saw him before," said Stuart.

" Oh yes, sir. He's quite all right now." As we got up she said, " Of course I may be able to get more out of him *gradually* like. But I don't like to badger him, see."

" No, don't do that," said Stuart. " But if he does tell you any more about it, let us know, won't you ? "

As we walked down the street Stuart said, " Isn't that maddening ? A year or two older and he could have told us the whole thing."

" He tried hard, poor little devil," I said.

" Oh rather. But you see they don't really understand what words mean. I still don't know whether he ever *saw* the thing, or whether he just knew it was there in the grass."

" I don't think he did. My guess is that she saw it, crouched down and called him, touched it, and up it went. She wouldn't pick it up if she were crouching down over it."

" No. Probably not."

We walked on for a bit.

I said, " The mother's a good person."

" Marvellous," said Stuart. " She has been all through."

" Where's the little kid's body ? "

" The doctor's been doing a p.m. We might go and see him. He may have something for us."

We saw the chap who had done the post-mortem. Stuart had already told him that fragments were important, and he had a couple of dozen steel splinters, but they were very small. It looked as though most of the casing of the thing had been plastic and that was always the devil. It goes almost to powder.

I asked him if he could give a guess at the position the child had been in when the thing exploded, from the nature of the injuries. It was pretty vital to us to know whether she had picked it up.

He shook his head a bit doubtfully. He was a rather nice, slow old Scot. He said, " It's verry difficult when injury is so widespread. I could do no more than make a guess at that."

" Would you think she was holding it in her hand ? "

The old boy thought for a bit and looked at his notes.

" I would guess that she was not," he said at last. " Mind you—she might have been. Explosion is a queer thing. There is a hand completely destroyed and one that isn't. But the head and thorax and the lower limbs are more damaged than the abdomen, and there's little damage, relatively speaking, to the pelvis. Now had the lassie been holding it and looking at it, why is the tibia more damaged than the abdomen ? "

" Does it fit with the idea that she was crouching over it, and put out a hand to pick it up ? "

The old chap thought. " It might. Mind you, this is the purest speculation. But it might. That might do something to protect the abdomen and expose the knees."

" But of course you can't tell us whether she actually touched it ? "

The old chap shook his head. " No one can tell ye that now. Did ye see the poor lassie's body ? "

" I did," said Stuart briefly.

" Then ye'll know . . ."

" Yes," said Stuart. " We can't expect much detail."

We sat down in a little room they had given Stuart, and thought. I said, " The devil of it is that we don't really know whether she touched it or not. And until we know for sure that she did, it may be a time fuse."

"It might still be a time fuse even if she did," said Stuart. "Be a bit of a coincidence though." He shook his head. "I'm fairly sure from the other cases that it's not a time fuse, o' boy. The snag about this is that each time the person who found the thing has been killed before they had time to show it to any one else. That wouldn't be likely to happen with a time fuse."

"Damn !" I said suddenly. "I am a dummy. I didn't ask Mrs. Davis if she was carrying metal."

"I did," said Stuart. "She was wearing a bracelet and she had metal protectors on the toes and heels of her shoes." He was a very competent bloke in a quiet way. I found myself beginning to like him a lot. He sat for a long time thinking, looking very young and damned tired.

I said, "When did you eat last ? "

"I don't know," he said vaguely. "I don't think he heard much what I said.

He looked up and said, "This is a devil, o' boy. Any theories ? "

"Well," I said slowly. "Let's see what we've got. We don't know how the things got there, but they're pretty obviously not ours, and they've come so far after planes have been over. The thing's probably mainly plastic, and it goes up darned easily. Probably not a time fuse. My guess would be magnetic or trembler."

Stuart nodded. "It's not a lot to go on, is it ? "

"Unless Bobby can tell us more ? "

"I doubt if he can ? "

"Then it's darned difficult to know what we can do until . . ."

"Until some more kids are blown to bits ? " said Stuart bitterly. "Damn it, o' boy. I've seen five dead children this week, and it's getting me down." He got up and walked quickly over to the window.

"Can you issue a warning ? " I asked.

"We can. We have. But we can't kick up too much fuss or people will get the wind up. Or so they tell me. Anyhow, you know what kids are. It's all very well to tell people not to mess about with anything they find, but it's too wide. For all we know the damn' things may look like a—a handbag or something." He turned and faced me. "Look, o' boy, we've *got* to get hold of one of these things, and damn' quick. We've got to find one, put a cordon round it and then take it apart."

I said, " Yes. That's going to be fun too, isn't it ? The taking it apart game ? "

Stuart shrugged. " You don't come into that. It's my job. In fact you don't come into the thing at all unless you like. I only got on to Mair because I used to know him and thought he might—might be able to help."

I said, " Bunk. Of course I want to be in on it."

Stuart looked at me for a moment. Then he just said, " All right, o' boy. Then let's try and hatch some sort of plot."

We got it fixed up eventually. I was to go back to town, and Stuart was to notify me as soon as he got another case, and we would get together as fast as we could. Meanwhile we would both think about it, shove down our ideas and exchange notes. It was too late to get back to town that night, so I stayed in a pub and went off early the next morning. Stuart came along and saw me off. He didn't look as though he had slept much.

V

ABOUT three days later I got a telegram from Stuart which simply said, " Police Station Llanfaris North Wales." But before I could do anything about it another came which said, " Don't come, Grenade." After that I heard no more of him for some while. It was just as well, because the figures of the Reeves trials were in and I was working like a navvy on the report.

It had come out very much as I expected from seeing the trials and from casual glances at the figures as Till was working on them. The long and short of it was that the Reeves had certain advantages over what we'd got already —particularly in engaging a target moving fast across its front—because it fired on a predicted line instead of off a graticule. But it was a heavy brute to handle for its hitting power, and as Holland had said, the layer's job was very tricky compared with an ordinary anti-tank layer's. For the life of me I couldn't see that there was anything to shout about. It seemed very doubtful to me whether it was a practical proposition for ordinary catch-as-catch-can anti-tank stuff.

I ended up, " A decision is therefore required as to whether the advantages set out above outweigh the disadvantages sufficiently to justify all the normal difficulties of a change of weapon. It is understood that whatever decision is reached large scale production of the predictor sighting gear, which is the biggest production problem, could not be arranged in less than nine months to a year."

I read the whole thing through. It seemed quite a reasonable statement of the case, so I passed it through to the Old Man.

Joe said, " R.B. won't like that. He's been selling the thing all round the place."

I said, " That's his funeral. I told him to wait."

" Bet you he tries to get the Old Man to stop the report."

" He may try, but the Old Man won't play. He knows R.B."

Joe said, " All right. Nous verrons."

We saw soon enough. I think Joe probably knew more than I did about how far the Old Man and Waring were committed.

Mair must just have glanced through the report and passed it on to Waring. Anyhow, about three o'clock Waring rang and asked me if I'd come down. When I got to his office he had the thing in front of him. He just said straight away : " Look here, Sammy—this report of yours."

" Yes ? " I said.

" Well, damn it all, you're just knocking the thing for all you're fit. What the hell's the idea ? "

Waring had rather thick lips, and when he was angry they went loose and his eyes flashed in a queer way.

I was genuinely surprised. I said, " Knocking it ? How ? "

" You're saying it's no damned good."

" No, I'm not," I said. " I haven't said anything about its being no good. I've merely given the results of the trials and summed up the advantages and disadvantages."

" Oh, I dare say," said Waring, throwing himself back in his chair and staring at me. " But it sticks out a mile that you don't think anything of it. It's a most biassed statement."

That got under my skin. " In what way is it biassed ? " I said pretty sharply.

" Well, all this about the time it would take to get into production."

" It's perfectly true. In fact, if anything it's under-estimated."

" But why on earth bring that in ? It's nothing to do with the trials."

I said, " Well, look here, R.B., this is exactly what I was talking to the Old Man about the other day. Just what is our job ? And more particularly, what is *my* job ? "

" What d'you mean ? " said Waring, not because he didn't understand but because he wanted time to think it out.

" Am I supposed to give all the facts, or some of the facts, or my opinions or your opinions or what ? "

Waring was silent for a moment. " I think," he said carefully, " that you're supposed to give the facts—to Mair."

" That's what I have done. I'd be interested to hear his views on them."

" But I don't think it's your job to interpret them," said Waring, still carefully. " Frankly, Sammy, I don't think you know enough of the background for that." He smiled brightly at me.

I said, " What do you mean by the ' the background ' ? "

Waring waved a hand. " Oh, all the political stuff. What other people think. What the official attitude is and so on."

" You think that alters the facts ? " I said bluntly.

He still smiled, but not too easily. " I think it alters the use one makes of them." He leant forward. " Supposing the Minister is really keen on this ? Do you mean to tell me that it will still take as long to get into production as though he didn't care a damn about it ? "

I said, " I dare say not. But is our job to tell the Minister the truth, or to tell him that what he wants to do is right ? "

Waring said, " I don't think that's a matter for you and me, Sammy. Certainly not for the technical side."

" The technical side being me ? "

" That's right," said Waring with his boyish grin. " If you want me to be blunt, I think the backroom boys should stick to their job."

" Which is to produce the answer you want even if we have to fake it ? "

" No, no," said Waring irritably. " Be reasonable, Sammy. Nobody wants to fake anything. But between ourselves the Old Man is rather on his ear about this. He was quite bitter about it. He seemed to think you'd done it on purpose."

" Done *what* on purpose ? " I said wearily.

"Knocked the Reeves." He grinned. "I think it might be worth while to make your peace when you get a chance. You know how he gets these ideas."

I said, "I think I know how he got this one."

"What d'you mean?"

"I think you sold him a pup, and made him sell it to other people."

"Nothing of the sort. He was keen on the thing and I've simply backed him up. What else could I do?"

"You could have backed *me* up and told him to hold his horses. I've told you this would happen till I'm sick of it. Now when it does happen, you want me to get you out of the mess by proving that you're right. Well, it can't be done."

"No, no," said Waring soothingly. "Of course not. It's not like that at all. It's just that Mair's a bit disappointed, that's all, and the whole thing happens to be a bit tricky politically speaking."

"But that's nothing to do with me."

"Of course it isn't," said Waring quickly. "That's all I was trying to say before. Don't worry about it. You've done your job and that's all that concerns you, as I told the Old Man."

He sat back in his chair and picked up the report. "Now," he said, with a comical grin. "The question is— what are we going to do with this?"

I said stiffly, "That's up to Mair. As far as I'm concerned the job's done."

"Yes. But he wants something done about it before he sends it out."

"What sort of thing?"

"He thinks the emphasis is in the wrong places."

I shrugged my shoulders and said nothing. The whole thing seemed so darned contemptible that there wasn't anything to say about it.

"I think we shall have to do something to satisfy him," said Waring shaking his head. "Or else he'll go messing about with it himself, and then God knows what he'll say." He looked up at me. "Will you do it, or would you rather I did? Sometimes it's easier for someone else. . . ."

I said, "Look, R.B.—if Mair isn't satisfied with that report he can alter it, and take responsibility for altering it. He's the boss. But I'm damned if I will, and if you're going to mess about with it I shall tell Mair that I wash my hands of it. Damn it all, you've never even seen the gun fired."

Waring hesitated. Finally he said, " Well, you can take that line if you like. But you'll find yourself pretty unpopular."

I said, " Fine. I'll go and see about it."

I got up and left him sitting there and went straight to the Old Man's room. He was just sitting at his desk sucking his pipe and staring out of the window. He looked round and said : " Hallo, Sammy."

I said, " I understand that you don't like my report on the Reeves gun." I was shaking slightly with sheer fury.

" The Reeves gun ? " said the Old Man, coming back to earth slowly. " Oh yes. Bit disappointing, eh ? "

" Just about what I expected," I said curtly.

" I hoped it would show up better than that," said Mair with mild regret. Anything less like a man on his ear I've never seen.

I said, " So did I. But I don't see that we can do anything about it."

" Well no—of course not. Anyhow, everybody knows that trials aren't everything."

It didn't seem to me that we were making a lot of contact.

I said, " Waring thinks you'll want the report altered before it goes out."

" Oh ? " said Mair vaguely. " Well, of course there have been various discussions already. I don't think you were there. Perhaps he's thinking of those. Have you talked to him about it ? "

" Yes."

The Old Man nodded. " Well, he can put you in the picture. He knows the situation."

I said, " He may know the situation but we're not reporting on a situation. We're reporting on a gun, and he knows nothing at all about that."

The Old Man looked at me sharply. I think this was the first time he'd realised that there was anything wrong.

He said, " No. Of course not. I'll tell you what—we might get him in and talk about it."

He rang for his girl and told her to get Waring. We sat in silence till he came. Waring didn't look at me.

Mair said, " Rob—the Reeves report. What's the position ? "

"You gave it to me last night and told me you thought it was too destructive," said Waring calmly.

"Yes," said Mair, frowning in a thoughtful way. "There was something about production time . . . ?"

I said, "I've pointed out that it would take nine months at least to get into production."

"That's right," said Mair. "I thought that might come out. It's nothing to do with the gun, and anyhow it's only a guess."

Waring said, "I think you felt at the time that in view of the previous discussions, we had to be careful about the wording in one or two places."

"Yes. We must be careful. It's a tricky situation." He glanced from Waring to me and back. "Of course Sammy wasn't at that meeting, so he doesn't know quite where we stand."

"In view of what the Minister told us . . ." said Waring raising his black eyebrows and smiling significantly.

"Oh yes," said Mair smiling back. "There's no doubt that it needs careful handling."

I was fed up with it. I said, "Will that alter the rate of fire, the number of times the target was hit, or the penetration? Because that's what the report is about."

"No, no," said Mair. "It's purely a matter of presentation."

He was just going on when his girl came in and said, "Dr. James is here, Professor Mair."

Mair looked at his watch in a startled way and said, "Good Lord—is it as late as that?—All right, show Dr. James in."

He turned back to us and said, "Look—talk this over together you two, will you, and agree something? You can put Sammy in the picture, Rob. It's a very good and clear report. It's just a matter of presentation in one or two places . . ."

I said desperately, "You wouldn't care to write it yourself, sir, in the circumstances?"

"Oh no," said Mair. "No need at all. You and Rob can agree it. Only do it right away because the Minister's eager to get it." He smiled at Waring. "For reasons we know." His girl came in and announced James. We got up.

"Ah, hallo, James," said Mair, going forward. "Come in." He said to us over his shoulder, "Then I'll leave that to you."

56

When we got outside I said, " I'll send you down the figures right away."

" Figures ? " said Waring. " What for ? "

" To write the report. I've said all I've got to say about the bloody thing. If Mair wants it to tie up with something you and he have told the Minister, one of you must write it. As I don't know what you said, I can't help."

" Oh Christ ! " said Waring. " Don't get on your dignity, old boy. It's too childish."

I said. " You're telling me. The whole thing's childish, and a pretty deplorable sort of child."

" All we want to do is remain neutral. That's all. We just don't want the report to damn the thing out of hand."

" Why don't we ? "

" Because if we do we play right into the hands of people who'd like nothing better than to see us come a cropper."

" How ? "

Waring shrugged. " It's a long story. You know how these scientific boys love one another. Look here, come along to my room and I'll show you the bits that are awkward. It won't take five minutes."

" Nothing doing."

Waring stopped and looked at me for a moment. Then he shrugged his shoulders. " All right, Sammy. If you won't help, you won't. But I don't mind telling you that if we fall down on this it'll be bloody nearly the end of Mair. Please yourself."

It didn't amount to much, in fact. They wanted the production time bit cut out ; which was reasonable in a way. Apart from that it was just a matter of a word here and there.

Finally I said, " Look here, isn't the real answer to cut out the summary altogether and just give the figures ? Then they can make what they like of it."

Waring said, " If you're prepared to do that I've nothing whatever to say." He grinned at me and said, " I don't want to add any noughts—honestly I don't."

" It seems the quickest way," I said wearily. " At least we're on sound ground there." I knew exactly what it meant. The big boys never looked at figures and didn't understand them if they did. The thing would just mean nothing to them.

I said, " Well, if you want to save the Old Man's face that way, it's nothing to do with me. Personally, I think he was more use in the days when his face didn't matter. But it's up to him."

When I got upstairs Joe was rooting for something in one of the filing cabinets and singing, and Till was drawing a graph. I looked at them and thought they were pretty terrible. Joe's red hair was all over the place, the points of his collar were curling up, and he looked a lout. Tilly had his long red nose about two inches from the paper and his back all hunched up. I suppose I was in a bad temper.

About half-past six Joe slammed his stuff into a drawer and pushed off. He was always a prompt finisher. Tilly went grinding on as usual. I should have liked to go myself, but I knew Susan wouldn't be home till after eight, and going home by myself, feeling like that, was asking for it ; so I carried on for a bit. But about quarter past seven it got altogether too humpy. I rang Susan up and told her to pick me up at the Royal on her way home.

The first thing I saw when I got into the bar of the Royal was Joe and Pinker hobnobbing at a table. I hadn't even known they knew one another and I didn't like it much. I knew Joe would be telling Pinker all the latest scandal and that Pinker would love it. Pinker saw me and waved, so I went over. I thought Joe looked a bit guilty—like a sheep dog that's been caught doing something.

"What ho !" said Pinker. "We've just been talking about you."

"Oh ?" I said, looking at Joe. He looked rather silly and drank some beer.

"Have a drink ?" said Pinker. "What's all the latest dirt from the scientific front ? "

I said, "Our troops have made a tactical withdrawal to shorter lines."

"So I'm told," said Pinker. "Marchant here seems to think that a major clash is imminent."

You could always depend on Joe to shoot off his face.

I said lightly. "Oh, Joe's always looking for trouble."

"Well, it sounds to me as though you'll soon find it without much looking," said Pinker. "That boy Waring is riding for a fall. I can hear the boys clicking a fresh magazine into their gats for him."

I said, "Oh, R.B. can look after himself."

My beer came. I took a drink and said, "Fired anybody lately ? "

" Not in so many words," said Pinker. " But things are developing."

Joe fidgeted about rather uncomfortably for a time and then drank up his beer and said he must go. When he had gone Pinker said : " Is that boy any good ? "

I said, " Oh, Joe's all right."

" He seems a bit infantile to me. How old is he ? "

" Twenty-eight."

" I wish he'd have his hair cut," said Pinker.

I didn't say anything. I was wondering just how filthy Pinker would be about me as soon as my back was turned.

Pinker said, " Do you know Sir Lewis Easton ? "

" I know of him. Chairman of the National Scientific Committee."

" How do he and Mair get on ? "

" Oh, about the usual thing. You know how these eminent scientists are."

Pinker filled his pipe and looked at me with his hot angry eyes. " Easton's very powerful." He paused and then added, " He's in on this Reeves gun thing."

" How ? "

Pinker shrugged. " I think he and Mair have had a row about it."

" But what on earth does Easton know about it ? "

" Well, for that matter, what does Mair ? " said Pinker bluntly.

I said, " Mair knows the facts."

" Does he ? " said Pinker gently. " Does Waring let him see them ? "

I didn't answer. Pinker grinned.

" If you're not darned careful," he said, " Waring's bluff is going to be called, and Mair's backed it."

" Mair's got the Minister in his pocket," I said rather shaken.

" Maybe. But Easton's got a bigger card than the Minister, if it comes to a show down." He looked at me thoughtfully. " You ought to meet Easton," he said, a bit too casually. " He's a good chap. I think you two might have quite a lot to say to each other. He doesn't like General Waring."

I was wondering what the hell to say to that when Susan came in, and that let me out. I waved to her and she came across.

Pinker was always very queer with her. He was a dapper

59

little man with sleek black hair, always very well dressed, and he preened himself and grinned at Susan very charmingly as though he were half flirting with her. But I had a feeling that he was just going through the motions and that women weren't really much in his line. Susan was always certain that he was a nancy.

Pinker said. "Your chief's going up in the world, Miss Roberts."

"Is he?" said Susan innocently. "Where's he going?"

"That's what a good many people are wondering," said Pinker with a grin. "Anyhow, he seems to be pointed for the top all right. I expect you're kept pretty busy?"

"Moderately," said Susan.

"Do you do anything for him?" said Pinker, nodding towards me. "Or are you entirely with Waring?"

"Oh, we share things out," said Susan vaguely. "It depends who's busy at the moment."

Pinker showed no sign of going so I ordered some more lager and said:

"How's the Permanent Secretary?"

"Oh, he's all right. We're not going to nominate him for an almshouse. We're going to set up an almshouse for all our Grand Old Men while we're about it. The trouble is that it'll have to be so bloody big." He looked from one of us to the other with his angry, contemptous eyes. "Nothing makes me so mad as the sentimental Tommy-rot about these old men. They dodder about; they can't hear; they can't see; they can't think; they hold up everything; and then everybody says, 'Brave old chap! Marvellous how he manages to work at all. Good old boy! Hooray!'" He made clapping motions. "Why the hell doesn't someone tell them that if they can't do the job the fairest thing is to get out and let somebody younger in who can? This is a war, not a Veterans' Race at the village sports."

I said, "There's a lot in that. Some of them stay surprisingly good, though."

"But it isn't a question of being 'surprisingly good,'" said Pinker savagely. "It's a question of being the best man for the job or not. Why the hell should we have to keep somebody because he isn't actually ga-ga though he's ninety? Put him in a museum or have him as a sideshow at a fair but why let him mess up a vital job? These old boys are useful as daddies for people who don't want to grow up. That's about the size of it."

I thought that one was to my address and went a bit red.

Susan was sitting very silent. She had a way of looking at Pinker with her eyebrows slightly arched and her nostrils drawn up which made her face very cold.

" I mustn't bore you talking shop," said Pinker turning to her. He said it rather patronisingly. Susan looked at him and her eyebrows went up farther.

" Oh, it's all right as long as I don't have to take it down in shorthand and type it," she said very meekly indeed. " I'm quite interested in the war."

Pinker looked uncomfortable. " It's a relief to find somebody who is," he said a bit lamely. " I often say it's time some of our high ups declared war."

As Pinker went out Susan looked after him and said, " I make it a rule never to be catty about that man, because I won't compete with him. But if he weren't for that rule . . ."

" Quite," I said. " And yet you know there's a lot in some of what he says."

" That only makes it more irritating," said Susan illogically.

I said, " Anyhow, let's have another drink."

After we'd been sitting there in silence for quite a bit Susan said : " Has anything bloody happened, darling ? Or is it your foot ? "

I said, " Mixture of the two."

" Can you talk about it ? "

I thought for a bit and then said, " No. I don't think so. The Old Man's making a fool of himself over the Reeves gun and Pinker's just told me that people are on to it. I've been squabbling with R.B. about it. That's what's really biting me."

A chap at the next table was just being served with a double. I looked at it and found that I was sweating a bit.

I said, " Look—I'm sorry, but I must have a proper drink."

Susan said quickly, " Hadn't we better go home then ? You've got plenty there."

" I don't want it at home. I want it here."

She looked at me with the queer worried wrinkles at the corners of her eyes and said, " You won't like it, you know, darling."

" Hell," I said. " Of course I shan't like it. Do you think I drink for fun ? You push off home, sweet. I shall be all right."

Susan suddenly got up and held out her hand. She said, "Come on. Home. Much nicer really."

I looked for the waiter. He was just vanishing through the service doors.

I got up and followed her out without saying anything. When we got down into the tube Susan said, " Now we'll play the Train Game." The Train Game was a game we'd invented. You sat in the train and bawled things to each other about other people in the compartment. The game was to avoid being left shouting so that they could hear as the train stopped at a station.

There was a brass hat opposite us and we started a yarn about his being one General Debility who commanded the Parliamentary Division at Rorkes Drift. It didn't go very well, so we switched on to the other version of the game which was to talk about something very serious and look as though you were flirting violently. Susan was very good at this. We started to recite " Blest Pair of Sirens," doing line and line, with me looking very passionate and Susan being coy and occasionally indignant. General Debility didn't seem to notice, but there was an elderly woman next to him who drank it in. When we got to " Oh may we soon again renew that song," Susan made a face which could only mean that I'd just made an immoral suggestion, and for a moment I thought the old lady was going to weigh in and tell me I ought to be ashamed of myself.

When we got in Susan said, " Now food. And after that tell me about to-day." She looked at me a bit doubtfully.

I said, just to tease her, " I was promised a drink."

" Well, you can have a drink if you want one, darling. Or how about some of your dope, if it's bad ? "

I said, " Ask me to have drink, woman."

" Would you care for a drink, Sammy ? "

" A whisky ? "

" Yes."

I said very firmly, " No, thank you, Susan. I'll have some of my nice medicine."

She suddenly grabbed hold of me and started to cry. Susan always cried in a queer way, with very quick, quiet little sobs.

" Here, come ! " I said.

Susan said, " Take it off. Take the bloody thing off. You know that helps."

" But I don't like taking it off."

62

" You do when you're by yourself. Why *will* you always keep it on when I'm here ? "

I said, " Well, it's all right now. Honest it is. The Train Game always does it. Come and get the supper."

VI

I went in on Sunday. There was a lot of stuff piling up—particularly my low-temperature lubrication baby—and I wanted to get a clear run at it when there weren't many people about. Till had been working on the figures and I got them out and started to wade into it.

I was surprised and pleased at the way it seemed to be developing. It began to look as though we might really be on to something that the official boys hadn't thought of. I decided to have the afternoon and evening on it. The figures were in from Graveley on the Charles Mortar trials. There was nothing new in them, and I didn't see that there was much to add to my previous report. The most interesting thing in my tray was a letter from Stuart, enclosing his notes on the booby-trap business. It said :

" Dear Rice,—I'm sorry about my false alarm. It turned out to be a straightforward accident—a chap found a grenade, started to fool around with it, and got blown to glory.

" I enclose my notes. Not very useful I'm afraid. There has been nothing lately. Interesting, as there have been no Jerry planes over to speak of.

" All the best,

" R. Stuart."

I read through the notes. He was quite right. They were a very careful and intelligent analysis of what we did know, but we knew darned little. The most interesting thing was his conclusion.

" As you said, there are three main possibilities over fusing.

" (*a*) Time fuse.

" (*b*) Magnetic (metal response).

" (*c*) Trembler (movement response).

Photo-electric seems fundamentally improbable. One assumes that the thing will be designed so that there is the least

63

possible chance of its being found unexploded and examined. This seems to put a time fuse out of court. Moreover, all the evidence suggests that the things explode only when they are approached or touched. On the other hand, it isn't easy to see how a simple trembler fuse could be made to stand up to being dropped from a plane.

" Since one must guess, my guess would therefore be a metal-response electric fuse. All the subjects killed (with one dubious exception) are known to have been wearing metal.

" I should like your view on this. If you agree, I shall work out a drill for tackling the thing (when we find one), starting from a guess, that it depends on a magnetic field."

I wasn't altogether happy about this. Stuart was quite right in saying we had to start from some sort of guess. But I thought he dismissed trembler a bit too lightly.

Old Taylor was the obvious person to talk to about it, so I went downstairs. Taylor was in his den, filing a bit of brass. He came to attention, but I thought there was less snap in it than usual, and he looked darned tired.

I sat on his bench and said, " Look, Taylor—I want your opinion as a fuse-King." I looked round the bench and picked up an old wooden cigarette box. " If you wanted to blow me up, and you were going to use this as a booby-trap, what sort of fuse would you use ? "

The old boy looked a bit puzzled. " Using that, sir ? "

" Yes, supposing you decided that you'd do it by putting that box—filled with a charge—on my desk, so that it would blow me to glory and nobody would know what had happened. What sort of fuse would you use ? "

Taylor scratched his head thoughtfully. " There are s-several things I *could* do, sir," he said. " A simple clock of c-course ? "

" It would tick and I should hear it. Anyhow, it might go off when I was out of the room."

" Would you be l-likely to *touch* the box, sir ? "

" Probably. It isn't there as a rule. I should wonder what it was."

" It could be arranged so that the l-lifting of the lid operated the f-fuse, sir. That could be either electrical or ch-chemical or mechanical."

" Yes. But you couldn't be sure I should lift the lid. I might just shove it aside without opening it."

Taylor stopped scratching his head and started to

scratch his chin instead. " What you require, sir," he said with his slow grin, " Is something that will d-destroy you if you t-touch it, or even app-proach it ? "

" That sort of thing."

" If you can depend on *m-movement*, sir, why not a simple tr-trembler ? Otherwise, an electric proximity fuse—possibly with a photo-electric cell ? " His face lightened. Taylor loved photo-electric cells. " The placing of the hand on the box might a-activate the cell, sir ? "

" Yes," I said. " But look—you aren't placing it on my desk. You're throwing it in from the window, so that it gets a bit of a jar and you don't know which way up it lands."

Taylor frowned. " If I may say so, sir, it would be a c-clumsy way of destroying you."

" Yes. But how would you *do* it ? "

" I think by some s-species of electric proximity fuse, sir. Probably photo-electric."

" You could fudge up a photo-electric fuse in a thing that size, that would work any way up and not be broken by dropping it ? "

Taylor hesitated. " W-way up—yes. Damage—no problem. S-space . . ." He shook his head. " I'm a little d-doubtful."

We went on for some time. I didn't feel we got very far ; chiefly because I couldn't very well tell Taylor the whole story. But he said enough to worry me about Stuart's approach. I jotted down a few notes for Stuart, saying :

" You're probably right, but I don't think it safe to put our shirts on electric proximity. If the thing's big enough it could be photo-electric, and it could certainly be mechanical trembler. The jar on dropping could be overcome. I don't think we must forget the possibility of a *combination* of things. Jerry likes multiple fuses of different sorts." I rather wanted to warn him not to mess about with the thing, if he got one, without bringing us in. But I felt I couldn't very well say that. After all, he was an experienced chap, and it was his show.

In the middle of the afternoon, when I was buried in the low temperature stuff, Sergeant-major Rose did one of his entries. Old Rose was a regular whom we'd been given because he was category C. He was very regimental but he had a soft spot for me and always came to me with his troubles. I suppose he thought we were category C men together.

He said, " May I have a word with you, sir ? "

" Of course," I said, rather fed-up at being interrupted.
" Will it take long, sergeant-major ? "

" Well, sir," said Rose, " It's about Corporal Taylor——"

" What's he been up to ? "

" I've had rather a lot of trouble with him lately, sir.
I thought you should know about it."

" Trouble with *Taylor* ? " I said, surprised. " What sort
of trouble ? "

" Oh, just a series of little things, sir. Punctuality and
so on."

I said, " But surely old Taylor works like a slave ? "

" Yes, sir," said Rose, coming as near looking embarrassed as you could with that moustache and that face. " I'm
not *complaining*. Taylor's a good man. But—well I think
there's trouble at home."

" You mean with his wife ? "

" Yes, sir. She's no good. I think the man's worried to
death."

" I thought he looked tired to-day."

" He's looked terrible sometimes lately, sir. I thought
I ought to report it."

" Of course," I said. " I thought about it for a bit and
said, " You're sure it's his wife ? "

" It's all round the place, sir."

Old Rose lowered his voice delicately, which meant
coming down to an ordinary conversational voice. " Apparently she's carrying on all over the place, something
shocking. Drink and men and so on."

" Not with any of our other people ? "

" Oh no, sir," said Rose as though it was a silly question.
" Just fellows she picks up. Of course she's a foreigner, sir."

I said, " Is she a tart ? "

Rose shrugged a shoulder. " She acts like she was, sir.
It's my belief she was on the streets before Taylor met
her, and he being an innocent sort of chap, never knew it.
He's a very innocent chap, Taylor. I doubt he'd know,
sir."

" Well, I've only seen her once, just as I was passing
through the hall, but she didn't look much like the vicar's
daughter."

" Just what I said myself, sir. I took one look at her and
I thought ' Hallo ! ' "

I thought for a while and said, " It's a bit difficult to
66

see what we can do about it, sergeant-major. Any suggestions?"

"I thought you might have a word with Corporal Taylor, sir."

I was just going to say, "Wouldn't you do it better than I should?" Then I saw, of course, I was an officer—or the nearest thing we had about the place. This time I wasn't the adjutant. I was the company commander. Rose was ten years older than I was, and a married man. But that didn't matter. It was an officer who ought to speak to Taylor.

"Think it would be better if Professor Mair talked to him?"

"That's for you to decide, sir," said Rose rather stiffly. I could see he thought it was a let-down. I said hurriedly, "Perhaps it would be better for me to."

"I thought so, sir."

"All right," I said rather reluctantly. "I'll talk to him. God knows quite how you ask a man if his wife's a tart, but there it is. Thank you, sergeant-major."

"Thank you, sir," said old Rose, doing an exit.

After he'd gone I sat back and thought it over. The more I thought, the less I liked it. I didn't see what the hell to say, and I cursed old Rose for a buck-passer. There was no doubt that commanding a company with him as your C.S.M. would have been no joke. It didn't seem likely to get any easier if I left it, and it was a good time, with Joe and Till both away, so I sent down for Taylor. He came in, and I could see now that he did look ghastly.

I took a rush at it and said, "Look, Taylor—I understand that you're having a certain amount of trouble at home?" His mouth tightened up. It was a very raw spot all right. But he just said, "Yes, sir," quietly.

"What's wrong?"

"Oh—n-nothing much, sir," he said vaguely.

"Your wife's not happy?"

"That's right, sir."

I waited hopefully, but he wasn't going to talk.

"Your wife's not English, is she?"

"No, sir. That's the trouble." Taylor hesitated. "They take advantage of her."

"Who does?" I said.

"Oo—just p-people she has to do with, sir. Tradesmen and such. S-she doesn't understand all the regulations."

" Regulations ? "

" About shopping and f-food and so on, sir."

We didn't seem to be getting very far, and for the life of me I couldn't see how to put it. I said, " It's no worse than that—just that she hasn't quite settled down in England yet ? "

" That's it, sir," said Taylor, doggedly.

There was a pause.

" Well, look here," I said, feeling very uncomfortable, " is there anything I can do to help ? "

" I don't think so, sir, thank you."

" Sure ? "

" Quite s-sure, sir. Unless——"

" Unless what ? "

Taylor's face twitched slightly, and there was sweat on his forehead. " If you wouldn't m-mind, sir, if sometimes I was to g-get away a few minutes early. S-she's all alone, and if perhaps I could g——"

He suddenly got completely stuck.

Usually his stutter was the machine-gun sort but this time he just stuck completely and wrestled with it, " . . . go home a bit early," he got out at last.

I said, " Of course. I'll tell Sergeant-major Rose right away."

" That would be very kind of you, sir."

" Anything else ? "

" I don't think so, sir, thank you."

" I expect she'll get used to it soon, you know," I said.

" I'm sure she will, sir. It's happening already. Sh-she's much—much happier than she was."

I knew it wasn't true and that he didn't even think it was true, but there didn't seem to be much to do about it. I said, " That's fine. Well, do let me know if there's anything I can do, Taylor. And try not to let it worry you too much."

He stood there in silence, looking very ill and rather old. Then he suddenly said, " It has been worrying, sir. I'm afraid it may have been affecting my w-work."

I said, " Well, try and take it easy for a while, Taylor. And don't worry."

" Thank you, sir," he said in his polite way and went out.

Susan rang up at about five and said, " Look—Dick's in town."

I said, " Dick ? Have you grabbed him ? "

" Yes. He's coming round now."

" We ought to take the kid out. We've never given him the dinner we promised him on his D.F.C."

" I thought of that. But it's Sunday, and he's off again to-morrow."

" Where ? "

" I don't know. He'll be here in a minute, so get back as soon as you can."

I had meant to go on for a bit, but I'd only seen Dick twice since the war started. Once just after he joined up, and once when he came up to get his gong in the spring of 1942. We never even wrote to each other unless we wanted something, and as we were all that was left of the family I always felt a bit responsible for him.

Dick was at the flat when I got back. He looked bigger than ever. I never saw how they got him into the cockpit of a fighter. He had shaved his moustache off, which made him look about twenty.

I said, " What's the idea ? Running for your picture in the papers as our youngest squadron-leader ? "

After we'd talked for a bit I said, " We've never given you the dinner we promised you for being a brave boy."

Dick looked a bit startled and said, " Well, surely I don't get that until I've got it up ? "

" You have got it up," I said, pointing to the D.F.C. ribbon.

He looked at me and then went very red and said, " Oh, yes," in a sulky way. I couldn't understand for a moment, but Susan just said, " They haven't by any chance given you *another* thing, have they ? "

Dick hesitated and then said, " Yes " very sulkily.

" Good God ! " I said. " What ? "

" The D.S.O. That's what I'm up for."

" What for ? "

" God knows," said Dick, still sulky. " It's a complete mystery to me. Thinking of another chap of the same name presumably."

I said, " You've got it wrong, my child. Sue and I don't want a suitable par. for the evening papers. So cut out the modest hero act, you great lout, and tell us about it. Have you gone and been brave again ? "

Dick grinned his slow grin and said, " No. But I've

69

showed a fine sense of self-preservation and I suppose they thought it ought to be encouraged."

" How have you ? "

" Oh, some Yanks went over to prang Wilhelmshaven and we went with them to keep the flies off. There was a certain amount of roughness and one of the Yanks went lame. It so happens that I'd gone a bit lame too, so I teamed up with this Yank and we pottered home hand in hand."

He looked at his nails. " As a matter of fact I didn't see him home. He saw *me* home. If you're going to potter along at that pace you want to be in something that can fire all round. Anyhow we got back with both the kites held together with chewing gum. I think a good many of the holes in mine were made by the old Yank. His rear gunner took one chap off my tail so close that I thought he'd got my rudder."

" How many did you get ? "

" Three each. Two of mine just came and sat in the sights when they were looking at him. The other had a go at his belly and broke away underneath so that I could drop on him. My kite would go down quite fast but it wouldn't go up much."

Susan said, " Could you have got home faster by yourself ? "

" Well, yes. I could go faster than the Yank. But it's so bloody *dangerous* lame-ducking it home by yourself. You want something to take their attention."

I said, " Well, it can probably be faked up to make quite a reasonable sounding story if they put somebody clever on it."

Dick said, " It was the Yank of course. He made an awful song and dance about it when he got home. He'd got it thoroughly into his head that I'd stopped around because I liked the colour of his eyes. Nice chap though, and a darn good pilot. I don't know how he held his kite together. Pretty nearly everything that could be shot away, was."

We had supper. I noticed that Dick still ate very slowly. Susan and I both beat him to it by about five minutes. When he was a little kid they used to start him on a meal five minutes ahead of everybody else because he was so slow. He always reminded me of a big, handsome cow eating, brown eyes and all.

I asked him about his job, but he was pretty vague.

Apparently he was just being moved, but he didn't know where. I said, " Aren't you just about due to come off flying duties for a bit ? "

He just shook his head and said, " I don't know what they're going to do with me."

I was pleased with Dick on the whole—particularly as he gradually stopped being shy. He was rather a prize specimen —big and handsome and winning medals and so on—and when he was shy he tended to act like one and go all Public-School-modest. But when he warmed up and remembered that it was me, it was better. You could see he knew he was pretty good and got a kick out of it.

Susan was sitting curled up in the big basket chair, showing a lot of leg. I saw the kid's eyes going down there, and I wondered how that side of things was going.

I said, " You're not married by any chance ? "

He grinned and said, " No—just semi-detached as usual." He pulled out his wallet. " Like to see the latest model ? "

I looked at the photograph. She was a pretty kid and looked intelligent. Dick said, " Name of Sylvia."

" She looks very young."

" Oh, yes. But she's got old-fashioned ways."

" Going to do anything about it ? "

" What sort of thing were you thinking of ? " said Dick, with his lazy grin.

" Honourable intentions and so on ? "

" We're sort of engaged."

" What sort of ? Ring ? "

" She's got my signet ring."

I said, " Oh, God ! I should think that damn' thing's nearly worn out by now."

He grinned at Susan and said, " Well, I'm not set such a hell of a good example, am I ? "

He asked me about my stuff. When I'd told him a bit about it he shook his head and said, " I don't see how the hell you stick that game. I don't see how *anybody* sticks these Ministries and places. A pal of mine—Len Henshaw—he got a bit tired so they put him into one of these office jobs. He stuck it for about a month and then went and asked them if he could come back on operations for a rest. And Sue . . ." He looked at her with calm approval for a moment and then slowly shook his head. " Hitting a typewriter and living with you. What a life for a girl with legs like that."

71

I said, " For God's sake pull your frock down, Sue. The kid's been all eyes for the last half-hour."

Dick grinned and said, " Mean monkey." He'd said that every time I wouldn't give him something of mine ever since I could remember.

Just before ten o'clock Dick said, " Look—I'll have to go. He looked at me a bit doubtfully. Susan said quickly, " Why don't you go down with him and have a drink in the pub to see him off ? "

I said, " How about you ? "

" No—I'd rather not. But you go."

Dick put on his overcoat and hat. He really looked huge in the whole outfit.

Susan said, " Good-bye, Dick dear."

He said, " Good-bye, Susan," put out his arms in his slow way and kissed her soundly.

He turned to me and said, " That in your eye, Uncle."

As we went downstairs he said cheerfully, " I like kissing that girl Susan of yours. If she was around I should kiss her a lot."

I said, " Like hell you would. You go and kiss your own women, you big cheese."

We got into the pub and ordered pints. Dick was rubbing the end of his nose, so I knew something was coming.

I said, " Cough it up and be a clean old man, Dicky."

He said, " Look—this new job of mine——"

" Well ? "

" I don't know much about it and anyhow I can't talk about it. But it's funny business. Not straight flying."

" What sort of funny business ? "

" Just funny business. You know—false beards and stilettos."

" Oh, is it ? "

Dick took a large gulp of beer and nodded, looking solemn. I said, " God Almighty—what an agent ! "

Dick said, " No—fooling apart. Sammy—it sounds about the most bloody wild-cat thing ever and y'see——"

He stopped and thought for a bit.

" What ? "

" Well, I should think I stand a pretty good chance of being a complete write-off."

There was a bit of a pause. Then I swallowed and said, " Well, what you've been doing hasn't been exactly the safest job in the war, has it ? "

72

" No. But this is different somehow. Mind you, it sounds darned good fun. But it just struck me that we'd better get things fixed up a bit." He stretched his legs out about eight feet and said, " This young woman, Sylvia, now——" He put his fingers in his breast pocket and pulled out a letter. It was a bit crumpled. " Thing for her if anything goes wrong. Follow me ? "

I said, " Yes."

" I don't know how the hell you know if anything *does* go wrong. I s'pose they tell you I'm overdue, like a submarine." He paused and added hastily, " For Christ's sake don't give her that until you're sure, Sammy, or I shall look an awful fool."

He finished his beer, picked up both our mugs and wandered lazily over to the bar. I saw the barmaid smile at him. People always smiled at him. He came back and said, " Apart from that there isn't much. I've made a will leaving you my overdraft." He rubbed his nose and said, " It's really just as well there are only two of us. Makes it easy."

My throat was dry. I said, " Listen. I'm not going to have this."

" What ? "

" Why the hell should you go on this sort of thing ? You've done your share."

Dick said, " Don't be a b.f. It's the chance of a lifetime. Biggest bit of damn' silliness I've ever heard of." He smiled quietly to himself with pleasure at the damn' silliness of it. " Mind you," he said, " this is on the q.t. Very much on the q.t."

I said, " Of course. But look, Dick . . . "

" That girl Susan of yours," he said slowly, looking at me thoughtfully with his brown cow-eyes. " Now that's a nice girl. Why don't you marry her ? "

" Why should I ? "

He shrugged his shoulders. " Wouldn't she like it better ? "

" Maybe. But I think she'd be wrong."

" Why ? "

I said, " I'm not a very good proposition for anybody to marry."

" I don't know," he said lazily. " Women have funny tastes."

I said, " I'm not keen to be anybody's funny taste."

There was a long silence. Dick's forehead was wrinkled up in a painful frown. It took me back a long way.

He said, " Look, Sammy. I wanted to say a thing . . ."

I grinned and said, " I thought you were going to ask me to help you with your prep."

" Well, it's a bit difficult. But this foot of yours. Well, it's bloody bad luck ; but hell, it doesn't *matter*, you know."

I said, " Of course, it doesn't."

" No. Only sometimes it does seem as though I've had all the luck, and it isn't fair. I mean I know about you. And so does that girl of yours. I mean, *she* knows."

I said, " Poor old Sue. She bloody well ought to."

" What I mean is, I don't think you ought to let it get on top of you, Uncle."

" No," I said, " I won't."

" Well, that's all right then," he said a bit doubtfully. " But honestly I wouldn't."

They turned us out of the pub at half-past ten. I walked along to the tube with him. He said, " Bungho, Sammy. Give my love to Sue. I'll let you know when I'm down again and we'll have a meal."

I said, " Good-bye, Dick." We shook hands. I saw the clerk grin at him as he took his ticket, and then he went down the escalator and out of sight.

VII

IN the middle of the week, Pinker rang up.

He said, " You know I mentioned somebody the other day that I wanted you to meet ? "

" What—Lewis Easton ? "

" No names, no packdrill," said Pinker quickly. " Well, I'm meeting the bloke in question this evening. Are you free to come ? "

I hesitated for a moment. Easton was a very big shot and I should have liked to meet him. But I knew that he and the Old Man were at daggers drawn, and I wasn't sure what Pinker was up to.

I said, " What are you meeting him for ? "

" Oh, just for a chat," said Pinker. " We meet from time to time and plan a quiet murder or two. He's a useful chap to know. I've told him about you and he wants to meet you. Can you manage it ? "

"I'm not really sure . . ." I said, trying to make up my mind.

"It'll only be for half an hour."

"Look," I said using one of my usual rather gutless devices. "I'm not really sure yet about this evening. Can I leave it that I'll come if I can?"

Pinker made doubtful noises.

I said, "After all, I suppose you'll be going anyhow?"

"Yes," said Pinker a bit doubtfully. "Well, look here—come if you possibly can. It's rather important."

I said, "I'll do my best."

"Fine," said Pinker. "Seven o'clock at the United. See you then."

He rang off. He sounded rather irritated. I think he guessed I didn't mean to come.

Joe had turned in some notes on the Keystone Komics about using recoil to work a power traverse. I was rather out of temper with Joe altogether, and this thing didn't help. It was a sloppy sort of job. He'd just rung somebody up, got some vague information about work done several years ago that had been a flop, and then decided that this thing was no good. As far as I could see the previous people had been barking up a completely different tree.

I said, "This idea may be no good, Joe, but you can't prove it like this. You might as well say that aeroplanes are no good because the people who tried to work them with steam engines didn't get far."

"Waterlow says the whole field's been thoroughly explored," said Joe.

"Maybe it's been explored. But if so, where's the map?"

"How d'you mean?"

"What did they do, and what results did they get?"

"What I've put in my notes," said Joe with pointed forbearance.

I said, "Well, that's one small, very badly-designed experiment with inconclusive results."

"It's all Waterlow could give me," said Joe sulkily.

"Did you go and see him?"

"No. I rang him up."

"Well, damn it all," I said, "this chap's taken a lot of trouble and used a lot of brains. We can't just throw the thing back at him after five minutes telephone conversation with Waterlow."

" You can't expect me to spend weeks on it," said Joe off-handedly. " I've got too much to do to spend a lot of time on damn' fool suggestions like that."

Till looked up and said, " Doing what ? "

" What ? "

" What are you busy doing ? Telephoning your wife ? "

" What the hell's it to do with you ? " said Joe, getting angry.

Tilly just grinned to himself and went on working.

" If it comes to that," said Joe, very red in the face, " it doesn't strike me that if I had done more, any use would have been made of it."

" Why not ? " I said.

" It never is," said Joe loudly. " Anything which is produced by any of us is altered or shelved if it doesn't suit somebody else's book. We get no backing."

I never liked Joe when he was doing his loud-voiced act, and this made me pretty savage.

I said, " There's no need to shout it round the town. When have you produced anything which has been altered or shelved ? "

" Or which hasn't, for that matter ? " said Tilly nastily.

Joe looked from one to the other and then said suddenly, " I wasn't thinking only of me. It's the same with all the work that comes out of here. We're just treated like—like stooges."

I said, " Well, we shan't stop that by producing this sort of stuff. It doesn't consider the idea at all. Have you read it, Tilly ? "

" No," said Tilly with a grin. " But I was here when he did the work on it. Took about three minutes."

Joe didn't say anything. His under lip stuck out and he looked like a kid that was going to cry. It was always the same with him. First he shouted and then he deflated and went hurt. He muttered something about, " Better go if that's what you think."

I said, " What you'd better do is to go and see Waterlow and find out what *has* been done and when. You know that act of theirs. Nothing's ever any good if they did something remotely like it about the time of the Crimea."

There wasn't much in the Keystone Komics that week. The only good effort was a bloke who had invented a sort of underground tank or land submarine, which tunnelled along underground and came up in the enemy's rear. He hadn't gone into details of how it was to work. He just thought it was a good idea.

"He's been reading Jules Verne," said Joe.

I said, "What he's been reading is a life of Foch. Foch thought of that. It wasn't a bad idea then, when people had lines and rears and so on. Nowadays when you surfaced you'd be liable to find the whole shooting match had popped off into the next continent."

The rest were respectable, dull and pretty useless. It was amazing how many trained people made suggestions which were quite all right from an engineering point of view but just didn't make sense from any other—you *could* do it, but why should you? We called them the tame dog ideas. The wild cats were things that needed perpetual motion or a barrel two hundred yards long.

Joe was an unlucky cove in some ways. I've know plenty of people who were more stupid and lazier, and even a few who were as tactless, who never seemed to come to any harm. But whenever Joe made an ass of himself it always came back and slugged him within twenty-four hours. That same afternoon Waring suddenly said:

"Look, Sammy—I met Marchant coming in at about half-past ten this morning. It's your affair, but does that boy *do* anything? And if so, what?"

I said, "He looks after the Keystone Komics chiefly."

"Does he do a decent job on them?"

I was pretty fed up with Joe myself, after the Waterlow business, but I knew Waring had never liked Joe and I didn't want to give him an excuse for butting in.

I said, "Oh, Joe's not bad. He needs watching, but he can do very good work when he likes."

"Does he ever like?"

"Yes. Sometimes. He did a very good job on smoke."

Waring said, "Whenever I ask if he's any good, I'm told he did a very good job on smoke. That was about two years ago. Has he ever done a good job since?"

I said, "I find him quite useful."

Waring shrugged his shoulders. "Well, I can't help thinking Master Joe's a luxury and I'm not at all sure we can afford him."

I said, curtly "Well, you don't have to, do you?"

I was quite within my rights. The technical stuff was nothing to do with him. But for some reason that got under his skin. I saw his eyes flash and his lips go loose, and for a moment I thought there was going to be trouble. But he just said : "Oh no—it's your affair. I just thought that as there were just the three of you up there . . ."

I said, " I'll think about it."

Mrs. Taylor was in the hall when I came out. I suppose she was waiting for Taylor. When you came to look at her you could see that old Rose was right. She was talking to the hall porter, and using everything she'd got from the feet up. The porter was about five feet high with a face like a superannuated warlock. But that didn't seem to matter to her. She was chattering away and smiling and wriggling at him for all she was fit. I thought the old boy was looking a bit overwhelmed.

As soon as I appeared she turned it all on me. I should have liked to take a good look at her, but she wasn't the sort of person you could very well take a good look at. She smiled at me and said, " Good morning," with a queer accent which seemed half Cockney and half foreign. I just had time to see that she had very white teeth and a rather broad, almost negro-looking nose. I said " Good morning," and went on. As I went upstairs I remembered old Taylor's face, and the sweat on his forehead, and wondered how the hell he'd come to do it.

I had promised to send some stuff down to Waring right away, so I took it down and gave it to Susan. She was just drinking her tea, and like a fool I stayed and had a cup with her. It was the sort of thing we usually took the greatest trouble not to do, and of course it went wrong on us. I hadn't been there two minutes before Waring came out of his office. He was looking very sour. I think he was probably still in a bad temper because I'd bitten him about Joe. He just glanced at me without smiling and then said to Susan :

" Is that stencil cut yet ? "

He said it from the other side of the room, as though he was talking to a junior clerk.

Susan said, " It's in the machine now."

" How long will it be ? "

" About another half-hour, I should think," said Susan, glancing down at the copy.

Waring frowned. " Well, push on with it as fast as you can," he said, in a voice which meant, " Stop drinking tea and gossiping and get on with it."

I said, " . . . please."

Waring glanced at me but took no notice.

Susan looked a bit surprised, " I'm sorry," she said apologetically. " I didn't realise that it was urgent."

"Urgent?" said Waring angrily. " Of course it's urgent. If you take the trouble to read it through you'll see why."

Susan flushed, " When you gave it to me I understood that there was no hurry for it."

Waring said, " I told you there was no need to stay here all night doing it. That was yesterday morning. I certainly didn't mean that next week would do."

I had a curious sinking feeling in my stomach. I said, " Look here, Waring. Susan was working on that darned thing till eight o'clock last night."

Waring turned and looked at me in surprise.

" Well, what about it ? " he said. " D'you mind ? "

Before I could say anything Susan cut in quickly and said, " It's a fairly long job and I haven't been pushing it. It will be through in half an hour."

" Thank you," said Waring sarcastically. He turned and went back into his office and shut the door.

I looked at Susan and saw that she had tears in her eyes. I said, " The impudent bastard ! What the hell does he think he is ? " I started to go towards his door.

Susan said sharply, " No, Sammy."

I said, " Why not ? "

" It won't do any good. You're completely in the wrong." She pushed her cup aside and said, " Now go away and let me get on with this."

She looked down at the stuff, blinking a bit.

I said, " Look, darling—don't cry . . ."

" Oh, for Christ's sake . . ." she said crossly. " I'm not crying, I'm only furious."

" I'm not going to have that bastard talking to you like that."

" Then don't give him the chance."

" But he's only . . ."

Susan looked up at me and said, " Sammy, for God's sake go away before I throw something at you or him or some-body. I know it doesn't matter, and I know exactly what he is, and I want to get on with this. Now go away." She put her head down and started to type.

I went upstairs feeling sick. It always made me feel sick

79

if I got really angry. I didn't want to go back and sit in a room with Joe and Till, so I went into one of the little spare rooms and flopped down on a packing case, feeling utterly fed up with everything. It seemed to be one long succession of bloody things like this, and I was always left feeling that I ought to have done something about it and not seeing quite what. I couldn't make up my mind whether Waring had guessed about Susan and me, and was getting at me through her, or whether it was a coincidence. Anyhow, I was fed up with the constant scrapping and constantly heading him off my stuff.

I was still sitting there when one of the lab. orderlies came in. I got up quickly, feeling a bit of a fool.

He said, " Excuse me, sir—may I get something out ? "

He opened the case and started to root about, so I went back to the office.

There was a message asking me to ring Pinker.

He said, " Sorry to bother you, but the bloke we talked about can't make it until half-past seven to-night. That all right with you ? "

I suddenly realised that it was right in my hand.

I said, " Yes. That's all right. I'll be there."

I had meant to be a bit early at the United, but I had never been there before, and wandered into the Stewards which is next door. By the time I'd found Pinker and we had bought ourselves drinks, Easton was due.

Pinker said, " There's just one point about Easton—he's a wee bit heavy in the hand. You don't want to take any notice of that. He's a useful gun if he's pointed in the right direction. But he mustn't realise that he's being pointed."

" What particular way do you want to point him ? " I said.

" Oh, no particular way at the moment," said Pinker, squinting at the bowl of his pipe. " This is merely a reconnaissance of the site for the gun. The point is that he's got the National Scientific Council in his pocket, and from the look of it we may need their weight."

" Does that Council *do* anything ? "

" Not at the moment, because nobody uses them properly. That's Easton's big grouse. What he feels is that if there's to be a Central Scientific Council it ought to be in on a lot of these things."

" But how ? It doesn't know anything about them."

"Well, it certainly looks as though something needs doing," said Pinker. "All this squabbling and odd hole-in-a-corner stuff aren't getting us anywhere . . ." he broke off and said, "Ah—here's Easton."

We got up. Pinker and Easton shook hands and Pinker introduced me. I had never seen Easton before, though I had seen photographs of him. He was a big, portly man who moved and spoke rather slowly and pompously. He had a big white face with gold-rimmed glasses and his expression never changed. He didn't smile or frown. He just stared through his glasses at you as though you were a dullish newspaper.

Pinker was all smiles and rather obsequious. He said, "Rice is with Professor Mair's outfit, Sir Lewis, so he's got a fair amount of experience of the stuff we were talking about the other day.

Easton said, "Oh yes?" And looked at me as though I were a newspaper published by the Opposition. After a bit he said, "How long have you been with Mair?"

I told him. He nodded slowly.

"Were you engaged in his work on accelerating crystalisation?"

"No, sir. I was working in his lab. at the time but I was doing a job of my own."

"A job of your own," said Easton. "And what was this job of your own?"

"It was on temperature effects on fluidity. It was never published, but I'm finding it very useful now for some stuff I'm doing on low temperature lubricants."

"Now," said Easton, throwing back his head and staring up at the ceiling. "Will you enlighten me as to how you come to be doing work of that kind?"

I said, "I don't quite understand."

"Well," said Easton, "You tell me you are doing work on low temperature lubricants. I presume that this work is directed to the national effort?"

"Oh yes."

"Then who instructs you to do such work? Under whose supervision is it performed? Who finances it? Who directs you?"

"Well, as a matter of fact nobody instructed me to do this. It was an idea of my own."

Easton pursed his lips and nodded ponderously, "It was begun, in fact, through your own initiative?"

" Yes."

" You designed the work yourself without consultation with anybody ? "

" Yes."

Easton turned his head towards Pinker and spread out a hand expressively. He didn't say anything.

I said, " Of course that's unusual. Most of our work is stuff which the Ministry asks us to do."

" I see," said Easton. " You mean that the research departments of the Ministry make the request ? "

" Well no. More often I think it's arranged direct between the Minister and Professor Mair."

Easton stared at me expressionlessly.

" In fact, a completely unofficial arrangement ? "

" More or less. I'm afraid I don't know much about that side of it."

" No," said Easton, deciding to be just, even to me. " I don't expect you do. There is no reason why you should. Your duty is to carry out your instructions, and their origin is no concern of yours."

He sat for a bit and stared into the distance as though he had known it once but proposed to cut it now.

" Of course as you were saying, Sir Lewis, the thing cries out to be co-ordinated," said Pinker. " There's overlapping all over the place. Did I tell you that there are three sets of people working on sea corrosion, none of them knowing that the rest exist ? "

" I can well believe it," said Easton. " I should not be surprised if there were thirty." He brought his eyes back to me. " Do you read the reports of the National Scientific Council ? "

I hesitated and said, " I have seen one or two . . ."

" Reports are published monthly," said Easton. " The National Council, of which I have the honour to be chairman, publishes a report surveying all current research work, not of a Most Secret nature, of which it is aware. Do you see that report regularly ? "

" No," I said.

" Do you inform the National Council of your activities?"

" I don't personally. Professor Mair may. Of course the snag is that most of our stuff *is* ' most secret.' "

" There is, in addition, a Limited Circulation Bulletin which covers that aspect. Is your work recorded in that ? "

" I really don't know, sir. It's not my side of the house."

" But you would naturally expect that it would be ? " said Easton.

" I'm afraid I don't know enough about our relations with the National Council to know," I said rather uncomfortably.

Easton started to cut the middle distance again.

" Your relations with the National Council," he said ponderously, " and those of every other research organisation have been clearly laid down by the Cabinet. It is the remit of the Council to supervise, control and advise on all scientific work directed to the war effort, and to act as general advisers on all scientific matters to His Majesty's Government. That is the position directed."

That shook me. I'd never heard of Easton's council *doing* anything, let alone controlling all research.

" Of course it's rather a tall order," said Pinker quickly. " Presumably you'd have to de-centralise a good deal."

I said, " I don't quite see how you could have real centralised control. The field is so enormous."

" The extent to which the Council thought it desirable to de-centralise control of detail matters," said Easton coldly, " would be for the Council to decide. I was merely stating its terms of reference."

" Of course the *real* answer," said Pinker, starting his gun aiming process, " Might be to have an executive sub-committee of the Council, under your chairmanship, Sir Lewis, consisting of the chief people who are actually running research teams."

Easton stared at him blankly, " You mean men like Mair ? "

" Yes."

" Possibly," said Easton without enthusiasm. He turned back to me. " What does the rest of your staff consist of ? "

I told him. He didn't seem impressed.

" Now what's-his-name . . . ? " he looked towards Pinker. " The man you spoke of the other day ? "

" Waring ? "

" Yes. Now what are his qualifications ? Is he a physicist ? "

I said, " Oh, Waring's not primarily a technical man, of course."

" Then what sort of a man is he ? "

I hesitated for a moment.

Pinker grinned and said, " I think he's an advertising

man in private life, isn't he? Did science and then went into advertising. Isn't that it?"

"Yes," I said shortly. I wasn't in any mood to give Waring a testimonial, but by this time anybody Easton didn't like was a friend of mine.

"Advertising," said Easton.

"He's a very intelligent chap," said Pinker smoothly. "Though I don't think any of you would claim that he's an ace scientist, would you, Rice?"

I said, "That isn't his job."

"Which is . . . ?" said Easton.

"Oh, he does a lot of the contact work with Ministry departments and so on."

There was a pause. Then Pinker lowered his voice and said, "By the way, Sir Lewis—this is the man who did the work on the Reeves gun."

"Oh yes," said Easton, giving me an unusually flat stare. "You were responsible for the report that Professor Mair submitted?"

I said, "I wrote a report for Professor Mair. I don't know whether he submitted it."

"You have faith in the Reeves gun?"

That was a dirty one. I said, "I don't think I looked at it from that point of view. I'm not a soldier, and it's for soldiers to say what the military value of the thing is. I only report on what it will do."

"An admirable viewpoint," said Easton dryly. "Unfortunately your report does not appear to stick to it." He gazed at the ceiling. "You may be interested to know that a special sub-committee of the Council were given an opportunity to see the gun and reported in precisely the opposite sense."

I said shortly, "I don't know what was finally submitted, so I can't discuss it. But my report was simply a write-up of the figures from the official trials."

"Six of the most eminent scientists in the country," said Easton impressively, "were unanimous in condemning it."

"Did they see it in action?" I said, getting a bit fed up with it.

"They were given every facility," said Easton, obviously not knowing.

"The main thing is," said Pinker, "that these things ought to be ironed out before they go to the Minister. Otherwise we shall get to the point where people say, ' Oh, don't let's ask the scientists. They never agree.' "

Easton nodded, " Precisely. It was to avoid these purely individual expressions of opinion that the National Council was set up—so that science could speak with one authoritative voice."

I said, " Wouldn't it be better if the voice were a bit less authoritative and a bit better informed ? Sometimes I think we rather try to teach the production and services people their job."

Easton turned his head very slowly and gave me the flat hard stare that served him as an expression of anger, surprise, interest and amusement, depending on the context.

" You regard science as a humble handmaid, to speak when she is spoken to ? " he said coldly.

" No. But I don't see that a scientist's opinion is worth any more than any one else's when he isn't talking on scientific grounds."

" *Are* there grounds which are not, in the end, scientific?" said Easton oracularly.

" Is there any chance of getting this co-ordinating sub-committee, Sir Lewis ? " said Pinker, trying to get on with the gun aiming.

" I have given it some consideration," said Easton. " And I am considering appointing such a committee. There are difficulties, of course, which I need not go into. Unfortunately at the beginning of the war, Ministries had no proper scientific advice, and some very dubious appointments were made. It is difficult to put these things right, once they have started badly."

Easton went about eight o'clock. He shook hands with me and said he was pleased to have made my acquaintance. Then he took Pinker away and led him by the arm towards the door, talking on the way.

Pinker came back with a broad grin.

" Bit sticky, isn't he ? "

I said, " He's about the nearest thing to God Almighty I've ever met or ever want to. Why the Pete did you want to let me in for that ? "

" I thought you ought to meet him."

" Why ? It put me in a bloody awkward position, being cross-questioned like that."

" I didn't know he'd wade in quite so fast," said Pinker.

I said, " Anyhow, this business about the Central Council
is pure hooey. It consists chiefly of old boys of about eighty
who haven't done a job of work for thirty years."

" Oh, of course," said Pinker. " Don't worry. They
won't do anything. He knows that perfectly well. Easton's
a darned sight shrewder than he looks."

I said, " He needs to be. He's got a face like a discon-
tented cod."

Pinker said, " He liked you anyway."

" What's he like with people he doesn't like, then ? "

" Oh, terrific. He can be about as rude as anybody I've
ever met."

" Maybe. But can he stop when he likes ? "

" Oh, he's all right," said Pinker. " Quite all right when
you get to know him. The useful thing is that he's got a
hell of a pull high up."

" I don't call that useful. I call it terrifying."

" Oh, you don't have to worry about him," said Pinker.
" Get the co-ordinating committee and we can see that the
right people are on it."

" But why Easton to run it ? Why not Mair ? "

" Because, frankly, I don't think the boys would play
with Mair."

" Well, Mair won't play with Easton. He loathes him."

Pinker shrugged his shoulders.

I said, " Look—get this right if you must mess about
with it. Mair may be a bit wild-cat at times, but he's out
of the class of most of these blokes. That's why they don't
like him. He knows what their reputations are worth. Take
Easton himself. He's never done a damn' thing to justify
his standing. He's simply a social climber who happened to
choose the science ladder."

" Anyhow," said Pinker with a grin. " He doesn't seem
to like the boy Waring."

" Hell ! " I said moodily. " It's no good dragging people
in just because they don't like R.B. We can do that by
ourselves." I didn't like the sound of it at all.

VIII

THERE was no doubt that our name outside was getting more
like mud every day. When my low temperature lubrication
stuff came through I rang up little Knollys of the Arctic

Areas Research Lab. and suggested that I should come along and see him. He was a decent little soul and very intelligent, and I thought he'd be interested. He seemed a bit odd about it, but finally we fixed up a time. I'd known Knollys long before the war, and I was glad to see him. But he was very queer. He talked in a low voice, and once when somebody came in he jumped up and stood between me and the door in a guilty sort of way. Finally I got fed up and said, " Look—what's biting you ? "

Knollys grinned rather sheepishly, polished his glasses and didn't answer for a moment.

Finally he said, " Well, Sammy, you know how delicate the situation is."

I said, " What situation ? "

" Oh, you know—all the internal politics."

" I know about forty-seven different sets of internal politics, but I didn't know you came into any of them."

Knollys said, " Well, you know how Hereward feels about Mair and—and all of your stuff."

" As it happens I don't. What *does* he feel ? "

" Well, frankly, he seems to me quite unreasonable about it."

" You mean he hates our guts ? "

" Yes." Knollys grinned apologetically. " I've been specifically ordered not to contact you."

" But in God's name why ? "

" He just doesn't like your having anything to do with this stuff." Knollys pegged at his blotter with a pencil. " You remember I sent you a note on some stuff we'd been doing on grease packing ? Well, I got a raspberry for that."

" What did he say ? "

" Just said it was nothing to do with you and he didn't want you butting in."

I thought about it. " So you oughtn't really to be seeing me to-day ? "

" Oh, that's all right," said Knollys. " He's away to-day. I think it's a lot of rot myself."

I said, " It isn't easy to do anything to win this war, is it ? There are such a hell of a lot of people who'd rather lose it than let you help. Anyhow, read through this and see what you think."

When Knollys had read it through he looked up and said, " Look, Sammy—you're on to something good here."

" You think so ? "

"Unless there's a catch in it somewhere. I don't think we've ever tried it that way round."

'That's what I thought. You can't go on these figures of course. I just had to mock the thing up with our small chamber. What we want now is a proper try-out."

"Well, that's easy enough," said Knollys. "At least it would be if . . ." We sat and looked at each other for a bit.

I said, "Your boss won't play if you tell him where it came from?"

"I'm in a difficult position," he said.

"Any good for Mair to put it to the Minister?"

Knollys shook his head. "You could get it tried like that. But it would mean that every one was out to shoot it down. It wouldn't get a show."

"Look," I said. "Your boss may not love us, but damn it all, there's a war on. Surely he wouldn't go kiddish over a thing like this? It really matters."

Knollys shook his head. "He's very queer about things like this," he said a bit helplessly. "Very sensitive about his position and so on."

I said, "Well, *Christ* . . . !"

After a bit Knollys said, "Do you really want to get this through?"

"If it's any good. What I want at the moment is a chance to try it out properly."

"Well, the only way you'll do it is to let him feel he thought of it himself."

I said, "He'd never have an idea like that if he lived to be a hundred and two."

"I know. But we've found that it's easily the best way to get things done."

I thought it over. It was a bit of a pill, because it was my personal baby.

I said, "All right then. How do we do it? Send him the thing?"

"Oh Lord, no!" said Knollys hastily. "Nothing like that. Somebody will just have to drop a word and get him interested and let it incubate."

"But I never see him."

"No," said Knollys. He pegged at his blotting paper for a minute and then said rather awkwardly, "Anyhow, I don't think it had better be you or he'll be suspicious." He saw my face and said, "It's all awful rot of course, Sammy."

I said slowly, " What you're saying is that not only must it be his idea, but I mustn't come into it at all ? "

Knollys didn't say anything.

" Is that it ? "

" More or less."

I suddenly felt damned angry. I said, " In other words I have an idea—an idea that may really matter to chaps who're fighting this bloody war. And just because you've got a jealous incompetent as a chief I've not only got to hand it to him, but daren't let him know I've got anything to do with it ? Why should I give *him* ideas ? This is an idea for soldiers, and that bullock's too fat to get through the hatch of a tank."

Knollys looked upset. He said, " Yes. Of course I see that. But I was only thinking of getting it through, you see, Sammy."

After a while he said, " Of course you can try it the other way—taking it to the Minister and so on. But you know what that always means."

We sat in silence for a bit. I knew he was right.

I said, " It's a damned good idea too, you know that."

" I think it's a brilliant job," said Knollys, as though he meant it. " That's really what makes it so—so difficult."

After a while I said, " All right. There it is. I don't see what else there is to do. Now what ? Can *you* put it up to him ? "

Knollys went a bit red and said, " Well—hardly."

" Why not ? You're on his staff. It wouldn't matter coming from you."

" Yes, but damn it—I don't want to—to bag your ideas . . ."

I said, " If there's a coconut or a large cigar coming to anybody out of this and I can't have it, I'd rather you had it than anybody."

Knollys said, " That's awfully nice of you, Sammy. But . . ."

" Bunkum," I said. " I don't really care much, I suppose, as long as it's done." I got up and said, " I'll simply leave it with you then. If you do try it out I'd awfully like to know what happens, just for interest."

" Of course," said Knollys. He hesitated and then said, " It is all *rot*, you know."

Coming back I tried damned hard to feel that it didn't matter who did it, but it didn't work. I felt like a kid that had had a toy taken away, and there wasn't anything to do about it. I never could be grown up about things like that.

Whatever else you could say about Waring, he worked pretty hard. But he had a nasty habit of firing a lot of stuff at Susan about half-past six, pushing off out to dinner, and coming back about half-past eight expecting it to be finished. It was a damned inconsiderate thing to do anyhow, but it worked out as something worse than that for us, because it meant that I got home first and had about an hour to put in alone when I was feeling tired and fed up, which was always risky. Usually if I knew Susan wasn't going to be home till very late I stayed on too. But sometimes she didn't get a chance to let me know.

It was like that on the evening after I'd seen Knollys. I went home about half-past seven, feeling utterly hopeless about the whole job and the war and me and God knows what. All I knew in the world was that I wanted to have a drink and forget it. But that had been going pretty well for a long time, and I didn't want to spoil it, so I just started to get the supper, thinking Susan wouldn't be long.

I went right on and got everything ready, cooked the sausages and potatoes, and even boiled a cabbage. By just after eight o'clock everything was ready and there wasn't another damn' thing to do, so I sat down and waited. Then of course the fun began.

Usually if Susan was going to be late she rang up. I thought, " By quarter-past eight she'll either be here or have rung up, so it's only a question of ten minutes." I sat looking at the cupboard which had the whisky in it and worked out that I could quite easily not have a drink for ten minutes. Then if she didn't come and rang up instead I should know how long she would be and could work something out.

When it got to twenty-past eight and she hadn't come and hadn't rung up I was stymied. I was sweating a lot and it felt as though I shouldn't last much longer. Reading and the radio were no good, and thinking about the job only made it worse. I suddenly found myself hating Susan and telling myself that it was her fault. She knew it would happen, and yet she hadn't even taken the trouble to ring up about it. I thought, " She'll come in with her worried expression on, and she'll say, " Darling, I'm *so* sorry " in that way I hate, and fuss about, and it doesn't mean a damned thing." I remembered her dancing with Iles, and Dick kissing her. I knew she'd liked it. Why shouldn't she? I thought, "She tries, but she's just a bitch really, like any other woman. I'm a damn fool not to face up to it, and to make her." I began to see what a fool I'd been to let myself get used to relying on her so much. There was something bloody humiliating in sitting there sweating and shaking because some damn woman was half an hour late. Anyhow, it was Susan who'd always made the fuss about it. If she couldn't take more trouble about it, the quickest way seemed to be just to have a drink and be done with it.

I got the whisky out, but there weren't any glasses on the table. I decided not to go out in the kitchen and get a glass until I'd tossed a penny and it had come down heads three times running.

It took a surprising number of tosses. Tails three times came quite quickly, and heads twice; but never heads three times. When it did turn up at last I went out into the kitchen and got a glass and decided not to go back into the other room until I'd got heads three times again.

It didn't take so long this time I went back and sat down and counted the number of letters on the label of the bottle, and then the numbers of each letter. Then I squared the number of each letter in my head and then squared the total. I was still sitting there with the glass in my hand doing this when Susan came in.

She stopped and said, "Oh Sammy, darling . . ."

I got up. My legs were very shaky. I chucked the glass down in the grate and said, "Thanks for all your help," and went out. As I went down the stairs Susan came out on to the landing and said, "Where are you going?" I didn't look back or say anything.

It was blowing hard outside, and raining in the wind. I was wet through with sweat, and the wind made me shiver. I hesitated, and then started to walk towards Notting Hill Gate. After about a hundred yards I heard somebody running behind me. I turned round and saw Susan.

She said, "I did try to ring up, but there's something wrong with the line."

I said childishly, "To hell with the line," and went on.

Susan kept beside me and said, "You haven't drunk any, have you?"

"No," I said. "I haven't drunk any."

She made an odd noise and said, "Tell me where you're going, Sammy."

I stopped and looked round and said, " I don't know."
" Woman ? "
" Maybe," I said. I hadn't thought of it.
She hesitated and said, " Well, how about me ? "
I thought for a bit and said, " All right. There's nothing else in sight so I suppose you'll do. Come and have a drink."
We went into the pub and I ordered two bitters. We sat down. I felt like a limp rag.
I said, " I've just walked out on the bitch I live with."
Susan said, " Go on ? Why ? "
I shrugged my shoulders. " Well, you see, I drink more whisky than's good for me."
Susan giggled and said, " Oo ! I do love wicked men."
" She knows that and yet she just bloody well left me to sit and look at a whisky bottle and sweat waiting for her to come home."
" Oh Christ, I know, I *know* ! " said Susan, beating her clenched hands together and looking away. " And you just sat there and didn't. I'm a useless bitch, darling—a useless bitch."
I said, " So when she *did* come I swep' out."
" So I should think," said Susan indignantly.
" It appears, however," I said, " that she tried to ring me up and couldn't. So I can't even have the satisfaction of being bloody annoyed."
" Yes, you can. Of course you can. She ought just to have come home and to hell with it."
It was warm in the pub and I was beginning to feel better. I said, " As a matter of fact, that wasn't too bad an effort. I couldn't have done it a few months ago."
" No. But what the hell's it done to you, I wonder ? " said Susan, looking at me thoughtfully. " That's what always worries me."
" Well, we can't have it both ways, can we ? It's not much fun at the time, but it's the only way."
Susan said, " Look—are you having me back now ? "
" Oh yes."
" I mean—you haven't left me or anything ? "
I said, " Oh no. I never had, much. It was mainly that I wanted to get out of that bloody room."
Susan shook her head. " Oh, you had left me quite a bit, I think."
" Well damn it, I had to have somebody to go for,

darling. I'd been telling myself that it was all your fault for hours."

Susan said, " God, that was a nasty journey home. I had three shots at ringing up and got ' number unobtainable ' every time. Then I just bolted for it. I still hadn't actually finished."

" It's about time an ultimatum was presented to R.B. pointing out that you like to get home before midnight every now and again."

The pub was full of uniforms, as usual. In fact except for an old Frenchman who looked like Zola, and was always there, I seemed to be almost the only male civilian in the room. What with Americans and Poles and Free French and this and that I was near being the only Englishman too. There was one very big handsome Free French officer who came in wearing one of those dramatic cloaks. He had a whole chestful of medals. He was with an R.A.F. pilot who was rather like a smaller edition of Dick. The whole party made me feel rather shabby and shrivelled in a queer way. Especially after what had just happened.

I said, " The foreign invasion is spreading West. Up to a little while ago you hardly saw any of this lot out here. They just milled round within a hundred yards of Piccadilly Circus. I suppose they're beginning to learn that a three-penny bus ride takes fifty per cent off the price of the drinks."

I wished as usual that Susan hadn't been quite so obviously a pip. The uniforms always looked at her a lot, and then went on and looked at me and pretty obviously wondered why she was out with me.

I said, " Have you noticed Beau Geste ? "

Susan said, " In the cloak ? No. I've been busy not noticing him ever since he came in."

" Well, what you can feel on the back of your neck is him gazing at you with fiery admiration."

Susan said, " There's no doubt that having the French and the Poles round has brightened life. Englishmen never stare at you unless you're their type and they're trying to pick you up. The French and the Poles just look round them passionately anyhow, and if you happen to be the nearest thing in a skirt you get it all. It raises a girl's morale. Like being pinched by Italians."

" Do Italians pinch."

" Oh Lord, yes. They pinch your bottom. It's a compliment."

I said, " Seriously, have you ever been pinched by an Italian ? "

" Yes. Once. In Rome."

" What did you do ? "

" I said ' Ouch ! ' or words to that effect. It made me jump."

" What did he say ? "

" Oh, he did a very white-toothed grin and said something about ' Bella ' and went on. He was only registering good will."

I said, " It's odd, but I've never been any good at that sort of thing."

" What ? Pinching strange females ? "

" Not necessarily pinching them. I'm just no good at registering interest. It makes me shy. Now, young Dick can do it. He's miles shyer than I am in some ways. But show him a girl he likes the look of and he just wades in perfectly calmly and collects her. Using force if necessary."

Susan said, " Well, but . . . " and stopped.

I said, " Well, but what ? "

" I was going to say that's more his line of country than yours."

I said, " What you were going to say was ' Well, he's a big handsome kid of twenty-five and you're not very handsome, or very big, or twenty-five and you limp.' "

Susan blushed and said, " I wasn't going to say anything of the sort, ass."

" Liar ! " I said gently.

" I'm *not* a liar," said Susan irritably. She looked down at the table for a moment and then looked up at me angrily and said, " You mustn't do that stuff, Sammy. It's a maddening trick. You don't believe it yourself and you know nobody else does. It's a complete pose and a very silly one."

" All right," I said. " Forget it. I'm an Adonis and we all know it. Let's have another beer."

About ten o'clock I suddenly thought of the dinner.

I said, " My God—I cooked the supper and it's still in the oven."

We went back. The food was a bit dried up, but it was still eatable. I said, " What with the bottle on the table and a smashed glass on the floor it doesn't really *look* like a notable teetotal effort, does it ? " I put the whisky away. It seemed queer that an hour ago I'd been sitting there

94

looking at it like a rabbit looking at a snake. It didn't mean a thing to me now. But of course it was always like that.

By the time we'd had supper and I'd told Susan about Knollys, it was getting pretty late, and we were dog tired, so we went to bed. Quite a long while after, Susan said, " Sammy—are you asleep ? "

I said, " Yes, why ? "

" It's about what you said in the pub to-night. You know—about you and Dick."

" About my not being twenty-five and handsome ? "

" Yes, I think there's something important there."

I said, " You're telling me, darling."

" I mean what you say about it. I've often thought about this, and I believe it's what's wrong with you in lots of ways."

I said, " What is wrong with the poor is poverty."

" But you *aren't* poor. That's just the point. You've made up your mind that you can't do things, and so you don't even try. And if you do try, you start out thinking it won't come off."

" As far as I can see I'm usually right."

" Bunkum ! How about this evening ? "

" Well, this evening was hardly a triumph, was it ? "

" Of course it was. It was a grand show."

I said, " Well, if it's a grand show not to get drunk, the whole thing's easy. I shall now put up a series of grand shows by not murdering anybody, not burgling a bank, not seducing other people's wives, and so on."

Susan said, " Don't be an ass, Sammy. This is really important. The truth of the matter is that you've got lots of things—abilities and so on, as you quite well know. But for some reason you never think about that. You only think about the things you haven't got which some other people have."

I said, " E.G.—two feet."

" Yes. All right. Well, that means you can't be a professional footballer. But what the hell difference does it make apart from that ? "

I said, " This is the second time within the last few days that I've been assured that it doesn't matter."

" Who else said so ? "

" Dick."

" Well, he was probably saying more or less what I'm saying."

95

"Yes, darling. But there was less of it and I wasn't trying to go to sleep."

Susan didn't say anything. I think she was looking hurt.

I said, "Darling, it's all right—all your geese are swans. Of course they are." I put my arm round her.

"Yes, but I hate you to say things in that bitter way that you did to-night. If you say them enough you'll begin to believe them, which is too darned silly."

I said, "Now listen, honey. I said I was not twenty-five, which is true. Check it up at Somerset House if you like. I said I was not very big which is also true. I'm average size. I said I was not handsome. Well, I'm not. I have nice eyes and nice hands, and look reasonably intelligent, but handsome you could not call me. And I said I limp, which I do. So what?"

"I dare say. But you were making it a reason why you couldn't attract women. Which is bunkum. You're obviously attractive to women."

I said, "Now you're talking. Come here and say that again."

IX

THE next thing I heard from Stuart was a telegram which turned up just as I was leaving the office about half-past seven one night. It said, "Number fourteen General Hospital, Lowallen. Urgent."

I looked up Lowallen. It was a good hundred and fifty miles away and there was no train that would get me nearer than fifty miles away from it before the morning. But there was one at five a.m. that would get me there by nine.

I rang up the hopsital. It took me over two hours to get through. Stuart couldn't come to the telephone, but he sent a message saying that the early morning train would do, so I went on that.

The hospital was a good way out of the town, and I didn't get there until half-past nine. It was a brand new place in a big park. They were still building bits of it. As I walked across the park with an orderly to find Stuart I noticed that the leaves were falling fast. I hadn't even noticed they were turning. That seemed queer, because in peace-time they are one of the things I always look for.

Whatever Stuart had got it wasn't in a ward. It was in a

separate block. They wouldn't let me go in at first, but Stuart came out when they told him I was there.

I was rather shocked at the sight of him. He looked absolutely all in. His face was yellow and very drawn, and his eyes were bloodshot.

He said, " Hallo, Rice. It's good of you to have come."

I said, " Sorry I couldn't get down last night. There was no train."

" It doesn't matter," said Stuart wearily. " You couldn't have done anything."

" What is it ? Another kid ? "

" No, thank God. It's a soldier, Gunner. Not that that's so much better."

I said, " Is he badly hurt ? "

Stuart looked at me in half surprise. Then he looked away and said, " Oh Lord, yes. The only wonder is that he's still living. He ought to have been dead hours ago."

" Can he tell you anything ? "

" When he's conscious. There was about two minutes last night when he could talk quite sensibly, and another few seconds early this morning when he was half awake. But since then he's been right under."

I said, " You've been with him all night ? "

" Yes. It was the only thing to do. Come inside. I don't think he'll come round again, but you never know."

We went into the room, which was quite small. There was a screen round the only bed in it. A nurse was sitting by the bed reading. Stuart nodded to her and she got up and went out.

The gunner was lying propped up with a lot of pillows. You could only see one of his closed eyes and half of the lower side of his face, and that looked absolutely drained and like wax—even his lips. The rest was bandages. He looked a very small man.

I said, " How old ? "

" Twenty. Field gunner."

I looked at him and said in a low voice, " What chance?"

" Oh, none at all. I tell you, he ought to be dead now. The doctors are quite annoyed about it. Apparently pretty nearly everything that could happen to him has."

Stuart dropped into a chair rather wearily.

I said, " How much has he told you ? "

" Quite a lot. At least, a lot compared with what we knew before." He opened a notebook. " He was walking up on the old golf course with another chap from his battery. The thing was lying on the hard sand in a bunker. It was a cylinder, just over a foot long and two inches in diameter. At least, that's what I made of it. He said it looked like a big electric torch, with a cap on the end and all. The pathetic part of it is that being gunners, they thought it might be some sort of shell. It was about the right shape. Then they saw that it wasn't. Some of it was black and some bright red, but I couldn't get that bit very clear." He paused and frowned at his notes.

"Did they pick it up?"

"His pal did. They were quite sensible. I mean they didn't rush forward and kick it or throw it about. They didn't know what it was, and they thought it might possibly be something dangerous. This boy wanted to leave it alone, and report it. But his pal was afraid they'd be laughed at as cissies. Being gunners, again, they probably knew enough to know that most things don't blow up unless you knock them about or arm the fuse or take a pin out or something. So they decided to carry it back to camp. This boy's pal picked the thing up, and up she went."

"Immediately?"

"That I'm not sure about. He went under again before I got clear just what his pal did and at exactly what point the thing exploded. The other thing I couldn't get was whether the thing was just lying clear or whether it had marked the sand as though it had fallen from a height."

"It was hard sand?"

"Fairly packed. You know how a bunker gets when it isn't raked."

"Had planes been over?"

"They're over here all the time."

"The other chap was killed of course?"

"Oh yes. Frightful mess."

"Fragments?"

"A few. Nothing to help much. Incidently it's pretty certainly plastic. This boy thought it was a big bakelite torch at first glance."

Stuart paused and passed his hand over his eyes.

I said, "Look here, you're damned tired. Why not go and get a bit of sleep? I'll stay with him."

Stuart shook his head. "No. I'd rather stay now. I'm quite all right." He brushed his hand over his hair and shut his eyes. "What we've *got* to get out of him if there's the slightest chance, is exactly what the other boy did to the thing, and whether it had made a mark in the sand."

" You've got a lot out of him already."

" Yes, but those two things are vital. Sooner or later we're going to have one of these things to play with. We *must* know at least some of the things not to do. Did this chap pick the thing up, or did it go up as he put his hand near it or on it ? If he did pick it up was he holding the end or the middle ? Did he hold it level ? See what I'm getting at ? "

" Oh yes," I looked at the gunner and said, " I don't think you're going to get any more out of this poor devil though."

" Nor do I. But we mustn't lose any chance there is."

I said, " They were both carrying metal ? "

" Oh Lord, yes. Bags of it. So that's still in."

I thought about it and said, " I can't see why Jerry does this. You wouldn't think it would be worth his while."

" Worth his while ? Of course it is. Do you realise that every single one of these damned things he's dropped so far has killed at least one person, and sometimes more ? You compare that weight for weight and cost for cost with most bombs."

After I'd been there about a couple of hours, one of the doctors came in to look at the boy. He was a rather fat chap, very bald, with a red face and brilliant blue eyes. He had a hearty slap-you-on-the-back manner which he switched on and off like a motorist dipping his headlights. He switched it on while we were introduced, switched it off while he examined the boy and switched it on again as soon as he turned away from the bed and told us he thought the gunner was as near dead as no matter.

He beamed at Stuart and said, " I'm afraid it's no go, captain."

Stuart said, " You don't think he'll come round again ? "

" Very surprised if he does. Might do of course. But it's very unlikely. He's fading out. Just-fading-out." He beamed at us, looked back at the boy, switched off and looked as though he didn't like it at all. Then he came back to us, switched on and said, " A couple of hours—maybe more, maybe less. Extraordinary business he's lasted so long. Extraordinary thing, the human body." He switched off and thought about that one. Then he had another look at the boy, shook his head, switched on his headlights at us again and pushed off.

I said, " He seems a cheerful sort of cove."

" Yes. But he's all right," said Stuart. " He doesn't think it's very funny really. I talked to him last night."

" You'll hang on until the boy actually goes ? "

" Oh yes."

We sat for a long time in silence. Then Stuart suddenly said in a queer voice. " Look, Rice—I went to sleep last night."

" You mean while you were sitting up with him ? "

" Yes. I'd told the fool of a nurse to wake me if she saw me dropping off and she didn't. When I woke up his eyes were open and he was conscious. She hadn't even noticed." Stuart's face twitched. " He may have been conscious for a long time. I'd been asleep for half an hour." -

" I don't suppose he had," I said a bit awkwardly.

" But supposing he had ? He might remember that I wanted something from him and have wanted to tell me."

I said, " He would have spoken and she would have heard."

" He couldn't see her. She was sitting over there. Anyhow he could only mutter. When I woke up he was looking at me."

" And he went under again soon after ? "

" Yes. It was a matter of seconds. I didn't really get anything."

I could see Stuart was shaken up about it, but there wasn't anything to say.

They were very nice to us, and brought in some lunch on a tray so that we could stay with him. The doctor came back at about two o'clock, and while he was looking at the gunner I saw him stiffen. Then he suddenly said quietly :

" Here you are, Stuart," and stepped back a bit, holding the boy's wrist in his fingers. The one eye that we could see was open.

The doctor said, " Quickly."

Stuart leant forward close to the boy and said, " Look, old man—did Rob pick it up ? "

The eye moved round to him. You couldn't see any expression for the bandages. There was a sort of very short, quick panting noise.

"Did Bob pick it up off the ground? Try to tell us. It's very important." The quick panting went on. It seemed to be blowing the boy's lips in and out slightly. Once it stopped, and the lips moved as though he was trying to say something. But nothing happened.

Stuart said, "Did Bob pick it up, old man?"

The panting started again and the eye closed.

The doctor looked at Stuart and shook his head. He was still holding the boy's wrist.

Stuart's face was the colour of dirty paper. He looked at the gunner for a moment and then turned to the doctor suddenly and said, "Can I do any harm now?"

The doctor hesitated and shrugged his shoulders. I saw Stuart take a deep breath. He suddenly said, loudly and rather harshly:

"Peterson ' Open your eyes and listen to me."

The eyelid fluttered and half opened.

"Did Roberts pick that thing up or did he not?"

The panting stopped again. Stuart took a quick step, pushed the doctor away and took the boy's wrist in his hand.

"Come on now," he said roughly. "Tell me. Did Roberts pick it up? Come on, speak up, man."

For just a second there was a pause. Then the boy's lips moved and he quite distinctly framed the word "Yes."

"He did?"

The lips said "Yes" again.

"By the end or by the middle?" The lips quivered for a moment and then closed.

"By the end or by the middle?" said Stuart again loudly. He was leaning forward and the sweat was standing on his forehead. The boy's lips moved and he breathed something. I think it was "Sir." Stuart's face broke in a queer way. He didn't say any more for a moment or two. The boy's eye was still half open but you couldn't see anything but white now and the panting had stopped.

Stuart turned to the doctor and said in a level voice, "I can't feel any pulse now. I think he's probably dead."

The doctor took the wrist, felt for a moment or two and nodded. He bent over the boy and then straightened up and said:

"Yes. He's gone." He looked at Stuart and said gently, "You got some of what you wanted. He said 'Yes.'"

Stuart nodded. Then he said, "Excuse me a minute," in an odd voice and went out. The doctor said:

" Go and see he's all right, old man. He's had enough.
I must see to this."

I went after Stuart. Going out I took a last look at the
gunner. He was lying just as he had been when I first came
in, but he was quite different.

I went back to town the same night. There was no more
to do. Stuart promised to send me on a copy of his notes,
and we agreed that he must press for a broadcast warning
about the things, now we knew what they looked like ;
though we'd no guarantee that they were always like that.

I was beginning to be worried about Stuart. He pulled
together very quickly, and ten minutes after we came out
of the ward seemed quite all right. But there was some
funny stuff going on inside him. He was one of these quiet,
competent chaps who don't stay quiet and competent
without paying for it. It seemed to me that the whole thing
was going a bit queer on him, and leaving him with a feeling
that he had let somebody down. I wasn't sure who the
somebody was, and I didn't think Stuart knew either. But
it struck me that the job had to be settled soon, or it was
going to do him no good at all.

I got back to the office at four, and stepped right into the
middle of it. There was a message from Waring asking me
to go down as soon as possible, and as soon as I went in he
said :

" Christ, Sammy, where have you been ? I've been trying to get you all day. Get the stuff and let's push along
right away."

I said, " What stuff ? "

" The Reeves gun figures. Haven't your boys told you ? "

" Nobody's told me anything. I just got a message saying
you wanted me."

Waring said, " God, that boy Marchant is a lazy skunk.
I gave him the whole dope and told him to get on to you
wherever you were. There's a big meeting on the Reeves at
four-thirty at Gloucester House."

" Who's coming ? "

" Oh, a hell of a crowd. Apparently Lewis Easton and
the soldiers have both been shooting at it and the Minister's
told Jake Gladwin to hold a round table conference on it
to tell all parties where they get off." He grinned his cheerful
grin. " You're the evidence for the prosecution."

" Is the Old Man going ? " I said, not liking the sound of it.

" Yes, rather. I've told him that it's time he stopped not speaking to Easton and started to be rude to him instead. He's all steamed up to thump the table."

I said, " Look here—you do realise the situation don't you ? Nothing that we've got proves that the Reeves is marvellous."

" Oh, to hell with that," said Waring lightly. " The Minister's sold. Gladwin knows what answer he's got to get. This party is just to bump off Easton & Co." He glanced at his watch. " Nip and get your stuff, Sammy. We haven't got long. We can talk about it in the cab."

I had hoped that Mair would come with us, so that I could at least tell him where the danger spots were. But apparently he was going straight to the meeting from home.

On the way I thought it over, and the more I thought about it the less I liked it.

I said, " Look, R.B.—let's get this straight. If these boys start talking figures we're sunk. The one argument for the Reeves is that it's a damned good idea. But as it stands at the moment it *isn't* a damned good *gun*. See ? "

" Oh, it isn't perfect," said Waring. " We all know that. Where's the pilot model that is ? "

" It's not only not perfect. It's still fundamentally wrong in quite a few ways. It's nowhere near the pilot model stage really, and if they put it into production like this there'll be an awful mess. Does the Old Man realise that ? "

" Oh, he knows the position," said Waring rather irritably. " He's seen all the stuff."

I said, " I should have thought you would have been better off without me. Then if you're questioned on details you can ask for notice, whereas if I'm there you can't. I'd keep them off my side of the stuff if you can, R.B. Honest I would."

" Yes," said Waring. " I think you're right there. But anyhow I don't expect there'll be any question of detail. It'll just be the usual chit-chat."

The main conference room at Gloucester House was a big, high, dark place with a table about twenty-five feet long. It you were sitting more than half-way down the table you couldn't hear a word of what was said at the top because of the noise of traffic. We always used to say that most of the odd decisions that were made in the Ministry happened because a bus went by at a conference.

We were a bit late and about a dozen people had turned up already and were standing about talking. Lewis Easton was there, looking as fish-like as ever, talking to a big man with black hair and a blue chin, whom I didn't know. There were Colonel Holland, a brigadier and a gunner major, and about half a dozen of Gladwin's people from the Ministry. Neither Gladwin himself nor Mair had shown up yet.

The conversation died down as Waring and I came in, and there was a rather awkward silence for a moment. Then everybody started to talk again. You didn't have to be very sensitive to know that there were a good many guns pointing our way. Waring didn't seem to notice. He went over and started to talk to some of Gladwin's people. I said, " Good-afternoon," to old Holland. He nodded rather coldly without saying anything, and went on looking at me in a quizzical way as though he wasn't sure whether he wanted to know me or not. Finally he said :

" Well—come to show us the figures, eh ? " He turned to the brigadier and said, " This is the chap who proves that black's white to three places of decimals."

The brigadier said, " Are you one of Easton's crowd or one of Mair's ? "

" Oh, he's one of Mair's," said Holland.

" So many scientific lots, I don't know which are which," said the brigadier, turning to Holland. He said it quite pleasantly.

Before I could think of anything to say Jake Gladwin and Mair came in. Gladwin was a big man with a fat white face that was always sweating slightly. He came in and dived into the chair at the head of the table as though he was playing musical chairs and said, " Well, gentlemen, let's get started," in his high squeaky voice.

Mair sat down on Gladwin's right, and Waring plumped down next to him. I hesitated about where to sit. I never knew at meetings whether to bag a place near the Old Man at the top, or whether to reckon that we sat in rank order, which brought me pretty near the bottom. Easton and his pal and the soldiers all went and sat on the opposite side of the table rather pointedly. Luckily, Gladwin's people just went and sat in a heap at the very bottom of the table from sheer force of habit, which made the whole thing look funny.

Gladwin looked down the table and squeaked out, " Oh, come on, friends, come up higher. Shan't be able to hear you. Won't be able to hear me. Gather round."

Finally we got sorted out. I sat next to Waring, with the soldiers and Easton opposite and Gladwin's people scattered about.

Gladwin wiped the sweat off his forehead and said, " Gentlemen, I have called this meeting on the Minister's instructions to clear up the position about the Reeves gun. The Minister has his own views about the Reeves. But before making any final decision, he wants to be sure that the various points of view of you gentlemen are fully understood by us. There have been extensive demonstrations and experiments. The question now is, what have those experiments shown and what are we going to do about it ? " He gave his forehead a final mop and said in a loud crow, " That's all I want to say. Now you talk and I'll listen."

There was a pause. Then Gladwin said, " I believe Professor Mair has been interested in these experiments. Perhaps he'll give us his conclusions ? "

I looked at the Old Man a bit anxiously. The chances were that he would up and do one of his enthusiastic acts, which were always bad salesmanship. But he just went on filling his pipe and said slowly, " Well, in a few words, Mr. Chairman, I should say that the Reeves gun is one of the most promising developments I've seen—from some points of view. But that's only an opinion, and for my part I should prefer to hear other people before being too dogmatic."

Gladwin nodded. There was silence again. Then the brigadier said, " Well, frankly, Mr. Chairman, we don't like the Reeves."

" You don't, eh ? " said Gladwin. As he must have known they'd been fighting it tooth and nail for weeks, I thought he did pretty well to sound surprised.

" No. It has a lot of snags from the user point of view, and we don't think it has sufficient advantages to offset them."

" Well, of course that's the question," squeaked Gladwin. " What's the balance of advantage and disadvantage ? Everything has disadvantages." He sank back and mopped his forehead as though thinking that up had exhausted him. Nobody seemed to know the next line.

Easton had been sitting staring blankly at the window.

He turned and looked through the chairman and said, " It might possibly be of interest to the meeting, Mr. Chairman, to hear the views of the National Scientific Advisory Council, of which I have the honour to be chairman."

" Please," said Gladwin in a loud squawk.

" The National Scientific Advisory Council . . . " said Easton.

" Of which he has the honour to be chairman," Waring muttered in my ear.

" . . . is the body officially deputed by the Cabinet to offer advice on all major scientific issues. The Council appointed a special sub-committee to examine and report on the Reeves gun. Dr. Brine, who is with us here to-day, acted as convener of this sub-committee, which was given the fullest facilities for the examination of this weapon. I suggest that Dr. Brine should give the views of his sub-committee."

" Please," said Gladwin a bit pathetically, mopping away. I had the feeling that unless somebody really gave some views pretty soon, he would burst into tears.

The blue-chinned man stroked the blue part and said, " Well, Mr. Chairman, my colleagues and I approached this matter purely as scientists." He said it as though everybody else had approached it as income tax inspectors or jobbing gardeners. " And our conclusion was that scientifically speaking it was not a sound conception. Not at all a sound conception. In fact I'll go further and say that no scientist could feel happy about many of the principles involved." He sat back and looked pointedly at Mair. I glanced at the Old Man. His bottom lip was beginning to stick out—that meant he was bloody angry. The blue-chinned chap was obviously trying to be rude.

I scribbled on a bit of paper, " Ask if the sub-committee saw the gun fired " and passed it to Mair.

" I'm interested to hear that, Mr. Chairman," said the brigadier. " Because in our unscientific way that's what we thought."

" Just what scientific principles did *you* think were unsound ? " said Mair quickly.

The Brigadier hesitated and old Holland chipped in. " We're talking about different sorts of principles," he said. " We didn't like it because it had user snags. Dr. Brine is talking about principles of—of physics or something like that."

" Well, then, may we take Dr. Brine's statement first ? " said Mair, unfolding my note and glancing at it. " What didn't the sub-committee like ? " Before Brine could answer he added, " Perhaps first he could tell us who were his colleagues ? "

Brine said, " The sub-committee consisted of Professor Char, Dr. Goulder, Dr. Pease and myself."

Mair smiled. " One crystallographer, one vital statistician, one embryologist and one—let's see . . . ? " he looked inquiringly at Brine with a charming smile. It couldn't have been more beautifully done if he'd slapped his face.

Easton went very red and said icily, " If I might answer for Dr. Brine, he is, of course, one of the best-known organic chemists in the country."

" Right," said Mair. " Now we've got that straight." He leant back and added casually, " By the way—you did see the gun firing, I take it ? "

Brine hesitated. Then he said, a bit feebly, " We were not actually present at the trials."

" But you've seen the gun *fire* ? You didn't just look at it as a piece of furniture ? "

" No," said Brine defiantly. " We didn't see it firing."

Mair looked at him as though he were astounded. Then he said, " Oh . . . Well, well—never mind. Can we get back to what the committee didn't like ? "

It was very pretty. The wretched bloke Brine started off, but it was obvious that no one was going to accept him as evidence after that. What he said was quite all right though not very profound. But he was batting on a ruined wicket. Easton weighed in once or twice, but he was so darned pompous that he only made things worse. So far the Old Man had the meeting cold.

At last old Holland looked up and said, " Mr. Chairman, might we consider this from another aspect ? There seems to be some difference of opinion on the scientific side, and I for one am not competent to know who's right or wrong. But our objections to the Reeves aren't particularly scientific. Professor Mair may be quite right in saying that it's a grand idea, scientifically, but what we're interested in is whether it's a good *gun* as it stands."

This was just the line I wanted to avoid. I glanced at Mair, hoping he'd stall. But by that time he had his tail well up and he went in head first.

" Well now," he said cheerfully, " that's surely a matter

107

of fact. We've had experiments and trials. What do they say?"

The brigadier nearly saved him by shaking his head doubtfully and saying, "Of course trials are one thing, and service in the field is another. Far too many weapons are put out without proper user consultation. That's the trouble."

This was a grand red herring, because it woke up Gladwin's boys. They recognised the opening notes of one of the eternal rows with the army and started to rally round.

Styies, one of Gladwin's senior people, said, "One of *our* difficulties, Mr. Chairman, is that we can never get at the facts on which these user opinions are based."

"Hear, hear!" said another of the crowd.

"Our trials may not be very good," said Styles. "But at least they're an advance on looking at the thing, firing it twice and deciding that you don't like the noise it makes."

The brigadier went rather red and I thought we were safe. They'd quarrel happily now for an hour about whether the army knew what it wanted or not. But old Holland chipped in again and said, "Mr. Chairman, this is an old argument, and it won't get us far. Could we get back to Professor Mair's question—what do the results of the trials show?" He looked across at me and said, "I'm not a scientist or a statistician. But my reading of the figures I've seen suggests that, in practice, we don't *get* these advantages that have been talked about. I may be wrong."

"I think Colonel Holland's taking altogether too gloomy a view," said Mair, still in a high good humour. "Perhaps, Mr. Chairman, you'd allow Mr. Rice of my staff, to give us the facts. Mr. Rice has done all the statistical work on the trials."

"Please," squawked Gladwin.

Everybody looked at me. I took the papers out of my bag. I knew the stuff by heart. But it gave me time to think. My hands were shaking slightly. Looking at the figures it suddenly struck me that they probably wouldn't mean anything to the meeting, because nobody but some of Gladwin's boys would know the comparative figures for other weapons. I just started to read out the figures rather quickly.

It worked quite well. Gladwin leant back and mopped himself in a bored way, and Brine and the brigadier had that nice vacant look of people who are plodding on through the snow but have lost their way pretty thoroughly. I could see that Gladwin's crowd were a bit doubtful about what to do. They didn't like us, but if they shot at the thing they would be backing the army, which was dead against their principles.

When I finished there was a silence. Then old Holland suddenly said :

" That's fine, Mr. Chairman. Now may I ask Mr. Rice what it all adds up to ? "

I said, " I hardly think that's for me to say. I was merely giving the results of the trials."

" And on these results you think that the Reeves is a first rate weapon ? "

I hesitated for a moment and then said, " I think Professor Mair's already given the view of the section."

" And you share that view ? " said Holland quietly.

" Oh come ! " said Waring. " That's scarcely a fair question, is it ? "

" Why not ? " said Holland.

" Well, Mr. Chairman," said Waring. " I suggest that if Colonel Holland expressed a view, he'd hardly expect us to ask one of his junior officers if he agreed."

" Quite," said Gladwin. " I don't think you can ask Rice to argue with his chief, Holland."

Old Holland was still looking at me. He sat quiet for a moment and then he started to pat gently on the blotting paper in front of him.

" Mr. Chairman," he said quietly, " I want to be quite frank. We don't like this gun. We're told that those figures show that we're wrong. Professor Mair suggested that his expert should give us the facts. If Mr. Rice, who carried out this work, feels that his facts prove Professor Mair's case, I've no more to say. But surely I'm entitled to ask him what his figures mean ? " He gave his blotter a sharp pat. " After all, this is an important matter. We aren't debating, or defending a point of view. We're trying to get at the facts." He was still staring at me with his rather pale, washed-out blue eyes. His voice was very quiet. " If the Reeves gun is accepted, sooner or later men have got to fight with it. If there is anything wrong—if we've been too optimistic or anything has been glossed over . . ." He shrugged his shoulders. " *They'll* be the sufferers. We shan't."

There was a rather uncomfortable silence. This was the

first time anybody had said anything as though he really meant it.

"Well, well, Mr. Chairman," said Mair cheerfully. "Nobody wants to hide anything. If Colonel Holland would like Mr. Rice's views, I have no objection at all." He leaned back and gazed at me inquiringly.

"Well, Mr. Rice?" said Holland. He turned the light blue eyes on me again.

I hesitated, and then said slowly, "I agree with Professor Mair that the idea is excellent . . ."

"And the weapon?" said Holland.

"I don't think it's right yet."

There was a very faint rustle of interest.

"Would you be happy to see it accepted in its present form?" said Holland mercilessly. "On these figures?"

I could feel Waring's angry eyes on me. My throat was very dry.

I said, "No. I shouldn't."

Holland sat back in his chair. "Thank you," he said quietly. "That's all I wanted to know."

Easton said, "You agree, in fact, with the view of our sub-committee?"

"I don't know how your sub-committee arrived at its view," I said. "My opinion is simply based on the figures."

"I think it's rather important that that should be realised, Mr. Chairman," said Waring. "Mr. Rice is a technician and what he has given is purely a technician's view."

"Quite," said Gladwin, mopping his forehead very hard indeed. "The position's quite understood."

I looked round the table. It was understood all right.

Gladwin shut the meeting down as soon as he decently could and said something vague about reporting to the Minister.

As soon as we were outside afterwards I said, "I'm sorry, sir."

"Oh, that's all right," said Mair cheerfully. "I thought it was quite a good meeting. Made Easton and his sub-committee look pretty silly anyhow."

"Well, it didn't leave us looking very clever ourselves, did it?" said Waring bitterly.

"Why not?" said Mair in surprise. It was clear that he hadn't noticed anything wrong.

" Well, Christ . . . ! " said Waring irritably. " If you're
going to say one thing and Rice is going to say the exact
opposite . . ."

I said, " Well, what the hell was I to do ? I warned you
beforehand that we were on dangerous ground."

" You could have stalled," said Waring savagely. " As
it is, you've given old Holland and that other red-tabbed
stooge exactly what they wanted."

" I simply told the truth. I'm a physicist, not a salesman."

" Oh, *you're* all right," said Waring bitterly. " You came
out as the boy who couldn't tell a lie. The people who get
the sticky end are the Professor and I."

Mair was lighting his pipe. " Oh come ! " he said
calmly. " What's all the fuss about ? Rice was quite right
to give his views. I told him to."

" But in God's name *why* ? " said Waring explosively.

" Why not ? " said the Old Man in surprise. " We're all
entitled to an opinion."

You could see he didn't feel that anything awkward had
happened. He never did. But I knew he was wrong this
time.

X

ABOUT a week after our meeting on the Reeves, Pinker came
in. Joe and Tilly were both out. He looked round the room
and said, " My God, they do give you a bloody hole to
work in, don't they ? "

I said, " Not very grand, is it ? "

" Why don't you make a fuss about it ? " said Pinker.
" There are buckets of other rooms here, aren't there ?
That's one of the advantages of being an independent outfit."

I said, " I suppose we might do something about it. I
don't notice it much myself."

Pinker sat down, filled his pipe and said, " I've got a
bit of news for you. The Minister's on his way out."

" Our Minister ? "

Pinker nodded. He was looking at me with a slight grin,
obviously trying to see what I made of it.

I said, " When ? "

" Within the next few days. It'll be announced to-
morrow."

" Who are we getting ? "

" Pedder."

That was a facer. I said, " Good God ! That diehard?"

" Oh, he'll be all right," said Pinker calmly. " He'll do
as he's told. In his last job I'm told they had a marvellous
technique for dealing with him. They just used to tell him
that he mustn't bother with detail because his time was too
valuable. The old boy ate it, and they got him to the point
eventually where they only sent him about two papers a
week. They called it his ration."

" Is our Minister getting another job ? "

" I haven't heard. I think he's a bit unpopular in the
House at present, so they may be putting him back in store."

Pinker stuffed his finger into his pipe and said, " I think
with any luck we shall be able to put the Permanent
Secretary out to grass now. He would have gone long ago
if the Minister hadn't insisted on keeping him. If we cross
him off the inventory before Pedder takes over he'll never
be missed."

Pinker darted one of his sharp glances at me and said,
" What d'you think the effect of this will be on your outfit ? "

" You mean the Minister going ? No ideas."

" Well, you're his private baby, aren't you ? "

" I suppose so. Perhaps they'll just shut us down. As
far as I can see plenty of people would be glad enough."

" I doubt if they'll actually shut you *down*," said Pinker,
as though he wasn't at all sure about it. " But I think
there'll probably be—certain changes."

" Such as what ? "

Pinker waved his hand. " Your guess is as good as
mine," he said. He squinted at the bowl of his pipe. " I
understand that you had a rather sticky meeting about the
Reeves gun last week ? "

I said, " It was a bit difficult in places."

" So I heard. Had to tell your chief and Waring that
they were talking nonsense, didn't you ? "

" Oh, Lord, no ! " I said, quickly. " Nothing like that.
I thought the Old Man was rather good. He made mince-
meat of Easton."

" Yes," said Pinker doubtfully. " Of course that sort
of thing doesn't do him a bit of good." He shook his head
at me. " Waring shouldn't let him play politics. He doesn't
understand them."

I didn't say anything. I had an idea what was coming.

"Personally," said Pinker, "I shouldn't be surprised if old Pedder started asking, 'Why Mair?' I don't think he'll close the place down, but he likes everything done in form. And Mair's purely a personal appointment."

I said, "Well, the proper answer to the question 'Why Mair?' is 'Because he's about five hundred per cent. better than any one else you could get.'"

Pinker lit his pipe again and thought for a bit. "If Mair did go," he said, staring at me with his shallow brown eyes. "I think Waring would go too. He's got across too many people, that boy."

I said, "If Mair went and Waring went, they might as well shut down and done with it."

"Well, is that quite true?" said Pinker, looking at his pipe. "People have always told me that Mair messed about with fuses and acted as figurehead, that Waring did the talking and that you did the work?"

I said, "It depends what you call the work." I knew my face was going red, and felt a fool.

"This is even less to do with me than usual," said Pinker casually. "But I should have thought that if Mair and Waring did go, a new man ought to be able to carry on perfectly well—with you as his deputy." His eyes came back to me in a flat, non-committal stare.

I didn't say anything.

"To be quite frank," said Pinker, looking franker than possible, "That's why I wanted you to meet Easton. Easton's a very powerful man, and what's more, he's a buddy of Pedder's."

I said, "That was very nice of you." It seemed to be called for.

"I wasn't thinking of you," said Pinker. "I was thinking of the job."

"I shouldn't think either of my contacts with Easton so far will have done me any good."

"Oh, you're wrong there," said Pinker. "He liked you. He was particularly impressed by your performance at the Reeves meeting."

That was a bitter one. I had a sudden vision of Easton's fish-like face and of the Old Man lighting his pipe after, not realising that anything had gone wrong. I felt a bit sick.

I said, "You think there'll be a move to get rid of Mair?" Pinker blew out a cloud of smoke and nodded slowly. "Who will they want to put in?"

"I don't know. I should guess a chap named Brine."

"Oh—that bird?"

"Do you know him?" said Pinker.

"He was at the Reeves meeting."

"Oh, yes. I think Easton's been grooming him for the job for a long time."

"God!" I said in disgust. "What a swop for Mair!"

"You'd probably have to hold his hand pretty firmly," said Pinker. "Easton realises that."

I hesitated and then said, "Look—this seems to me a pretty rotten sort of business. Brine couldn't look at Mair's job really."

"He could with you helping him," said Pinker calmly.

"I doubt it. A lot of what the Old Man does is right out of my depth. And anyhow, damn it, why should I? I like Mair. He's good, and he's straight, and I've been with him a long time."

"Oh, I dare say," said Pinker rather impatiently. "Nice chap. Good husband and father. Admirable scientist for all I know. But he's got no tact. He's not the right man for a job like this." He shook his head with a frown. "It's no good being sentimental about these things."

"Sentimental, my boot. It so happens that I like Mair and don't like Easton or Brine. That's all."

"Damn liking them," said Pinker. "It's the job that matters."

"All right. Then it so happens that I think Mair is good and that Easton and Brine and Co. aren't in his class. It comes to the same thing."

Pinker hesitated for a moment. I could see that he was darned annoyed. But he just said, "Oh, well. Have a think about it and let me know how you feel. As I say, it's nothing to do with me. None of it may happen."

He got up and took his hat and case.

I said, "The Minister going is definite?"

"Oh, yes. That's fixed. But the rest is pure guesswork. All this is quite off the record, of course. I mean—I don't want any of it to get round to Mair. Or Waring."

I said, "Of course not."

"Righto," said Pinker putting on his gloves. "Well, if I hear any more I'll give you a ring. Till then—cheerio."

As soon as he'd gone I wondered if I'd said the wrong thing and ought to have stalled more. I was afraid of Pinker in a queer way.

I was still thinking about it when Knollys rang up. He said, " Look, Sammy. I'm frightfully sorry but I've made a pig's-ear of that low temperature stuff of yours."

I said, " How ? "

" I talked to the big white chief and he seemed very interested and asked a lot of questions, so like a fool I showed him your paper. It wasn't signed or anything, but he pounced on it at once and wanted to know who'd given me authority to do it and so on. Finally I had to tell him that you'd done it and passed it on to us in case we were interested. Honestly, Sammy, anybody would have thought you'd picked his pocket."

I said, " So now he won't do anything about it ? "

" Oh, worse than that. He went haring straight off to the Permanent Secretary to lodge a complaint that Mair's outfit is interfering in his affairs and doing things behind his back and God knows what. I'm afraid he means to make a row."

I said, " Oh, well. It can't be helped. Don't worry."

He said, " I'm frightfully sorry, Sammy. It is a lot of nonsense."

The balloon went up the same afternoon. Waring rang up and asked me to go down to the Old Man's room. The Old Man had a letter in front of him. He looked rather upset. He passed it over to me and said, " Do you know anything about this ? "

I read it. It was a lovely effort from Hereward. It ran, " It has come to my notice by indirect means that your organisation has been engaging in work falling properly within the scope of this department. I must point out to you that my terms of reference make it quite clear that *all* work of this kind must be subjected to my consideration and approval before it is begun. The matters raised by you are already fully in hand, and I am sure you will agree that this useless and unofficial duplication on a small scale of work for which I am responsible to the Minister must cease forthwith. I propose to take no further action in the matter provided I receive your personal assurance that these activities will cease at once, and will not be undertaken in future."

" What the hell's he talking about ? " said Mair. " Do you know ? "

I said, " Yes. It's my low temperature lubrication stuff."

" Low temperature lubrication stuff ? "

" Yes. I've been working on it for a long time."

" Well, it's the first *I've* heard of it," said Waring, looking at Mair.

" It wasn't in the sort of stage where you'd have been interested," I said. " I talked to Professor Mair about it a long time ago. You may remember, sir ? "

" I've got a vague recollection of it," said Mair. " But anyhow, what on earth have you been doing to Hereward to make him write a letter like that ? How did he get hold of it ? "

I explained what had happened.

Waring said, " But, Christ, Sammy, surely you know by now that you mustn't give these things to people like that ? Now we haven't got a leg to stand on. Hereward's quite right. It's clearly his job. Of course he'd kick up a fuss."

I said, " Well, what could I do with it ? "

" If it went out at all it ought to have gone officially from the unit."

" But it hadn't got far enough for that. And anyhow if it came officially from here, he'd certainly have put it in the waste-paper basket."

" That's his affair. It might very well have been decided that as a matter of tactics we wouldn't send it out at all. But this was asking for trouble. You can't just go butting in on somebody else's territory like that."

I said, " But every damned thing we do is butting in on *somebody's* territory. If everybody really did his job there'd be nothing for us to do."

" That's quite true," said the Old Man. " Our job is to give general advice."

" Yes," said Waring quickly. " When it's *asked* for. That's the point. If a department consults us—well and good. Or if the Minister asks us. But here nobody asked us. We've just put an oar in uninvited. And of course we've got a raspberry."

I said, " But the stuff is important. There's a grand job to be done and they're not doing it. It's all bunkum to say it's in hand. They aren't doing anything about it at all."

" How do you know ? "

" Because I talked to them about it."

" That may be," said Waring. " But it's nothing to do with you."

I said, " Even if it might shorten the war by six months ? "

" It's no good talking hypothetical cases," said Waring

irritably. " This is simply a matter of organisation. People are given terms of reference. Whether they're the right people or the wrong people is nothing to do with us. But as long as they've been given the job, we've no right to interfere just because we don't agree with what they're doing."

" Oh, wait a minute," said Mair doubtfully. " You're going rather far there. We've a perfect right to offer suggestions."

" If they're asked for," said Waring.

" Or if they're not," said the Old Man. " It's a free country."

" All right, then. We're entitled to offer suggestions. But we've no grouse if they're turned down. And certainly we've got no right to make unofficial contacts with junior members of other people's staffs."

There was a short silence.

I said, " Then it comes to this—if I get on to something good—even if I can prove that it would win the war—I can't do anything with it if the head of the department who ought to have thought of it chooses to ignore it ? "

" That's it."

" And you don't think I even ought to try ? "

Waring said, " Not in this sort of way, anyhow."

" How, then ? "

Waring shrugged. " If it's as valuable as all that you might try going over his head. You might have got the Professor to take this to the Minister for example. But personally I don't think it's any good trying to do these solo efforts."

" Expand that," said Mair. " I'm not quite sure what you're getting at."

" I think we should concentrate on things which we're *asked* to do and which we know somebody responsible wants done, and stop haring off on these ideas of our own. They always make trouble."

Mair brushed a hand through his thick silver hair. " I don't like to abandon our right to be constructive," he said doubtfully. " It's rather a limiting formula, you know."

Waring said, " I don't think a few limits would be a bad thing."

Mair sat silent for a moment. Then he picked up the letter and said, " Well, anyhow, what are we going to do about this ? "

"We shall have to eat humble pie," said Waring. "There's nothing else for it. We're completely in the wrong and there's nothing to be done but to admit it and apologise."

"Apologise?" said Mair, looking up with a frown.

I said, "What are we to apologise for?"

"For acting quite out of order and very discourteously."

"But I don't think you understand," I said rather desperately. "That stuff matters. His own people know that it's good and say it's never been tackled before. There's stuff there that I was working on before the war. What's going to happen to it?"

Waring said, "That's entirely up to Hereward. After what's happened, you can't expect him to be very enthusiastic, can you?"

I felt myself shaking a bit. I said, "It isn't a question of whether Hereward is enthusiastic or not. That idea might make all the difference to operating transport and guns in cold climates. Why should it be stopped because of his bloody dignity? The war isn't his private show."

Waring said, "My dear chap, we're not talking about how good or bad your idea is. It may be marvellous for all I know. But it happens to be about low temperature stuff, and low temperature stuff is Hereward's business. That part of the war *is* his affair, and it's no good making a fuss about it."

I didn't reply. I knew he was right in a way—in the bloody silly way that everything was arranged.

Mair said gently, "You're being logical, Sammy, and I'm afraid it isn't a matter of logic."

He smiled his pleasant smile and said, "I'm all with you myself. It seems to me to be a lot of damned nonsense. But I'm afraid Waring's quite right. From the Civil Service point of view we're in the wrong. And until we can get the Civil Service to declare war on our side, there's nothing to be done."

Waring said, "Oh, nobody denies that it's a farcical situation. But we've got to make the best of it. If the organisation's bad, the only thing to do is to make it work as well as it can—not just to kick it and then complain because you hurt your toe."

He paused for a moment and then added, "Do you think it might be best if I went round and saw Hereward and explained? I know him quite well. He's all right if he's handled gently."

Mair said, " If you like I'll see him myself."

" No," said Waring hurriedly. " I don't think we should admit that it's important enough for you to go. I'll drop in to-morrow and say that there's clearly been a misunderstanding. We can probably clear it up without having to answer his letter."

" All right," said Mair. " If you think that's the best way."

Waring glanced at me and said, " I shall probably have to take the line that this is private work of Sammy's, most of which was done before the war, that he just gave it to Knollys for interest, and that Knollys thought it was done officially for you."

He grinned at me and said, " You don't mind my saying that, Sammy? It's more or less true, anyhow."

I said wearily, " No, I don't give a damn what you say." I had a pretty clear idea of what Waring would really say to Hereward. Holding the baby didn't matter. The bitter thing was that there should be a baby to hold.

I said, " You'd better tell Hereward that I'm just an ignorant stooge who didn't realise that this was a war to get him a knighthood."

With that we came away. I was feeling furious about the whole thing, and wondered whether to go for Waring as soon as we were outside. I was just deciding that it wasn't worth while when he settled the whole thing for me. As soon as he'd shut the Old Man's door behind him he said cheerfully, " If you ask me, my lad, I think you're very well out of that."

I said, " What the hell d'you mean? "

" Well, it was bloody silly of you to give that stuff to Knollys and put us in this jam. If I'd been in the Old Man's place I should have been livid with you."

I said, " You certainly did your best to *make* him livid."

" I was thinking about this outfit's relations with other people," said Waring coldly. " Somebody's got to, after all."

" You seem to think our relations with ticks like Hereward are more important than the work we do," I said bitterly.

" Well, good God, o'boy, of course they are! " said Waring in genuine surprise. " What on earth's the good of doing work if you get everybody up against you? Nothing ever gets through." As we turned into his office he said, " You *must* realise, Sammy, that you can have ideas that'd win the war four times over and it still won't do anybody any good if you can't sell them."

Susan was sitting at her desk. I saw her head come up as we went past. Waring said, " We're not in a university department, you see."

Susan was looking at us with interest.

I said, " Nor in an advertising agency, though I often wonder about that."

That rang the bell all right. Waring half stopped and looked at me. His black eyes flashed and his face went a queer sallow colour. Then he just stepped aside, waved me into his office and followed me in. He didn't shut the door.

Waring said, " Look, Sammy. You may reckon that you're a great big scientist and that I'm just a commercial stooge, but the plain fact is that if you people on the technical side make a mess, I have to clear it up. I don't mind that. It's my job. But don't start being patronising about it, for God's sake."

I said, " Right. And the equally plain fact is that the stuff you build a reputation on comes chiefly out of my head. I'm not a politician or a salesman, thank God. But neither am I a kid of ten."

Waring looked at me for a moment in silence. Then he suddenly broke into a broad grin and said, " Not ten, Sammy, eight. Ten's what you are when you're not cross."

I wasn't sure whether to hit him or to laugh. A moment before he'd been looking like the devil, and there he was sitting back with his *enfant terrible* grin and not a feather out of place.

I said, " It's all very well, but this isn't good enough."

" You mean all this work of yours being wasted ? " said Waring seriously. " My dear old horse, it's a bloody scandal. Don't think I don't see that, for Pete's sake. That's why I said what I did."

I thought that was a bit quick even for R.B.

I said, " Hey—half a minute. I thought you were worrying about the department's relations ? "

" But it's the same *thing*, Sammy ! " he said banging his fist on his blotter. " Can't you see ? Look——" he leant forward confidentially, " In this place we've got you. We've got the Old Man himself. We've got Till. We've got half a dozen people who are turning out work that really matters. It's my job to put that work across. That's all I'm interested in. All I kick about is when we do something which means that the work you do will be wasted instead of being used and reckoned to your credit."

He shook his head. " Seriously, Sammy, that's all I'm after."

I hesitated for a moment and then said, " Of course, I know that. But I still don't see what I could have done about this."

" But, of course—— ! " said Waring. " I couldn't say so in front of the Old Man, but if you'd told me about it I could have put it to him that it was a thing to take straight to the Minister. We could have gone straight over Hereward's head. *Then* he could have kicked as much as he liked and we could just have said we were sorry and that it was an oversight not to have consulted him."

" That wouldn't have done our relations with him any good."

" Maybe not. But the stuff would have gone to the right place by then. I don't mind who we quarrel with as long as we can cock a snook at them."

We went on talking for a bit. Then Waring said, "What's the time ? Four o'clock ? Let's go and see if La Susan has rustled up any tea." We went out into Susan's room. The door had been open all the time. Susan was just pouring out the tea.

Waring said, " Pot of tea for two, miss," in Cockney.

Susan said, " It's just ready," without looking up.

We all took our tea. This was the first time for some while that I'd seen Susan when Waring was there, and it felt queer and uncomfortable. Waring said, " What I have to put up with in this place—— ! Did you hear Sammy calling me an advertising agent ? "

Susan took some sugar and said, " As you were both shouting at the tops of your voices I could hardly help it."

" *He* was," said Waring. " *I* was calm, cool and good tempered. Wasn't I, Sammy ? "

Susan looked at me expressionlessly. I said, " I don't know. You were being bloody annoying, anyhow."

" For your own good, Sammy. For your own good." Waring turned to Susan. " Y'know, Sue, I'm a much misunderstood man. I'm not appreciated. That's my trouble."

" Never mind," said Susan gently, without smiling, " I appreciate you."

" My God, what a menacing remark ! " said Waring in horror. " Well, you damned well keep it to yourself or I'll stop your beer money. *See ?* " He struck an attitude. Susan went on drinking her tea. She was still looking at him with her big grey eyes wide open and quite expressionless.

" As I was about to remark when I was interrupted from the back of the hall," said Waring, " I am a misunderstood man. Take this man, Sam." He pointed at me. " I labour for that man. I toil on his behalf. I nourish him in my bosom. And what do I get ? Friendship ? Kindness ? An occasional beer, even ? No. Abuse. Scorn. Accusations of being an advertising agent."

I said, " I don't see why you should take that so hard, R.B."

" Oh, no," said Waring, shaking his head. " To you it may seem nothing. But to a man who has been—ahem—in the advertising business there could hardly be a more deadly insult."

Susan had turned away and was standing looking rather moodily out of the window.

" I didn't mean that you weren't a very *good* advertising agent," I said, trying rather desperately to play up to his fooling.

" You mean that if I am an advertising agent I'm the sort that charges fifteen per cent instead of ten per cent ? "

" Something like that."

Waring sighed, " To a man who has been in the advertising business," he said pathetically, " it's bad enough to have your alleged friends call you an advertising agent. But to be likened unto a fifteen per cent agency—— ! " He shook his head, sighed again, clapped his hands and said, " Ho, Slave ! Tea ! "

I finished mine and said, " I must go and do some work."

XI

Two DAYS later Joe came charging in, very excited, with the morning paper. Pinker had been dead right about his facts. The Minister had gone. Pedder had got the job. There was no mention of another job for the Minister. The only thing that hadn't come off was the sacking of the Permanent Secretary. The paper said nothing about that so evidently Pinker hadn't pulled it off.

The change-over didn't get very big headlines and there was no comment. I had hoped that some people would be pretty horrified and point out that to appoint Pedder to anything was a retrograde step. But nobody seemed to care a hoot. Pedder was a good party man, so the government Press didn't mind ; and the Minister was a good party man too so the Opposition weren't interested. I suppose they took the line that all good party men were alike—as long as it was the same party.

Joe said, " How much difference is this going to make to us ? What's Pedder like ? "

I said, " Pretty average stooge, I believe. He's failed at pretty nearly everything at the Postmaster-General level so now they've promoted him."

" D'you think he's ever seen a calculating machine ? " said Tilly looking up.

I said, " I shouldn't think he's seen a typewriter yet. You mustn't rush these old boys."

" The main thing," said Joe looking very cunning, " is whether he's a pal of the Old Man's ? "

" Well, he isn't. At least, I don't think so."

Joe shook his head and looked very solemn.

I suppose Mair must have been told about the change beforehand, but apparently Waring hadn't. He came into the Coach for lunch looking very worried.

He said, " This is the bloody part of being one of these unofficial outfits. If the man who backs you goes, you're sunk. Now you'll see why I worry about our relationships, Sammy."

" Do you think it will really make a difference to us ? "

" *A* difference ? It'll make *the* difference. Listen—I knew last night that the Minister was going. Nobody had told me, but I guessed and I guessed right."

" How ? "

" Simply because of the atmosphere in departments I talked to that day. You couldn't miss it. As long as the Minister stayed and people knew the Old Man had him in his pocket, we could get anything. But the moment the word goes round that the Minister is off, they politely tell us to go to hell." I suppose he saw that I looked doubtful, because he went on, " I tell you, Sammy, that's how these boys' minds work. The pukka Civil Servant kow-tows to his Minister until he nearly makes you sick. But he doesn't worry. He knows that one day the Minister will be flung out on his neck. But the Civil Servant won't. He's there for keeps." He tapped nervously on the bar with his fingers. " I've tried and tried again to get the Old Man to get together with the Permanent people, but he wouldn't do it. Now we're left flat."

I said, " What d'you think will happen ? "

" God knows. I can't see the Old Man staying. I doubt if they'll give him the chance."

" Will you stay if he goes ? " I said, thinking of Pinker.

Waring looked at me for a moment without speaking. " I don't know," he said at last. " I certainly don't suppose they'll give *me* any choice. I've done too many tough things for the Old Man. No. It looks like the old age pension for me all right."

The whole place had gone very jumpy. There was a queer feeling of sitting on a bomb with a time fuse. No one knew when it would go up, but everybody knew that it must be sooner or later. I couldn't settle down at all, and about tea-time I rang up Susan and suggested that we should go out instead of having supper at home. For some reason she didn't want to go to the Royal, so we went to Noble's instead. Susan turned up looking worried, and I thought she seemed very quiet.

I said, " Anything wrong, darling ? "

" I'm not sure. Look, Sammy. I want to talk to you about this business of the Minister going . . ."

I said, " Oh God—need we talk about that ? I've had nothing else all day."

" I know. I'm sorry," said Susan. " But there's just something I want to ask you." She looked at me with the queer worried wrinkles. " Do you know anything about it that I don't know ? "

" What ? Why he's going and so on ? No."

" Did you know beforehand ? "

" Well—yes. Up to a point. Pinker told me yesterday."

" Did R.B. know ? "

" I don't think so."

" Pinker hadn't told him ? "

" No. In fact he made me promise not to tell him. Pinker can't bear R.B."

" It's mutual," said Susan. " At least it was. I wish to God you'd told me before."

" I meant to. But I haven't seen you to talk to since he told me."

" Just what did he say ? "

I told her. When I came to the bit about Mair and Waring going she sat up quickly looking rather startled.

I said, " What's funny ? I think probably they *will* both go. R.B. thinks he'll be chucked out, I know."

Susan said, " Wait a minute." She thought for a bit and then said, " Look, Sammy—there *is* dirty work at the cross-roads. I'm sure of it."

I said, " Of course there is. The whole thing's dirty work."

" Yes—but you don't know this bit. Pinker rang R.B. up this afternoon and they've gone out this evening."

" Pinker and R.B. ? "

" Yes. That's why I suggested that we came here instead of to the Royal. They've gone there and I didn't want to meet them."

That shook me rather. I said, " I don't like that. Maybe it's just my nasty mind, but . . ."

" Oh, be your age ! " said Susan impatiently. " It's perfectly obvious what's happening. They want to get rid of Mair, but they want to have someone left to run the show. Pinker tried you and you wouldn't play so now he'll try R.B. Of course he will."

" He might. But I should rather doubt it."

" Why ? "

" Well (a) he loathes R.B. and (b) R.B. couldn't do it and (c) I don't believe Pinker's in a position to do that sort of thing anyhow."

" Bunkum. People like Pinker don't let things like that stand in their way. He won't care who it is or how good he is as long as it's somebody who's their nominee."

I said, " R.B. told me at lunch-time he thought he'd have to go if the Old Man went."

Susan said, " He might if they flung him down the steps. Otherwise he won't. Why should he ? "

" Well, if they put in some awful stooge like Brine, who knows nothing about it . . . "

" Well ? " said Susan. " How much does Mair know about most of it ? "

" At least he's good."

" You always say so. R.B. thinks he's a menace off his own ground."

She shook her head and said, " I think it's an awful pity you let Pinker think you were tied to Mair."

I said, " Well, damn it all, darling, you can hardly

expect me to come in with a cove like Pinker in doing the Old Man dirt."

"It's no question of *your* doing him dirt. If they are going to get rid of him they will. You can't stop them."

"Maybe not. But I needn't actually help them."

"But what the *hell's* the good of that?" said Susan furiously.

I was startled. She seemed genuinely angry.

She said, "You really are hopeless, Sammy. You seem to go out of your way to make—to make yourself useless."

I said, "How d'you mean?" rather crossly.

"Well, take this thing. It's quite obvious that Mair's going. You've got the place in your hand because you're the only person who knows anything about it. They come and more or less offer you the job of running it, and you turn it down. Now they'll go and get someone else, and you won't like it."

I said, "You don't know what you're talking about. I wasn't offered anything."

Susan made an impatient noise.

I said, "Anyhow, if they put this bloke Brine in, it would be pretty hopeless."

"So you'll resign if Mair goes and he comes?"

I hadn't actually worked it out as far as that. I said, "I'm not sure."

"Well, I'll tell you," said Susan. "You won't. You'll let all this happen, and then when it has you'll see that it will be a mess if you go, so you'll hang around hating it and expecting everybody to be sorry for you."

I said, "I certainly shan't expect anything of the sort."

"Oh yes, you will. You do this all the time. You put yourself in bloody situations and then tell yourself that life is very hard. I've seen you do it."

I said, "Oh, for God's sake stop grousing at me, Susan."

"No," she said. "I'm going to tell you this. You think what you've done about this is rather good and honourable and loyal. Well, it isn't. You've just done what was the easiest thing for you and let everything else go to hell."

I said, "Look here, you're talking bunkum and you'd better stop."

"I *won't* stop!" said Susan passionately. "It's true. You won't face things—not real things that are difficult. You just work on little easy things, like whether you like people or have known them a long time or something. You

126

just want to be safe. When it gets difficult you run away."

I said, " Shut up, you little bitch ! "

" Well, it's true, isn't it ? "

I said, " I happen to care about the quality of the work the place does."

" And you think it'll do better work with Brine in charge and R.B. running him than with you running him ? "

I hesitated and said, " That isn't the point."

" But it *is* the point. There isn't any other point. Oh, Sammy, you're such a *fool* . . ." Susan suddenly stopped, bent her head down and started to rake in her bag for her handkerchief. She said " Damn ! " in a smothered voice.

I put the brakes on hard and said, " Pull yourself together, Sue. You're making an ass of yourself."

She didn't say anything. She sat there raking in her bag for a moment and then suddenly got up and went out.

I sat there for a long time, thinking she might just be in the lavatory. But she didn't come back. So I got my hat and coat and started for home. I had to go past the Royal to get to the Tube, and on a sudden impulse I turned in there. Lord knows why, except that I was scared about something and had some queer idea about feeling safer if I saw Pinker and Waring together.

I went and looked through the glass doors of the big downstairs bar. For a moment I thought they weren't there. Then I saw them at a table right up close to the door, and dodged back in case they should see me. For a moment I thought of just barging in and trying to have a show-down. I watched them for a minute. Waring was leaning forward and talking hard. Pinker was looking thoughtfully across the room and sucking his pipe. I saw him smile his contemptuous smile at something Waring said. Waring laughed too. They looked very much together. It had never struck me before, but when you came to think of it they were made for one another. I turned away and went home.

When I got back to the flat Susan was there. She was sitting looking into the fire, quite calm again. She just looked up as I came in and said " Hallo " quietly.

I was feeling pretty jumpy and damned annoyed with her. I said, " Well, that was a pretty performance, my dear."

" Yes. I'm sorry," she said, not very apologetically.

" Next time you just decide to go home when we're out together, I'd be obliged if you'd tell me, and not just leave me sitting and wondering whether you're coming back."

Susan said nothing.

I said, " From the way you were acting I thought you might have gone and thrown yourself into the Thames or something."

She looked into the fire and smiled. It was a rather contemptuous smile and I didn't like it. I chucked myself down in a chair, picked up a book and pretended to read.

We sat there for quite a while. Susan still didn't say anything, but just went on looking into the fire. After a bit it began to get on my nerves. I couldn't quite make out what had happened to her. Usually if she flared up at me, she was very apologetic afterwards. Finally I threw the book down and said, " You know it strikes me that if you really think I'm such a poor sap as you said to-night, you'd better leave me."

Susan looked at me thoughtfully for a moment and then just said, " The same thought had occurred to me."

I hadn't expected that. After a moment I said, " Well ? And what did you decide ? "

Susan leant back in her chair, shut her eyes and frowned. " I hadn't really decided anything," she said calmly. " I can't make up my mind whether I do you more harm than good by being here." She opened her eyes and looked at me inquiringly. " What do you think ? "

I swallowed and said, " I hadn't realised that you thought of yourself as a sort of charity. If you do there's only one answer."

Susan smiled and said, " Darling, don't let's be proud. It's so difficult if everybody's proud. The only reason why I stay here is because I want to, as you very well know. The question is whether it's a good thing from your point of view."

I said, " I think you're talking a lot of nonsense. What in God's name's got into you, Susan ? "

" I may have put it in an irritating way," she said, as though she hadn't heard. " But what I said to-night was true, you know."

I said, " Well, if you're now going to say it all over again, I'd rather you didn't."

" No. I'm not going to say it again. But what are we doing to do about it ? "

" I don't see that there's much I can do about it now, even if I wanted to."

" I don't just mean over Pinker, I mean over everything."
She suddenly leant forward. "Look, Sammy—it's like
this. You've got to make up your mind whether you want
to spend your whole life being a person it's too bad about,
or not. See what I mean ? "

I said, " You mean I'm too sorry for myself ? "

"Yes. And more than that. You're too willing to let
things go wrong and then be sorry for yourself about them."

I thought for a long time. Then I said, " What you don't
understand is that I can't just be a different sort of person
because I want to."

Susan said, " But you could try."

I suddenly felt very tired and hopeless. I said, " It's odd
that you should think that I don't try. That's the only thing
I mind really—that you should think I'm just lazy or a self-
deceiver or something. I know I'm not effective in the way
some people are. But I don't particularly like it, you know."

" No," said Susan. " You hate it. I know that. That's
why I wish you'd—you'd try harder. Or—oh, I don't know
what I mean."

" No," I said roughly. " You don't. You talk a lot but
it doesn't really mean anything. Far better if you kept your
mouth shut."

Her head came up, and for a fraction of a second there
was something in her eyes. Then it was gone. She just
nodded and said : " Perhaps. But I doubt it."

After a while she said, " You were nice and tough with
R.B. the other day."

" When we came into your office squabbling ? Well, he'd
been bloody rude to me."

" Why don't you do that more often ? "

" Be rude ? I often am. It doesn't do a lot of good that
I can see."

" I don't mean just being rude. Being—tougher with
people. You see he gilly-gillied you in the end even there."

" How did he ? "

" He had you eating out of his hand in five minutes. I
heard the whole thing. I've seen him do it a dozen times."

I said, " Well, damn it all. I could scarcely go on
quarrelling if he didn't want to."

" Why not ? Why should he decide whether you shall
quarrel or not ? Why shouldn't you ? "

" I don't want to. I never do want to quarrel with
people. I loathe rows."

" Why ? "

" Well, don't you ? "

" Not particularly. Sometimes I love them."

There was a long silence. Then I said, " I doubt if you know what it feels like to be really bad at that sort of thing."

" What does it feel like ? " said Susan gently.

" Well, it makes me tremble and it makes my hands sweat and it makes me feel sick. In other words, I just feel scared stiff."

" What of ? "

" God knows."

" Of them ? "

" Partly. Partly not. I don't really know."

" Do you always feel like that ? "

" Yes. If I'm angry at all. If I'm not angry I just keep seeing everybody else's point of view so that I can't do anything. That was the trouble with Waring the other day. As soon as I wasn't angry I could see that he was right in a way."

Susan looked at me for a moment in silence. Then she said, " Oh well—let's forget it. How about some food ? "

We had supper and sat and read. It was a bloody business. We both knew perfectly well that what we had been saying was too important to leave like that, but there didn't seem to be anything useful to say. About half-past ten Susan pushed off to bed and I sat and thought about it. I tried to imagine myself handling things differently—going to see Waring and telling him where he go off ; taking Pinker out for a drink and telling him I'd changed my mind ; seeing the Old Man and making him go to the Minister about my low temperature stuff. But it wouldn't fire. I would have given a lot for a drink. I thought, " That's the trouble. There are too many bloody things to fight at once, and I haven't enough guts for all of them. In fact I haven't got any guts at all."

About midnight I gave it up and went to bed. Susan seemed to be asleep, so I didn't put the light on. I undressed and got into bed and lay on my back thinking.

After a bit Susan said in an awake voice, " Darling, you must go to sleep. You'll be dog-tired to-morrow." I didn't say anything. She put her arms round me and said :

" It's all right really, you know."

For some reason that did it. I said, " It isn't all right. It's bloody well all wrong," and started to cry.

130

Susan said, " Oh, Christ, darling, don't. It's all right. No one shall make you. I'm an ass to worry you about it."

We lay for a minute or two. After a while I began to feel better. I said, " Listen—how much of this sort of thing can you stand ? "

" As much as you like."

" Well, I don't like it. Something's got to be done."

Susan said, " All right. But not to-night."

I hesitated and said, " All right. Not to-night. But soon."

The last thing I remember is taking her arms from round me and putting mine round her, which was how we usually lay. I must have been nearly asleep, but I know it seemed very important to get that right.

The next ten days or a fortnight were pretty intolerable. Everybody was on the jump. I only saw the Old Man once or twice but I thought he looked very grey and old and worried. He went to see the new Minister once, but I didn't hear anything about it, or anything from Pinker, so I just put my head down and went on with the work and tried to forget it all. It was the only thing to do.

I couldn't make out about Waring. If he had got together with Pinker and Easton there was nothing much to show it, except that he didn't seem as worried as most of us. He was just the same as usual—very in and out, either clowning about or furious with everything and everybody.

The only time he showed signs of knowing anything was when he tackled me about Joe. He asked me if I'd thought any more about it and said all his usual piece about Joe being lazy and useless. When I tried to stall him off he said, " Well, the fact of the matter is—we're going to have to do a clean-up. I don't want this to go any further, Sammy, but this place is going to be put under the microscope pretty thoroughly. And if there's any dead wood about, we want to get rid of it before that happens."

He thought for a minute and then said, suddenly, " Is there any reason from your point of view why Marchant shouldn't go ? "

I said, " I've already told you there is."

" Yes, but could you manage without him ? "

" Well, yes. You can always manage without anybody."

" Right," said Waring. " Then I suggest that he *ought* to go before this inquiry begins."

I said, " But look, R.B.—we can't very well just chuck Joe out."

" Why not ? " said Waring calmly.

" Well, damn it—he's been in the outfit from the start."

" That's nothing to do with it."

" . . . and he's only just got married. What's more, it would probably mean that he'd be called up right away."

Waring said, " Why not ? I shouldn't think that'd do him any harm."

" Well, it wouldn't do most of us any harm if it comes to that," I said, rather curtly.

" He's had his chance," said Waring. " If he hasn't succeeded in making a job for himself which makes it worth while to keep him, it's his affair."

I said, " I don't agree with you and I doubt very much if you'll get the Old Man to agree. He rather likes Joe and he was one of his own boys."

Waring opened his lips to say something and then shut them again and shrugged his shoulders.

Two days later the Old Man called me in and said, " It's been suggested that Marchant ought to go. What do you think ? Waring says you say you can manage without him ? "

I said, " Well, sir, I can manage of course, but . . ."

The Old Man smiled, " Exactly," he said rather wearily. " That's how I feel about it. But if we keep him, can we justify it ? "

" To whom, sir ? "

" Oh, to anybody who likes to ask," said Mair rather bitterly. " I gather we're going to be asked a lot of questions and that we shall be expected to justify our existence. Can we justify Joe's ? "

I said, " It depends who's asking the questions."

" We don't know that yet," said Mair, passing his hand across his closed eyes. " I dare say it'll be difficult enough to convince some people that the section ought to exist at all." He sat in silence for a moment. " Anyhow," he went on. " You'd rather keep him if we possibly can ? "

" Of course."

" Good. So would I. I wouldn't say old Joe was much of an asset, but I don't want to break the team up, unless I'm forced to."

He didn't say any more. There were a lot of things I would have liked to ask him but I didn't like to. He looked so damned tired. As I got into the office Joe was just

132

saying to Till : " For two pins I'd go and see the Old Man
and chuck my hand in."

He was always saying that as soon as anything happened
that he didn't like.

Tilly just said, " And do what ? " in his sardonic way.

" Go carry a rifle," said Joe off-handedly.

" I doubt they'd give you one," said Tilly looking up
and pointing at Joe with his red nose. " They'd be afraid
you'd shoot somebody."

" Well, I don't know," said Joe. " After all, I'm a fit
man. I often wonder if I'm doing the right thing in staying
here." He looked at us in turn rather pityingly and said,
" Of course, it's different for you two."

He was always a tactful cove. Tilly said, " Well, I
wouldn't stay if it gives you a bad conscience." He believed
in taking a firm line with Joe.

XII

EASTON and his boys didn't lose any time. About three
weeks after Pedder became Minister, Waring called me down
and said : " Sammy, it's more than my job's worth to show
you these, but I think in fairness you ought to see them."
He chucked across a letter. " Exhibit A. Letter from the
Minister to the Old Man."

It ran :

" Dear Professor Mair. Following our very pleasant
discussion the other day I have given a good deal of anxious
thought to the position of your Research Section, and have
sought the opinion of my official advisers on scientific
matters. It is my view (and theirs) that the value of your
contribution to our councils could be greatly increased if
the position could be regularised, and the functions and
status of the Section more clearly defined. As you will be
aware, the Cabinet has appointed, as my official advisers,
the National Scientific Council ; a strong representative
body of eminent scientists, with great technical resources.
It seems to me, and I hope and believe that you will agree,
that the time has come when some process of affiliation or
merging should now take place between the activities of the
National Council and yourselves.

The arrangement I had in mind is something like this

133

—that you yourself should join the Executive Committee of the Council, which sits under the chairmanship of Sir Lewis Easton. I have Sir Lewis's assurance that you would be a most welcome addition to their strength. Meanwhile, your Research Section, possibly strengthened and enlarged, would come under the general direction of the Council, who would proceed to appoint a Director who would carry on the day to day work, reporting through the Council to me.

I am convinced that this plan, or something like it, is in the best interest of the work which we all have at heart, and it is my profound hope that you will find yourself able to accept it.

In the meantime, may I, on behalf of myself and my Department, offer you sincerest thanks for the invaluable contributions which your Section has made to many of our most important problems.

" Yours sincerely,

" CARL PEDDER."

I looked up and said, " And very nice too. In other words, ' Hand over or get out ? ' "

" Exhibit B," said Waring, chucking across another letter. " The Old Man's reply."

I read :

" Dear Minister. When, at the request of your predecessor, I left my University department to form this Section, I pointed out the existence of a number of Committees and Councils who were intended to advise him on scientific matters. He replied that he already received far too much advice, but lacked anybody to do hard practical and disinterested *work* on specific problems. In the light of this statement, I have never considered that the work of my Section overlapped with that of the National Scientific Council. My staff consists of young men, doing practical work on the problems confronting your Ministry. The National Council consists of eminent elderly men, able perhaps to advise you on broad issues, but quite unsuitable, and in many instances incapable, of designing, controlling and carrying out practical researches.

Moreover, if our work is to be of value, day to day contact with various departments of your Ministry is the first essential, and I fear that the necessity of reporting through a Committee, whose members were not directly in touch with the work, would be completely stultifying.

For these reasons, and others which I need not touch upon, I do not feel able to fall in with the arrangement you suggest. It would, in my view, be far better for me to sever my connection with your Ministry and return to my own work, leaving you a clear field for any changes which you feel to be necessary.

"Yours sincerely,"

"R. H. N. Mair."

I said, "Well, that appears to be that." My throat felt very dry.

"I'm afraid so," said Waring. "I tried to stop him from sending it, but he wouldn't listen."

"There wasn't much else he could do, was there?"

"Oh, I don't know," said Waring. "Pedder's letter was perfectly pleasant and reasonable. He could have compromised if he'd wanted to."

I said, "Oh come, R.B.! After having the Section taken out of his hands and given to Easton's gang?"

"Well, he would have been on the Committee."

"That seems to me the dirtiest crack of the lot."

Waring shrugged his shoulders. "I don't understand these big scientific boys," he said rather irritably. "They're like a lot of kids with their bloody squabbles."

After a pause I said, "Well, what happens now?"

Waring hesitated. "I don't know," he said. "There's been no reply from Pedder yet."

"You think he'll let the Old Man resign?"

Waring looked up in some surprise. "Of course. Why should he try to stop him?"

"He might have thought it was a pity to let him go," I said rather bitterly.

"Oh, he'll accept his resignation all right," said Waring. "The question is, what will happen then?"

I said, "What d'you think will?"

Waring looked at me rather uncertainly and then started to draw squares on his blotting paper. I thought, "So it's all fixed."

"*I* don't know," said Waring. "Your guess is as good as mine."

"Will they disband the Section?"

"I shouldn't think so," said Waring, still drawing squares. "Not entirely, anyhow. They'll probably do the sort of thing Pedder suggests."

135

" Bring in a new director and put the whole thing under Easton's outfit ? "

" Something like that."

" Who will the director be ? "

" How should I know ? " said Waring irritably. " You know these people better than I do."

" Somebody like Sturges, I expect," I said watching him closely. " Or Brine."

" No idea," said Waring chucking down his pencil. " I suppose we shall hear soon enough." He got up. " Well, there it is, Sammy. I thought you ought to know. Don't say anything to anybody about it, will you ? "

I said, " Well, that's rather a point, R.B. If the Old Man's going, oughtn't Joe and Tilly to be told soon ? "

" Why ? "

" They're both his people. We all are. They may not want to stay if he's being chucked out."

" Oh bunkum ! " said Waring in surprise. " He's not being chucked out. It's his own choice." He looked at me sharply. " You don't feel like that yourself, do you ? "

I said, " It depends who's coming. If it's some awful stooge there wouldn't be much point in staying."

Waring said, " Well, I think that's nonsense, Sammy. To be quite frank I think a shake-up like this may be a very good thing. We shall know where we stand. Mair can walk out in a huff if he likes, but I can't see why any one else should. He's a nice old boy, but we don't *belong* to him after all."

It was on the tip of my tongue to say, " You may not belong to him, but he made you." But it wasn't worth it. I could see just what had happened.

I took Joe and Tilly out for a drink and told them. Maybe it was a breach of confidence but it was only fair. I thought Joe would want to resign on the spot, but for once he didn't. He just kept quiet and looked rather white.

Tilly poked his glasses further back on his nose and said, " Well, what do we do ? Go or stay ? "

I said, " I don't know. It all depends who we get. I've got an idea we shall get Brine."

Tilly said, " What's he ? "

" Organic chemist. Quite good, I believe. I don't know much about him."

" *Organic chemist !* " said Tilly expressively. " Probably knows no statistics whatever."

" Probably not."

Tilly shook his head. He divided people into statisticians, people who knew about statistics, and people who didn't. He liked the middle group best. He didn't like real statisticians much because they argued with him, and he thought the people who didn't know any statistics were just animal life.

Tilly said, " Well, I'll leave it to you, Sammy. If we ought to resign, you tell me and I will."

" We may not get the chance," said Joe uneasily.

" Well, that's all right," said Tilly nastily. " You're young and fit, aren't you ? You told us so the other day." He turned to me and said, " And our colleague, Mr. Waring ? How does he feel ? "

I said, " He seems quite happy. He told me he thought it would be quite a good thing."

" For whom ? " said Tilly politely.

" He didn't go into that."

Tilly put his mug down and said, " Then we may take for granted who he had in mind."

On the following Monday Mair sent for me. He greeted me with, " Hallo, Sammy ! Come in and sit down. I want to have a crack with you." I thought he looked very cheerful and about ten years younger than he had been looking lately, and for a moment I thought perhaps they'd asked him to stay after all. But he went on, " I've decided to go back to the department, so I shall be leaving the Section in about a week's time."

I tried to seem surprised about it. It didn't sound very convincing, but I don't think he noticed.

" Yes," he said cheerfully. " I think it's time I had a change. So I've been to see the Minister and it's all fixed up. I shall go at the end of the week."

Mair lit his pipe. I said, " What will happen to the Section, sir ? "

" Oh, it'll carry on," said Mair, pressing the tobacco down with his forefinger. " There's no question of scrapping it. In fact I expect it'll grow. There'll be a certain number of changes of course. After all, the conditions are very different from when we started. A new broom will probably be a good thing."

I didn't say anything.

" The idea is that the whole thing shall come under the

137

National Scientific Council," said Mair. " I've seen Easton
about it. They're putting in Brine in my place—you know,
the chap who was at that meeting. Big fellow who looks as
though he doesn't shave."

I said, " Good God ! "

Mair looked at me quizzically. " Why good God ? " he
said. " Don't you like the sound of it ? "

I said, " Frankly, it sounds perfectly bloody."

" Oh, but why ? " said Mair reasonably. " Brine's a
good chap. It'll give the place some official standing." He
put another match to his pipe. I knew he was looking at me
closely.

" I think the whole thing's an absolute disaster," I said.

" Oh, you mustn't think that," said Mair. " It isn't true.
And even if it were true it wouldn't help. The main thing
is that the work must go on. Personalities don't matter. The
work does." He smiled that very sweet smile that wrinkled
up his whole face. " That's what I wanted to talk to you
about. We've been a good team and done some good work,
and I don't want my going to hinder that work in any way."

I hesitated and then said, " I think I ought to tell you
that—that I know a certain amount about what's happened."

" Oh, you do, do you ? " said Mair with a grin. " Well—
perhaps it's all the better if you do." He leaned forward.
" Now, look here, Sammy—I've had you ever since you were
a pup, and I know how you probably feel about it. But
you've got a job to do, and whether I'm here or somebody
else is here makes no difference. The work that science does
in this war—or at any other time—depends on you and
people like you." He waved a hand. " Directors and
professors and so on don't matter a damn. They may think
they do but they don't. By the time a man's fifty he's
probably done most of the best scientific work he'll ever do.
These eminent scientists—they're just living on the past—on
the work they did when they were young, unknown men.
All they're good for now is to quarrel and fight and worry
about their reputations, or getting a knighthood, or some
bloody silly thing like that." He wagged a finger at me.
" Now, that's not science. It's nothing to do with science.
It's just a matter of cliques and intrigues and politics, and
it's no damn' good to anybody. I want you to keep clear
of that stuff. You just go on—do your work—draw your
conclusions and shove them down. And don't give a damn
who likes them and who doesn't."

138

He paused for a moment and sucked at his pipe.

"Now," he said, " I've seen Brine. I've told him about you, and I've told him that he can rely on you completely. He doesn't know much about it, of course, Sammy, and I've told him he'll need to lean on you pretty heavily. Don't be afraid to have your own opinions, and don't be afraid to give them him. He's not a bad chap. But limited, like these chemists always are. But he might be a lot worse. Anyhow, I've done my best for you there."

I said, " That's very kind of you, sir." There was a pause, and then I said, " How about all your fuse work ? "

" I shall take that with me. The Minister's very keen that I should carry on with it. I shall take old Taylor with me if I can. There's some fuss or other about letting me have a uniformed man but I expect we shall get it straight eventually."

" And apart from that we shall just carry on ? "

Mair frowned slightly. " Well, of course I can't guarantee that. It won't be my show any more. I suppose it'll be up to Brine and Easton what the Section does now." He grinned. " I expect they'll have to muck it about a bit, you know, just to show they're in charge. But I don't suppose they'll stop any of the stuff which is actually running."

He got up and said, " Well, there you are, Sammy. That's all. Just keep going. Do all you can to help Brine. And remember—don't get mixed up in the political stuff. It never did any one any good. Leave that to us old chaps who're not fit for an honest job of work any longer."

The Old Man went at the end of the week. I thought we ought to have taken him out or something, but it was a Saturday, and he was catching an evening train, and what with one thing and another the idea fizzled out.

He came round at lunch-time on Saturday to say good-bye. There was something very depressing about it all. I hated saying good-bye to the old boy, and apart from that I couldn't for the life of me imagine how the place could carry on without him. He'd built it round himself, and without him it would be no shape under heaven.

He went on being very cheerful and saying that Brine was a good chap and so on. But I had a shrewd suspicion that the whole thing hadn't been as friendly as he made out. Otherwise I should have thought Brine would have come before he went. As it was, Brine didn't show up until the

Wednesday, so for three days we were Nobody in Particular's Research Section doing damn all.

However, on the Wednesday Brine turned up. He came in the morning, and as Susan said Waring was out of his office all the morning, I suppose they were together. Anyhow, after lunch Waring came round with Brine in tow and introduced us all to him.

Brine looked much the same as when I had seen him last —a very big, hefty chap, rather bald, with a projecting blue chin and eyes a long way back in his head. He looked about fifty, but it was hard to be sure of his age to ten years. He was quite pleasant without being exactly cordial. When we shook hands he said, " Oh yes—I've seen you before of course." Apart from that he just said " How d'you do ? " to the others, shook hands, looked round the room, and went away again with Waring.

Tilly looked after him for a moment and then said, " You say he's an organic chemist ? "

I said, " Yes."

Tilly just nodded without saying anything, as though he could well believe it.

Joe said, " Golly—what a tough ! "

For the next day or two we neither heard nor saw anything of Brine. He spent all his time with Waring. I rather expected that at some point he'd come round, or call me in to talk about the jobs that were on hand, but he didn't. We were a bit puzzled, because we didn't see how he could be finding anything out.

Tilly said, " I expect he's getting the dope from Waring."

" But R.B. doesn't know anything about most of it."

" What's that got to do with it ? He'd tell him something."

Finally, we got a notice round. It said, " The Director wishes to be given a *short* description of the investigations on which you are at present employed, including a statement of how they came to be initiated, and the results so far achieved. Lists should reach me by 9 a.m. on Monday. (Signed) R. B. Waring."

This gave me a bit of a jolt for three reasons. Firstly, it was sent to Joe and Tilly as well as to me—there was no suggestion that I should report for all of us, as I usually did. Secondly, Waring usually didn't come into technical things much and I didn't see why the stuff should go to him instead of direct to Brine. Thirdly, the note came round at about four o'clock on Saturday, so it looked as though we should have to spend Sunday on it.

Of course Joe had gone home, and when we rang him up he wasn't there, so it looked as though I should have to do his. Then Tilly said, " It's impossible to separate my stuff from yours. I'm either doing nothing or mixed up in everything. I shall just refer him to your list."

Finally we decided to do one statement, which we would all sign, pointing out that we worked as a group and couldn't split it up so as to make sense.

I worked all Sunday on the thing, and even then it wasn't very satisfactory. It was an incredibly difficult thing to do so that anybody would understand it. Some of the things were clear-cut enough. But with most of them it was difficult to say who *had* initiated it, or just exactly where it was at the moment. Sometimes we were doing the whole thing. Sometimes we were doing one bit and about a dozen other people were doing others. Sometimes the job was something which would take about a week, and sometimes it had gone on for three years and would go on as long as the war lasted. As for results, it depended entirely on what you called a " result." If we examined a new fuse and reported on it, was that a " result? " And if not, what was it ?

I managed to get hold of Waring at home and asked him if he knew exactly what Brine wanted, but he only seemed to have a very vague idea. He just said, " Oh, he only wants to know what sort of thing we're doing. Just very briefly." That was all I could get out of him.

Finally I just did the best I could and bunged the thing in. Presumably he'd want to talk about it when he had read it anyhow.

Just as I was leaving on Sunday evening, old Taylor came in. I hadn't seen him for a long time, and it gave me a shock. His face seemed to have sunk in off the bones, and he looked as though he hadn't slept for a week. He said, " Could I trouble you for a moment, sir ? "

I said, " Sure, Taylor. What is it ? "

" I understand, sir, that the f-fuse work is being transferred away from here ? "

I said, " That's right. Professor Mair's taking it over in his own lab."

" Exactly sir. Well, before he l-left Professor Mair very

kindly said that he would take me with him, sir, to continue the fuse work."

"Yes. That's what he told me."

Taylor stared at me through his glasses—a rather odd stare. "They won't let me," he said in a queer, flat voice.

I said, "You mean they won't let you go?"

"No, sir. I've just heard. They won't let me."

"Really? Why not?"

"They *say* it's because he can't have a uniformed man there, sir." Taylor paused and then added, "That's what they *say*."

I said, "But that's just damned silly. If you were allowed to do the work here, why not there?"

Old Taylor was still staring at me in the same way. I could see his chest rising and falling very fast as he breathed. He seemed to be waiting for me to say something else.

I said, "Well, that's awfully bad luck, Taylor. I know Professor Mair will be very disappointed. Perhaps he'll be able to fix it later on. Meanwhile I suppose you'll just have to hang on here."

"I'm not to be let to stay here," said Taylor in a low voice.

"What?"

"No, sir. I'm to g-go. And I'm not to go to the Professor. I'm to g-go back to duty, sir." He got it out as though he were struggling for breath.

I said, "Well, I'm damned!"

Taylor suddenly began to speak very quickly, in a low voice. I noticed that he didn't stutter at all.

He said, "I can't do it, I can't go back to general duty. They'll post me away, and I can't leave home, not with things like they are. I'd rather do anything. They don't know, sir. I can't leave home, not now."

I was a bit alarmed at how he looked and the way he said it. I said, "But, after all, if you'd gone with Professor Mair you would have left London, wouldn't you?"

He shook his head. "Ah, but I could have found somewhere to live there. I should have known where I was going to be. It's different. If you're on general duty you may go anywhere any time. You're always moving." He stopped and then said, "I couldn't. Not with things as they are."

I looked down at my blotter and said, "I suppose the fact is that you—that you don't want to leave your wife?"

He looked at me with the glassy stare and said " Yes " almost inaudibly.

I said, " They might not move you out of London."

" I've been told, sir."

" What ? Where you're going ? "

" Yes, sir. They're sending me up north."

" Who told you ? "

I saw an odd, rather puzzled look come over his face. He hesitated for several seconds and then said, " It's right, sir. They're sending me up north."

" But who told you ? You haven't had any orders yet ? "

" No, sir. But I've been told."

" Who by ? "

He hesitated again and then said, " Sergeant-major, sir."

I thought for a bit and then said, " Well, look here, Taylor—I'll see what I can do. I don't suppose it'll be much. You know what these things are. But I'll do my best."

He looked at me and said vaguely, " I can't leave home, sir."

" Well, I'll tell them about it and see if we can arrange something." As he still stood silent, I said, " Would you like me to do that ? "

Taylor didn't answer for a moment. Then he started slightly, pulled himself up to attention and said, " Thank you, sir. It's v-very kind of you," in his old voice, and went out.

The next morning I got hold of Sergeant-major Rose and said, " Look here, Sergeant-major, what's all this about Corporal Taylor ? Is it right that he's being posted away ? "

" Yes, sir."

" To the north ? "

Rose said, " I don't know where, sir. But he's going back to duty."

" You haven't told him he's going north ? "

" No, sir. I've heard nothing about that."

I said, " He's got it into his head that he's being sent north."

" Of course somebody may have told him down at the barracks, sir."

I said, " Well, he seems to be in a frightful state about it, and he's looking like death. He seems to think he can't leave his wife."

Rose hesitated for a moment and then said confidentially, "Well, if you asked *my* opinion, sir, I should say the man was being driven off his head. That's what *I* should say."

"He certainly seems very queer."

"I've reported it, sir."

"Have you?"

"Yes, sir. I've told the M.O. that I don't think he's normal in his mind."

"What did the M.O. say?"

"He saw him, sir. But he was all right then. Of course he *is* all right at times."

I said, "D'you think there's any way we could arrange for him to be kept in London?"

Rose shook his head dubiously. "You can't pick and choose in the army, sir. There's a good many would like to be at home, if it was as easy as that."

"But it's a damned silly business anyhow. He'll be precious little use on general duty, and he's been very valuable to Professor Mair. Why waste him like this?"

Rose said, "That's the army, sir." It was his standard reply when you complained that anything was silly. It wasn't a criticism or an excuse or a justification. It was just an explanation.

I said, "Well, I think I must tackle the Director about it. It's a bit awkward, as he's only just come. But I don't see that any one else can do anything."

"No, sir," said Rose. "It'd have to be taken up from the top. Be all right *then*, I dare say."

XIII

SUSAN had a day off on Thursday, and went down to see her mother. She didn't much want to go but she hadn't been down for months, and we thought we'd fit it in with a night when I'd said I'd go round and see Knollys. It never looked like being a jolly day for the start, and as time went on it just stopped trying.

The fun began bright and early. Joe and Tilly and I had just finished our usual Komics meeting when Waring rang up and said the Director wanted all of us at once.

We trooped down to his room. It was the same room that the Old Man had used, but it looked very queer, because Brine had shifted all the furniture around and got himself

a different desk. Waring was sitting beside him. They were
discussing a file. When we went in Brine looked up and said :
    " Ah—here you are. Get yourselves chairs and sit down.
Shan't be a minute." We sat down, and he and Waring
went on talking for a few moments. Then Brine chucked the
file back into his tin tray, leant back in his chair, rubbed the
bluest bit of his chin and said :
    " Well, now gentlemen . . ."
    He looked round at us for a moment with quite a pleasant
smile, as though he was just checking up that we were the
right people. I glanced at Joe and Tilly and hoped I didn't
look as queer as they did. Joe looked like an untidy thirteen-
year-old and Tilly was doing his Ugly-Man-in-a-Fair act.
    " I haven't called you together before," Brine went on,
" because before having a general talk about the future, I
wanted to put myself right about what you all did. I've now
had a chance to look through this document you produced
for me, and I think I've got the general picture." He smiled
rather bleakly and added, " Up to a point anyhow. You'll
forgive me for saying that it's not a very *coherent* picture, but
still—there it is."
    He seemed to expect someone to say something so I said,
" I think we all felt that it was a bit scrappy, sir. But it isn't
easy stuff to get down . . ."
    " Oh quite," said Brine, waggling his fingers quickly as
though he were trying to shake something off them. " I'm
not complaining about the document. It gives me just what
I was after. If it's scrappy, it's because the *work* is scrappy."
    He stroked his chin again, looked down at his desk,
looked up again and said, " That's what I want to talk
about." He leaned forward, looked at each of us in turn,
leant back again and waded in. " Now," he said, in his deep
bass voice. " This list that you've given me contains twenty-
four major items—activities—pieces of work—whatever you
like to call them. In addition, stuff which has come in during
the few days that I've been here touches on another eight
subjects. That makes thirty-two. Now, with the greatest
respect to all of you, I simply can't believe that a Section
of this size, with these resources, can have anything useful
to say or do on thirty-two different issues."
    There wasn't a lot to be said to that. It was a thing
we'd all been saying long enough. But the Old Man never
would refuse a job.
    " Thirty-two different issues ! " said Brine. " No wonder

you find it a bit difficult to make the thing into a coherent story."

There was a pause. Then I said, " Of course, sir, you realise that on a good many of those things we're not doing the whole job. We're only giving some small bit of help to other people."

" Oh, I quite realise that," said Brine. " But it doesn't alter my point. It's all much too widespread and vague."

He picked up the paper again. " That's one thing. The next is this—there are six or seven things here where the initiating branch is given as ' Section.' What does that mean exactly ? "

I said, " Those are things originally proposed for research by us."

" In other words nobody asked for them to be done. You just thought them up ? "

" Yes."

Brine shook his head slowly. " Well, y'know . . . ," he said dubiously. " It really doesn't look as though you needed to propose *new* work. Surely your job is to tackle the things you're *asked* to do."

This seemed to me to be going a bit far.

I said, " I think most of our best jobs have been on things that we *did* propose ourselves."

" Ah, you may think so," said Brine. " But does anybody else ? Just glancing through these it looks to me as though most of them are a pure duplication of somebody else's job. Look at this for example—Ricochet Penetration. Now, you don't tell me there aren't people whose job it is to deal with a thing like that ? "

" I think the point there was that Till hit on a rather effective new way of calculating probable velocities after glancing impact."

" Oh, I dare say," said Brine rather impatiently. " But in that case his job was to hand the thing over, as a suggestion, to the right people, not to start messing about with it here."

I looked at Tilly and said, " I believe you tried that ? " Tilly just nodded.

" Well ? " said Brine, " what happened ? "

" Nothing, sir," said Tilly respectfully. Brine looked at him rather sharply. I could see that he was annoyed.

I said rather tentatively, " I think that's really the trouble. If . . . "

" Well, well," said Brine breaking in rather rudely. " I don't want to spend a lot of time arguing about it. The main fact's quite clear—we're trying to cover far too wide a field, and the first thing to do is to cut it down. Perhaps later on when the Section's been strengthened we can spread our wings. But for the time being I don't want to see any of you trying to run more than one, or at the outside two jobs at once."

Nobody said anything.

" Now," said Brine. " I've been through this list with Mr. Waring, and I've told him which of these issues seem to me our legitimate work. Those are the things which I want you to concentrate on, and I want it to be clearly understood that no time is to be spent on anything else without direct permission from me." He paused and added, " Or, of course in my absence, from Mr. Waring." He turned to Waring and said, " And I want to be notified as soon as may be."

My face went hot and I could feel both Joe and Tilly looking at me. For the life of me I couldn't see how to put it. Finally I just said : " From Mr. Waring ? "

" Yes," said Brine. " If I happen to be away and he's acting for me. I don't suppose it will arise, but it might."

I swallowed and said, " Mr. Waring is to act for you in —in *technical* matters ? "

Brine gave me a cold stare and said, " Of course. As my deputy he will be in control in my absence."

I looked at Waring. He was staring down at the carpet a bit uncomfortably. I thought of what the Old Man had said, " I've told Brine he'll have to lean on you pretty heavily . . . "

I said, " Oh, I see. We hadn't actually heard of the appointment before."

Brine was looking at me in a rather irritated way. He sensed that there was something wrong, but he either didn't know what or didn't care. He said shortly, " Well, that will be the arrangement."

I said, " May we see which items you've selected to carry on with ? "

" Yes—if you want to," said Brine rather grudgingly, as though he thought it was a waste of time. He passed over my list. " The things with the headings underlined."

Joe and Tilly leaned over and looked too. It was just as I expected.

I said, " Of course, sir, four of these are things where we do very little really. On this rubber substitutes work for example—it's practically all done by the Ministry. Till just does the routine calculations for them because they haven't a statistician or a calculating machine. But it isn't two hours work a month."

" I know that," said Brine.

" Are we to drop all the inventions stuff, sir ? " said Joe in an injured way.

" Certainly," said Brine. " I can't conceive why it was ever started. It's nothing whatever to do with us."

" People send and ask us what we think," said Joe defensively. " Departments of the Ministry, I mean."

" I know," said Brine grimly. " I've seen some samples. Everything that's too nonsensical to go anywhere else comes here. Sheer waste of time."

I was looking at the list. It was heartbreaking. I didn't regret the Keystone Komics, and there were half a dozen other things which could well be dropped. But he'd cut out all the fuse stuff, all the radio, all the weapon trials, all the ballistics stuff—everything where we'd ever done any good or had any real contacts or reputation.

I said, " What are we to do about jobs in hand ? I'm thinking of things like weapon trials. The Reeves gun for example . . . ? "

" The Reeves development has been discontinued," said Brine calmly. " So you won't have to worry about that."

" And the Charles Mortar ? "

" What's that ? "

" The experimental Air Mortar."

" Who asked us to tackle it ? "

" I don't know, sir."

" Well then, we'll keep out until we *are* asked—officially."

I said, " I think E.W.E. may be expecting something from us . . . "

" I haven't the faintest idea who E.W.E. are," said Brine curtly.

" Experimental Weapons and Equipment."

" Well, if they're expecting something we'll wait till they ask for it."

" And the work for S.W.D. ? "

" Who are they when they're at home ? "

It went on like that for about twenty minutes. He'd no idea what the things were, or who the people were, or what we were doing, or whether it mattered. All he knew was that he was going to stop pretty nearly the lot. Finally I just gave it up. It was no use trying to tell him and he only got annoyed.

Brine said, " Well, is that clear ? "

I hesitated and then said, " I think I ought to tell you that the things you've left on the list won't keep us employed for more than a week a month."

" Ah," said Brine, leaning back with a smile and flicking things off his fingers. " That's what I was waiting for you to say. Because *now*, having disposed of that lot, I've got some work that *does* need doing." He picked up another sheet of paper. " I've been talking to the Executive of the National Scientific Council and I've asked them for topics for consideration. These are what they've given me." He read from the paper. " First of all, the effect of hydrogen ion concentration in quenching fluids in the hardening of molybdenum and tungsten steels."

He looked up, with the air of a man who'd given us a present.

" How about that one ? "

There was a pause. At last I said, " Of course . . ." I was just going to say that none of us was a chemist or a metallurgist ; that we weren't equipped for that sort of thing, and that it was clearly a job for one of the big labs. anyhow, but Brine didn't give me a chance.

He said, " No—not you. Someone else for a change. You." He pointed at Till.

Tilly sat up with such a jerk that his glasses nearly came off. I'd never seen him look so startled in his life. He just stared at Brine like a cod fish and didn't say anything.

" Not an easy one, is it ? " said Brine smiling. He seemed to imagine that Tilly was busy thinking it out.

Tilly shook his head. " Far from it, sir," he said respectfully. I didn't suppose for a moment that he knew what hydrogen ion concentration meant.

" Well, have a think about it," said Brine, " and come and talk to me sometime. I've got my own ideas about that one, though it isn't really my line of country. Now then . . ." he consulted his paper again. " Ah—now this is a real beauty for somebody. ' The stability of the ring structure of organic vesicants.' Now we know a certain amount about that already." He looked round at us and said, " I think we may probably have to get somebody in to tackle that.

There's a student of mine who's been working right next door to it. Number three . . ."

He went on like that through six items. All of them but one were chemical, and the other was straight crystallography. Every single one was clearly somebody else's job—so clearly that even I could have told him whose, though I didn't know much about the chemical side. If they weren't actually being tackled it was for the very good reason that they were all very vague, long term things—the sort of thing you potter about at for four years and write a Ph.D. thesis on.

I didn't say any more. For one thing I'd been more or less told to shut up, and for another there wasn't anything to say anyhow.

Finally he gave Tilly another snorter to think about and dismissed us. I gathered that he thought Tilly was the side's real research man. Anyhow he didn't give Joe or me any presents in that line. But as we came out he called Joe back.

Tilly and I went upstairs in silence. When we got into our room we looked at one another and then Tilly began to laugh. He very seldom laughed, and when he did it was a peculiar affair in which he didn't smile but just opened his mouth and made a clucking noise.

After a while he stopped, poked his nose at me and said, "Hydrogen ion concentration," and laughed some more.

I just said, "Oh God!" and sat down at my desk.

After a while I said, "What the hell are we to do now?"

Tilly said, "Hydrogen ion concentration and the stability of rings of something, and if we want to do anything else we must get permission from the Director, or, in his absence from his deputy, Mr Waring."

"Of course he doesn't understand the position at all," I said, trying to be reasonable. "He's thinking of a university department with people working for Ph.D.s. The whole thing's fatuous."

"Well, you can't blame *him*," said Tilly. "He said he'd agreed it all with his deputy, Mr. Waring." The mister part of it seemed to have hit him hard.

I said, "I wonder if we ought just to walk out right away? Perhaps that's what he meant us to do?"

"That's up to you," said Tilly characteristically. "I'll do whatever you say." He sat down at his desk, pushed his glasses up on his forehead and started to punch his machine.

I don't think he was calculating anything in particular. It was just that the noise comforted him.

I was still sitting trying to think what to do next when the door burst open and Joe came blundering in. His face was as white as a sheet and his eyes were like saucers. He said : " Hey. I've been flung out ! "

I got up and said, " *What ?* "

" I've been sacked."

I looked at him for a moment. Of course, now the Old Man was gone Waring would have been able to do it.

Joe said, " He's just told me. The big—the big bastard." Then his face suddenly puckered up like a baby's and he started to cry. Tilly stopped punching his machine and stared at him in his misty way.

I said, " Oh come, Joe, never mind, old boy. What did he say ? "

Joe gave a loud snort and sat down at his table. " He said that we were stopping all the work I was concerned with and that he didn't think I should be s-suitable for the new stuff and that he didn't think he could afford to carry me." He produced a filthy handkerchief and blew his nose messily.

" It's just that he wants to work in some bloody people of his own," he said bitterly.

I said, " Was Waring there ? "

" No. He'd gone." He looked at me pathetically and his face puckered up again. " What the hell am I to do, Sammy ? " he said miserable. " I can't go home and—and tell M-Madeleine . . ."

Tilly said, " You might try ringing her up." I don't think he ever regarded Joe as a human being. Joe raised his head and said :

" You *bloody* bastard ! You bloody red-nosed bastard ! "

I said, " Don't be a cad, Tilly."

Joe said, " It's all very well for him. He hasn't got a wife, and anyhow he's not fit. If I can't get another job they'll call me up."

Tilly opened his mouth to say it and then caught my eye and shut it again. I thought for a moment and then said, " Look—I'll go and talk to Waring."

I went downstairs. Susan wasn't there but Waring was in his office. I went straight in and said :

" Look, R.B.—this business about Joe . . ."

He said, " What business, Sammy ? "

" He's just been fired."

Waring looked genuinely surprised. " Fired ? Already?"

" Yes. Brine's just told him."

He looked a bit blank and said, " Oh . . . "

I said, " Damn it all, it's a bloody dirty trick. The kid's heartbroken."

Waring tapped his front teeth with a pencil and said, " Well, Sammy—you know what I think about it."

" Maybe. But that was no reason for going behind my back and getting him chucked out the moment the Old Man had gone."

" But I didn't get him chucked out."

" Oh come ! " I said irritably. " If you didn't, who did ? Brine's no idea whether he's any good or not."

" Sammy," said Waring seriously. " I give you my word that I neither suggested that he should be chucked out nor even implied it. All that happened was that Brine asked me what various people did and I told him, as best I could. It wasn't easy to say what Joe does. You've often said so yourself. Then, when he was looking at your list he said, ' I don't see much about Marchant,' and I said, ' No. I think he's a sort of odd man.' That's all."

I hesitated for a moment and said, " And you mean to tell me you didn't say what you've often said to me and to the Old Man—that Joe was lazy and a luxury and so on ? "

" No," said Waring. " I honestly didn't."

He suddenly broke into his boyish grin. " To be quite frank, Sammy, I probably should have if he'd asked me, but he didn't."

I didn't know what to think. He said it as though it was true, and there was no particular reason why he should lie about it. I said, " Then didn't Brine tell you he was going to sack him ? "

Waring shook his head. " Not a word. In fact I'm rather annoyed that he didn't."

" Well then, can we go and see Brine now and say we don't think Joe ought to be fired ? "

" Oh, half a minute," said Waring with a shake of his head. " That's another thing, Sammy. You were accusing me of having him fired and I tell you I didn't. But I don't think I'm prepared to go and kick up a fuss if Brine's decided to fire Joe himself. How can I when I think he ought to go ? "

Of course he had me beautifully.

I said, " Well—don't you think it's a bit tough ? I mean —he's married and so on."

" He's a darn sight *too* married," said Waring. " That's part of his trouble. Why not suggest that he tries to get Mair to take him on ? Mair likes him. He'd find him a job."

I could see that I wasn't going to get any change.

I said, " All right. Then I must go and see Brine myself."

Waring shook his head. " I don't think I would, old horse. Not on that."

" Why not ? "

" Because I doubt you'll do Joe any good and you might do yourself harm." He tapped his teeth. " His nibs is a queer bloke and he needs handling. Very touchy at the moment about his authority and so on. I think you'll only get a raspberry."

I laughed, " That'll matter a hell of a lot now, won't it ? I've had nothing but raspberries all the afternoon, so one more's neither here nor there."

" How have you ? "

I said, " Oh, cut it out."

" No, but seriously ? "

" Well, for one thing. I understand that if I want to start a new job now I've got to get your permission."

Waring laughed. " Yes—that was rather good, wasn't it ? " he said lightly.

I said, " I didn't laugh much. Nor did you, I noticed."

" Oh, but you don't want to worry about that, my dear man," he said cheerfully. " It's just that he's got no idea how we work. He'd have been just as likely to say I must get permission from you before I contacted anybody."

I said, " Well, you might try suggesting *that* next time."

" But my dear old horse," said Waring looking puzzled. " There's nothing to feel like this about. All he's trying to do is to see some sort of *shape* in the whole thing. You must admit that it's not an easy place for an outsider to under- stand. I don't see that it matters a cuss, as long as *we* know how the thing really works."

" Well, it won't work like that. Not with me in it anyhow."

" Of course it won't. But he can't know that yet because he doesn't know any of us or what we can do." He grinned and said, " As a matter of fact when he came to that bit I nearly butted in and pointed out that I wasn't a technical chap. But then I thought he'd only get more mixed up than ever, so I thought it was best just to let it pass and arrange everything quietly between ourselves as we've always done."

I had the old helpless feeling that talking to Waring always gave me. I said, " How about this change-over in the work that he's proposing ? You realise that a lot of the stuff that he's suggesting is just impossible for us ? "

" Oh well," said Waring. " I wouldn't know about that. That's purely your side of the house. It certainly sounded pretty frightful."

" He said he'd agreed it with you."

" With me ? " said Waring in surprise. " My dear old Sam, you couldn't agree most of that with me. I haven't even heard most of the words for years. No. All he agreed with me was that the programme needed cutting down. Which it certainly did. You've always said so yourself."

" But why cut out everything any good ? "

" I tell you, o'boy, that's nothing to do with me. I'm only a poor bloody salesman nowadays." He frowned slightly and added, " As a matter of fact I told him I thought he ought to have a session with you on the whole thing. I don't know why he didn't."

I said, " It wouldn't be a bad idea. Try suggesting it again. Tell him he'll recognise me all right. I'm the one with the limp."

Waring said, " Look, o'boy. I know he's got under your skin. But give him a chance. After all, he's barely in the saddle yet."

I came away a few minutes later. There was nothing to do about Waring. He wouldn't fight. Why should he when he'd got it all in hand ? He might quite easily be telling the truth about Joe and about telling Brine to see me. There was no need for him to press now. He could sit back and let the thing work itself out in the only way it could.

I hesitated at Brine's door, and wondered whether to tackle him straight away, tell him what I thought, and walk out if he didn't like it. But somehow I just couldn't face any more of it at the moment.

I didn't much like the job of going back and telling Joe it was no good, but as it turned out it didn't matter. By the time I got back Tilly had him back to normal, and when I came in they were looking at a big dent in the ceiling that

Joe had just made demonstrating how to slope arms with a piece of brass curtain rod.

I told Joe what Waring had said. I rather expected that he would say that Waring was a liar right away, but he didn't. He seemed to think it was just Brine. He knew Waring didn't like him, but of course he didn't know anything about Waring trying to get him sacked before.

I suggested that he might write to the Old Man, and try to get a job with him, but he didn't seem as keen on that as I had expected. Apparently sloping arms with the curtain rod had made him come over all military again. He probably half wanted to join the army really and half didn't, both halves being very strong. There were a lot of people like that.

That was the morning. I had lunch with Tilly and we talked things over, as far as you could talk anything over with Tilly. I was wondering whether the thing to do wasn't to ring up the Old Man and see if he'd take us back into the Department. Tilly thought that was a grand idea, but somehow I didn't like it much.

I said, " It seems so damned feeble just to walk out, and leave R.B. and Brine to muck the whole thing up."

Tilly said, " No worse than staying and watching them."

" If we're going to do any good what we want is more contact with Brine."

" Do you ? " said Tilly pointedly.

" Yes. Half the trouble is that we haven't seen enough of him."

" Well," said Tilly, poking his glasses. " Personally I've seen plenty. But I leave it to you."

When we got back I decided that the only thing for it was to barge in and see Brine, tell him about Taylor and use that as an excuse for a general quack.

I don't know why, but ringing Brine up made me feel a bit nervous, particularly when he picked up the receiver and said, " Yes ? " impatiently almost before I heard the ringing tone.

I said, " This is Rice here, sir . . . "

He said, " Who ? Oh yes, Rice. Yes ? "

" I wondered whether you could spare me a minute if I came down ? "

He hesitated and said, " Well . . . I'm rather tied up. Is it urgent ? "

" It is rather."

He hesitated again, " Can you give me any idea what it's about, Rice ? '

I said, " It's about Corporal Taylor, sir . . . "

" Taylor ? " Brine said, " But surely that's all fixed up, isn't it ? "

I was a bit puzzled. I said, " You mean he's going ? "

" Going ? He's gone. The commandant rang me up this morning."

I said, " Oh—I'm sorry. I didn't realise that. He's been posted away already ? "

" Posted away ? " said Brine, obviously irritated. " No. Taken away to hospital. Tried to murder his wife or something. Anyhow they've rung me up and said he's been taken to hospital."

I hesitated and then said, " Oh . . . I'm sorry. I didn't realise that. Sorry to have wasted your time."

" That's all right," said Brine rather grudgingly. " That's all I know. Rose will tell you about it, if you ask him." He rang off.

I went and saw Rose. It was quite true. Taylor hadn't done her much harm luckily. Her version was that he'd come in, looked at her in a queer way, and suddenly grabbed her by the throat. She'd got away and yelled for help, and the neighbours had come in. I think there was probably more to it than that really, but anyhow it was pretty clear that poor old Taylor wasn't safe so they'd taken him away.

I said, " That's my fault."

" *Your* fault, sir ? " said old Rose inquiringly.

" Yes. I said I'd see the Director about it yesterday and I didn't. I knew Taylor oughtn't to be about."

" Well, come to that, sir, so did I," said Rose reassuringly. " That doesn't make it your fault. After all the doctor'd seen him. Nobody's to blame—except that whore of a woman. She was the trouble, sir. If you ask me it's a pity poor old Taylor *didn't* finish her—except for his own sake." He paused and then said, " You hadn't said anything to the Director ? "

" No."

Rose hesitated and then said, " Oh well—even if you had it wouldn't have been in time. It was the doctor ought to have seen."

I didn't say any more. But he knew I'd let Taylor down.

He'd pass the buck to somebody else on principle of course. But it didn't make any difference.

After that lot I couldn't face an evening with Knollys, talking about viscosities. I rang him up and spun some yarn about working late and got out of it, and went home about half-past six. It never occurred to me that it might be a bad thing to do. For once I wanted to be at home by myself. I was even glad in a way that Susan wouldn't be there.

We had a wire cage letterbox. There was a telegram in it. I never had the slightest doubt what it was, and I was right. It was from the Air Ministry and it said that Dick was gone. It didn't say he had been killed in action. It just said he had " lost his life while employed on special operations." I put it back in its envelope and went into the living-room.

There was a note from Susan on the table which said, " Hope you had a nice evening. Now go straight to bed, darling. Good-night. See you to-morrow. S."

After that it all got very queer for a bit. I got out the whisky and had a drink, but the taste of it nearly made me sick so I didn't drink any more. I sat down and tried to think, but I kept switching about from one thing to another and never getting anywhere. What shook me was that I couldn't even keep my mind on Dick. As soon as I started to think about him I switched over to thinking about Taylor and Brine and Waring and God knows what. There was a piece of black polished linoleum over in the corner of the room and I had a queer feeling that I could see Pinker out of the corner of my eye, crouching on it and watching me. The feeling was so strong that I turned and looked, but of course there wasn't anything there.

I made another effort, and remembered that now I must send Dick's letter to his girl. I got up to get it, and then the telephone rang.

XIV

WHEN I picked up the telephone I had a fleeting hope that it was Susan. I suppose that confused me because at first I couldn't catch what the chap at the other end was saying. He had to say his name three times before I realised that it was Stuart. He said, " I've got one, old boy."

I said, " My God—have you ? In one piece ? "

" Yes. In fact I've got two. Complete, undamaged, and in mint condition."

" Where ? "

" I'm at Luganporth. They're down on the sands about two miles away. I've got cordons round them."

" On the *sands* ? "

" Yes. Couldn't be better, could it ? I think they must have been jettisoned."

I said, " You've seen them ? "

" Yes. I've taken a fairly respectful sort of look."

" Like we thought ? "

" Fairly. Bit bigger. We were a hundred per cent wrong about one thing though."

" What ? "

Stuart said, " Tick-tock, tick-tock."

" Time ? "

" Apparently."

I said, " Are you sure ? "

" Oh, yes. I heard it myself. Look, o'boy—I take it you want to be on in this ? You don't have to, of course, but——

I said, " Of course I do."

" Right. Then this is the idea—I shall give them until to-morrow to do their stuff by themselves. Then, if they haven't I shall have a go."

I said, " How early can I get down ? "

" Wait a minute. As we've got two the obvious thing is to try them in series. I'll have a go. Then if I make a pig's ear you'll know some of the things not to do with the other. Agree ? "

" You'll wait till I get down ? "

" Depends what time you arrive. But anyhow I'll see that absolutely everything's recorded."

I thought for a moment and then said, " I'd much rather you waited till I got there."

" Why ? " said Stuart. I heard him chuckle to himself.

" Two heads are better than one."

" Yes. But we can't do a joint thing, o'boy. Otherwise if it goes wrong there won't be anybody to cope with the other one."

I said, " What are you going for ? "

" Stopping it if it hasn't stopped. Then try electro-magnetic. Then photo-electric. Then trembler. In that

158

order. After that I shall get annoyed and hit it with a hammer or something."

"Look," I said. "For God's sake wait until I get down. I've got a lot of things to suggest."

"Fine," said Stuart. "You can try them on Number Two. But Number One's mine. Damn it, I found it."

He sounded extraordinarily happy. I said, "I'll get down by the first train. There might possibly be one to-night."

"I doubt it. It's a God-forsaken bit of coast."

"Then first thing to-morrow. How far is it from here?"

"Oh, quite a step. Four hours, I should think. Tell you what—I'll have the thing's liver grilled for you for lunch."

I said, "Be careful, Stuart, for the love of Mike."

"Laddie," he said cheerfully. "I propose to be so careful that it'll hurt. See you to-morrow."

"Yes. And wait if you can. Seriously."

"Well—we'll see. Cheerio till then."

I said, "Cheerio. And good luck."

We hung up. I went straight on and rang up about trains. There was nothing till six in the morning and that didn't get there till one-thirty. There was a fast one at nine that got down ten minutes later so I decided to go on that.

It was only when I'd done that and chucked some things into a bag ready for the morning that I began to think about the thing, and then very suddenly it went bad on me and I got scared. When I was talking to Stuart I hadn't been thinking at all and I'd even been a bit annoyed that he wouldn't wait for me. But when there was nothing to do but wait till the morning it was quite different. I kept thinking, "He'll kill himself and then I shall have to tackle it alone." My hands began to sweat. I looked down and saw my foot and thought that I shouldn't be able to wear it because it was metal. I wondered for a moment whether that would get me out of it; or if I could arrange it so that I told somebody else what to do.

Then it occurred to me that if I told Brine he would stop me, because it wasn't really our job. I wanted somebody not to let me do it. That was what I wanted. I tried to tell myself that they'd never let me—not with my foot, and it being nothing to do with us.

I must have gone on sitting there for over an hour, sweating and shaking and generally in a funk. Then I thought perhaps it would be better if I went to bed, but it wasn't. I just lay with my eyes shut, and thought about it. I could see the bloody thing lying on the sand looking small and quite harmless, ready to go off, and I knew I should never be able to touch it. Some people are good when they're frightened and go steadier than usual. But I knew that I just shook and got helpless and clumsy and couldn't use my hands properly.

I tried telling myself that Stuart would deal with it and that there wouldn't be anything for me to do, but that didn't work. I just came back every time to the thing lying there on the sand waiting for me.

I must have been gradually going to sleep in spite of it, because I remember deciding that though Stuart would be killed and I should be killed too, there was nothing that could be done about it, and started to think about how to tackle the thing. The last thing I remember is thinking that I should want wooden clamps like you use in a lab., and wishing that I'd suggested them to Stuart. Then I went to sleep and slept all night. I'd noticed before that however worried I was, only certain sorts of things would keep me awake— the sort of things which I thought about and thought about and couldn't get any further. As soon as I could think about anything that led anywhere, I could go to sleep.

It was still pretty bad the next morning, but in a slightly different way—partly because I can never see things so vividly in daylight as at night and partly because I hadn't that inevitable feeling about Stuart. I still thought that he might probably get blown to glory, but the night before there had seemed to be no question about it. It was difficult about the office, and about Susan. Nobody would be at the office before my train went, but I could hardly go off without saying anything. Finally, I rang up Tilly at his home and told him where I was going, but didn't tell him any details. I told him not to tell anybody unless I was wanted.

The only thing to do about Susan seemed to be to leave her a note. I knew she was coming back to the flat about lunch-time, before she went in. I went to get out some paper and came on Dick's letter to his girl. I don't know why, but when I saw it, I just began to laugh. It seemed damned funny, somehow, that I should be going to write one to Susan before I'd even posted his. I had a silly thought for a moment that I might just have crossed the address out and put Susan's name instead and left it at that.

It was while I was standing there, grinning to myself, with this letter in my hand that I first saw about this thing and what it meant. I'd been too busy being frightened before. I took a piece of paper and wrote a note to Susan. I said, " A lot of things have happened. Dick's been killed. Stuart's got two of his things and I've gone down to help him with them. It seems to me if I get blown up that might be quite a good thing, and anyhow it'll put me alongside Dick which is good enough for anybody. If I don't, then I shall have done a thing. See? Anyhow, I love you. I am frightened, but not as much as I was. I did have a drink last night but only one. Good-bye pet. Sammy." I wasn't quite satisfied with it, but it was high time to go for my train so I just wrote underneath, " You can say what you like but this is quite a *difficult* thing, and if I do it I shall probably be quite different and bully everybody."

It wasn't until we were nearly half-way there that it occurred to me that Stuart might have waited to tackle the thing until I came, after all. For some reason that panicked me again. I knew I would far rather he'd tried it and been killed and left me to do it than that I should have to tackle it with him. I felt pretty sick and went along to the lavatory, but I hadn't any had breakfast and though I retched quite a lot it didn't really do any good. I stood for a long time in the lavatory, hanging on to that hand-grip they always put in train lavatories, and wishing the train would stop rocking. The lavatory had walls covered with silvery metallic-looking stuff. I thought, " If I were any good I should be worrying about Stuart." But I wasn't. He was a good chap, and normally I should have cared a lot what happened to him. But I seemed to have gone cold and frightened inside and however much I thought about it, it was always me I was worrying about. I looked at my face in the lavatory mirror. It had that pulled in, chinless look that always made me look weak and timid. I thought, " Portrait of a hero being sick at the thought of it."

Just as we got to Luganporth, I realised that Stuart hadn't given me an address and that I'd no idea where to go. But there was a sapper lieutenant on the platform and as soon as I got out he came up and said, " Mr. Rice ? "
I said, " Yes."
He said, " My name's Pearson, sir. I have a car here for you." It was always queer to be called sir by subalterns.

He was driving the car himself. He didn't say any more until we had started and then I said, " Has Captain Stuart done anything yet ? "

He looked at me as though he were surprised and then said, " Oh, yes." He looked away and said, " Rotten business." After a moment he added, " I thought you knew, but of course you couldn't. You were on the train."

I said, " Is he dead ? "

" Oh, yes. He was killed instantly." He was silent for a bit and then said, " Apparently they thought he'd done it. I wasn't down there myself, but the people who were thought it was all finished. Then something went wrong, and it went up."

My throat was very dry, but otherwise I felt quite calm. I said, " Any one else hurt ? "

" No. He was working on it alone. Nobody else was near."

I said, " Damn it. He was a good chap."

The sapper said, " Yes. He had guts."

We drove for about a quarter of an hour in silence. The only thing I remember about the drive is doing my old trick of thinking that perhaps I was still asleep at home really. It wasn't that I was surprised about Stuart, but the thing had a queer, flat, obvious feeling.

We went down a narrow, very steep road marked " Dangerous for motor traffic " which led down to the sea. There were a couple of small bungalows beside a cove, and three or four cars outside. For some reason this rather startled me. I had never thought that there would be a lot of odd people about. I had just imagined Stuart quite alone, with nobody else concerned at all. Pearson parked the car outside one of the bungalows and said, " The C.O. told me to take you straight in, sir."

We went in. The bungalow wasn't furnished much. I should think they had just bagged it for the job. It only had two rooms. In one of them a lieutenant-colonel was sitting at a trestle table. Pearson said, " Mr. Rice, sir," and he got up and shook hands. He was a tall, very broad chap of about forty-five with a face like a prize fighter and rather incongruous baby blue eyes. He said, " Ah—here you are. How d'you do ? My name's Strang." He turned to Pearson and said, " All right, Don. Thanks very much." Pearson saluted and went out. We sat down. Strang said, " You've been told what happened ? "

I said, " I know Stuart tackled it and that it went wrong."

" Yes. That was early this morning."

" I should like to know exactly what happened," I said after a pause.

" Well, of course, we don't know what went wrong," said Strang. " That's the trouble. The only man who could tell us that is Stuart and he's dead."

I said, " Yes. I really meant before that. What he did beforehand. How he tackled it."

" Oh, we've got all that, of course. They're transcribing the shorthand notes now. You'll be able to see them soon."

" Did he have somebody making notes, then ? Or did he——"

" He had a field telephone," said Strang shortly. I had never thought of that and felt rather a fool.

" Anyhow," said Strang, brushing some papers out of the way and putting his elbows on the table. " We can go into all that later. What I've got to get settled is where you come into this."

He looked at me thoughtfully with the baby blue eyes. " I believe you've been working on this thing with Dick Stuart for some time ? "

" Yes."

" You're a fuse expert ? "

" I've done a lot on experimental fuses."

He nodded and said, " Of course, strictly speaking, Dick had no right to bring you in at all. Not that that matters. You can't worry too much about the official channels in a job of this kind. But it puts me in rather a spot."

I knew what he was getting at, and tried desperately to see what it was I wanted and what to say. But it wouldn't come clear and before I could say anything Strang went on, " Dick told me last night," he said slowly, " that he'd arranged with you that he should try it and that if it went wrong you were to have a go."

I said, " Yes."

" Well, if he'd arranged that with one of our people it would have been quite all right. Somebody's got to do it. But I'm not sure how I stand with a civilian like yourself." He stared at me for a moment and then said, " He ought to have had somebody else working with him on it. But he was so damned cagey and independent about it and we were so short of chaps that we just let him carry on alone. Now, we're caught with our pants down, with nobody knowing anything about the damned thing."

There was a long pause.

"Of course we've got plenty of people who're only too keen to tackle it," said Strang. He smiled slightly and jerked his hand towards the door. "There's young Don Pearson—the boy who drove you out. He's longing to go and hit the thing a few good clips with a hammer and a cold chisel. But it isn't quite that sort of job."

He stopped again. I knew he was waiting for me to say something. I looked out of the window on to the beach. It was flat, calm, and the tide was right down. The sea looking incredibly peaceful.

I cleared my throat so as not to croak and said, "I had a fairly definite plan mapped out with Stuart. I think if I could see his notes I could probably—I should probably be all right."

Strang's face changed in a queer way. He smiled and said, "Oh, I'm not worrying about *you*, old boy. I'm worrying about me. If I let you do it and you happen to blow yourself up, what's your family going to say to me? And your boss? And God knows who?"

I said, "I haven't got a family. And my—and Professor Mair knows all about it."

"I see. So you think it's all right at your end?"

"Yes."

Strang thought for a moment and then shook his head. "Well, I think I shall have to cover myself at mine. I mean I shall have to talk to *my* master. You see we can't take any chance of having it said that as soon as there was a dirty job to be done we called in a civilian."

I said, "I don't see that being a civilian's got much to do with it. Civilians get plenty of dirty jobs. Why shouldn't they? Anyhow, it's a pure trick-fuse job."

There was another pause and then Strang said, "So you think on the whole you stand a better chance of getting away with it than any of my boys? After all, that's the real point. We've got to get the damned thing apart, and it's purely a question of what's the best way to do it."

I said, "Yes. I'll do it."

"Do you want to work alone or do you want help? I can get you plenty of people if you do, and they'll do exactly what you say."

"I'd rather do it alone."

"Well, think about that when you read Dick's notes. I think there was one place where he was saying he needed three hands." He sat back in his chair and thought.

Then he said, "Right. Well, then I shall get through to my master and tell him the situation. I shall tell him I've talked to you, that you're willing to do it, that it's all right with your Professor, and that on the whole I think we ought to accept your offer."

He suddenly smiled very charmingly and added, "With great gratitude, I may say."

I felt myself going a bit red and muttered something vague.

"Right," said Strang, getting up. "Now it'll take me some time to get through, and while I'm doing that you'd probably like to have a look at Dick's notes and the transcription of the shorthand. It ought to be finished by now." He let out a terrific bawl of "Sergeant Wilks!" A sergeant came in and Strang said, "Go in next door and see if those notes are finished, will you? And bring them in to me."

When the sergeant had gone he turned to me and said, "Just one other thing while we're waiting. Morbid subject, but I ought to mention it to you. You're not married I take it?" For some reason that struck me as wryly funny. I said, "No, I'm not married."

"And no dependents? I tell you why I ask you—because if they agree to this they'll almost certainly make you say that the whole thing is done at your own risk."

I said, "Well, that's all right."

"Good. Only I've had this before. It always sounds damned mean and ungracious but it's the Treasury. If ever the Services want a civilian to do anything risky for them, they aren't allowed to do anything for him—not to insure him or to promise to give his people compensation if he's killed. It always makes me livid, but there it is. It's the damned mean red-tapey way things are done, and I thought I ought to tell you about it."

I said, "It does sound a bit hard. But it doesn't matter in my case. I haven't got anybody like that."

They gave me the other room in Strang's bungalow, with just a trestle table and a chair, and brought in Stuart's notebooks and a lot of typewritten sheets, which were the transcription of what had come over the field telephone.

I was itching to read the transcription, but I thought I'd

165

better begin at the beginning, so I started with the notebooks. Apparently there had been about half a dozen cases of the things before anybody realised that they weren't just dud shells or bombs of our own that had been left about. Then there had been another five before Stuart was put on the job, which was about a month before he had got in touch with us. It seemed that the outfit Stuart belonged to was a special affair called C.S.B. The things themselves were called " booby traps " at first, and later L.O.U.s. It was odd to read the bit about meeting me and about our expeditions. He had been damned nice about me and made it read as though I had done a lot more than I had. Several things that he'd got down as my suggestions were things I could have sworn he'd thought of himself and mentioned to me. There was a copy of the letter and telegrams he'd sent to me, and of my replies. The whole thing was very orderly, and there was a complete analysis of how reports of the things being found tied up with reports of enemy aircraft being over. There was only one case where one was reported where there didn't seem to have been a plane. I read on through right up to the stuff we got out of the gunner in hospital. After that there were only two or three rather scrappy notes about warnings having been broadcast, then a gap, and then a section headed with a date three days before, which was the stuff I was really after. It ran :

" At 1900 hrs. C.S.B. was informed by telephone that an R.A.F. officer on leave, walking with his wife on the beach about two miles from Luganporth, had found two objects corresponding to the broadcast description of L.O.U.s. Orders were issued through Command to the nearest unit to place cordons round the objects with a radius of three hundred yards from their position, as nearly as Squadron-Leader Lacey could estimate it. Strict orders were issued that no one should approach the objects more nearly than this. In the meantime I started for Luganporth by car, arriving at about 0430 hrs. on the 25th. There was a considerable amount of mist on the shore and as Squadron-Leader Lacey and Mrs. Lacey could not give the location of the objects with certainty to within 100 yards, it was not felt advisable to try to operate until morning.

" With the first light Lacey could get his bearings more accurately, and the objects were located without difficulty. They were about a quarter of a mile apart, both lying on

166

sand above high-water mark. The cordons had been placed with great accuracy, considering the vagueness of the directions.

"I decided not to attempt to neutralise the objects until the arrival of the C.S.B. party with the field telephone, and as soon as the light was good enough, I stripped and approached them with the intention of getting photographs. Those taken are attached. It will be seen from the rule shown beside them that they are somewhat larger than we had supposed, being about fourteen inches long and two-and-a-half inches in diameter, except at the cap, which is somewhat larger. (cf., the evidence of Gnr. Peterson.) Both were embedded to nearly half their depth in the sand, which was fairly firm, though B (the more westerly) appeared to have struck a piece of shingle which was beside it. It seems a reasonable conclusion that they had been dropped from a fair, though not enormous height, which corresponds with the idea of jettisoning from a damaged enemy A/C."

I stopped here and had a look at the photographs. The things were very much as I'd thought of them—a thickish cylinder with a cap on the end—not unlike some sorts of incendiary. The photographs were very good and clear. They had been taken from a range of about six feet. I supposed Stuart had either forgotten the metal in his camera or else had decided that that much metal at six feet was safe enough.

I went back to the report and found that he had thought of the metal.

" Having taken the photographs I left the camera away from the objects and took a closer look at A, without, however, touching it. Whilst I was examining it I thought I detected ticking, and on putting my ear close to the object I could clearly hear the ticking, without having to use a stethoscope. Similar examination of B showed that it was ticking also. This was unexpected, since it suggested a time fuse, and we had rather abandoned the idea that they might be time bombs (see above).

" I reported the ticking to Lieut.-Colonel Strang who had now arrived with the C.S.B. group, and after some discussion it was agreed that since, if the L.O.U.s were time fused, they would be liable to detonate at any time, we should leave them untouched for twenty-four hours. It was felt to be very unlikely that they would have a longer fuse than the thirty-six hours which would then have elapsed since they were found. If no explosion had taken place by then, I was to approach them. If the clocks were still going I was to endeavour to stop them with the E.M. apparatus. If the clocks had stopped we should assume either that the fuse had missed or else that it was now set and liable to detonate on some stimulus."

The report broke off here for a few lines. Then there was a note about telephoning me and our conversation. Stuart hadn't said anything about my asking him to wait till I came. Then the whole thing suddenly turned into a letter to me :

" Dear Rice,
" In case you want it (which I sincerely hope you won't !) here's the set-up I'm going to use. The story up to date is above, and later on you'll get the running commentary from the ringside. But this is what I aim to do, as I see it at the moment (2200 hrs. on the 25th).

" (1) I shall tackle A. Rather mean because I think it's lying a bit better, which means you may get B.

" (2) I shall get going as soon as there's plenty of light.

" (3) Shorts and sweat shirt, so that there's no risk of catching clothes in things (and my God will it be cold !). Field telephone laid on to shorthand writer.

" (4) I have dug a slit trench about thirty feet away, which is as far as my reaching rods will go. Get into it and try dangling metal all round the thing with the reaching rod to see if it will go for electro-magnetic.

" (5) Assuming it won't, I shall then try shading it in various places with the reaching rod in case it's some trick photo-electric thing.

" (6) Assuming it still won't, I shall then try slightly warmed stuff against its surface to make sure it won't go from the warmth of one's hand if touched. (I know all this sounds damn funny and that I shall look an awful fool doing it, but you told me to be careful.)

" (7) All being still quiet, I shall then arise from my funk hole and positively go up to the thing. I shall listen for the clock. If it's still going I shall get the portable E.M. apparatus which will be about 50 yards away, and try to stop it. I don't like this bit at all, but I don't see quite what else to do. If Jerry's put the clock in just to frighten us, which he's quite capable of doing, then he's no gentleman. But if it's got a job to do we *must* stop it before going any further. The snag about the E.M. is that it will probably stop the clock, but if the thing's got another sort of fuse too, it may blow it. Which will be annoying.

" (8) Anyhow, assuming that the clock has stopped itself or that I've stopped it, I shall then assume that we're most probably dealing with some sort of movement fuse—probably trembler, and that the problem is how to keep the damned thing still while I work on it.

" (9) I've thought it over, and for the life of me I can't think of anything much better than a big pipe wrench, and even that will be damned difficult to get round because of the sand.

" (10) If I can get it firmly in that I shall then scrape away sand round the cap end, and see if I can shift the cap with another wrench. This bit is pure guesswork of course, but the balance of probability seems to be (*a*) that the cap comes off (after all, Jerry must fill the thing, and fit the fuse somehow, and I can't see where else he could), (*b*) that the fuse is in the cap.

" (11) If I get the cap off, then we shall see what we shall see. . . . If the cap doesn't come off, or I can't get it off, then I think I shall get a bench out there with a vice and try lifting the thing very carefully in the exact plane in which it is lying, until I can get it into the vice and have a look for other ways. I don't think this will happen, because if the cap won't come off and the whole thing is as light on the trigger as it seems to be, I shall almost certainly send the balloon up in trying to shift the cap.

" I think that's all. I'll do a running commentary from the ringside and you'll have that. Cheerio, old boy, and thanks a lot. See you at lunch.   " DICK STUART."

Underneath was written. "If you *do* have to have a go at B, remember to take a handkerchief for your hands. They may get sweaty. And keep your head down if you do the reaching rod stuff again. Yours *might* be different from mine." There was another gap and then the last sentence, " I've dug a trench for yours too, you lazy hound." Just as I'd finished reading this, Strang came in. He said, " Well, I've talked to my master. I don't think he likes the idea much, but he says that we can go ahead, as long as you're quite clear that your people know the sort of job it is. I told him I'd talked to you and that you seemed to have had it all fixed beforehand with your Professor and Stuart. So there we are."

I said, " Right."

" By the way," said Strang suddenly. " You did have lunch on the way down, of course ? It's only just occurred to me——"

" Oh, yes," I said quickly. " I had lunch on the train."

" That's all right then," said Strang. " It just didn't enter my head to ask you before."

He looked rather doubtfully at the papers and said, " Well, now we're rather in your hands. Like to think about a programme now, or would you rather finish reading that stuff ? "

" I think I'll get through this first. I shan't be long now."

" All right," said Strang. He looked at his watch. " It's about half-past three now. Supposing we have a cup of tea in about an hour and then you tell us how you want to operate ? "

When he had gone I turned to the transcript of the short-hand notes. They were a queer mix-up of what had come over the telephone with the shorthand writer's own notes. The first sheet began : " 0645 hrs. wire tested and found in order. Capt. S. went out and we saw him get into slit trench 0647. Well, here we are at Wembley, it's a lovely day with sun and a slight breeze blowing from the pavilion end, the ground looks in beautiful condition, there must be quite 100,000 people here, the King hasn't come yet. 0648 I am putting the reaching rods together and baiting the hook with a large spanner. Capt. S. is humming. Sergt. Groves has the glasses and reports he can see him fitting the joints. One won't go in. It has gone in now. 0651. Well, here we go. Sergt. Groves reports Capt. S. bringing spanner over object. Says something, can't catch it. 0653. Well, it won't rise to a spanner just ignores it. Now trying another fly. Sergt. Groves reports fitting shade to rod. 0655. Here we go again with the shade. 0656. No go isn't interested in that either. How about the warm tube. 0659. This is a bit tricky. I nearly poked the damn thing then. Anyhow, it doesn't seem to mind the warmth. Hell—now I suppose I shall have to get out of this nice safe hole and make a frontal attack. 0700. Sergt. Groves reports Capt. S. out of trench. 0701. Listen you boys back there, this wire of yours is a bloody nuisance. Capt. S. looking down. Having trouble with the wire. Says, oh curse the stuff. 0703. Capt. S.

now near object. Kneeling down. Sergt. Groves says his head right down listening. 0704. Glory be it's stopped. The clock is not, repeat not ticking so the fuse has either missed or is now fully set. Where's that wrench. Oh, hell I've only brought one wrench. 0705. Look chaps, I seem only to have one wrench. Sergt. Groves says he's left it in the trench. Sergt. Groves reports Capt. S. gets up and goes to trench. Oh, no—here it is. Thing weighs about half a ton. Sergt. Groves reports Capt. S. going back to object. Kneels down again. Still having trouble with wire. Says something don't catch it. 0707. I'm now going to try to fit the wrench on to hold it steady. 0708. Sergt. Groves reports working with wrench. 0712. Says, Christ. 0715. Whistles. Says well it's on. If it is a trembler it's a damned insensitive one. I shook it badly once. The wrench is now clamped across the thinner end, so that I can steady with my left hand. Not that my left hand is much of a way to steady anything. 0717. I shall have five bars rest I think. Will one of you back there bring me out a cigarette and a match. Don't come towards me until I get well away. Capt. S. takes off transmitter and starts to walk out to left. Sapper Reece goes out with cigarette. Gives to it Capt. S. Capt. S. sits down and lights it. Sapper Reece comes back. Says Capt. S. says it's going well but this is the tricky part. Sapper Reece says he seems all right but sweating a lot. 0725. Capt. S. gets up, goes back. Sergt. Groves says putting on transmitter. Can you still hear me, mother? Kneels down again. Now holding it steady with the wrench in my left hand. I am going to work the sand away from under the cap end so that I can get at it with the other wrench. 0726. Capt. S. humming. 0729. I think that's all right. Oh, God, this is where I need three hands. I shan't be able to tighten the wrench up. Sergt. Groves reports Capt. S. kneeling upright looking at object. 0730. What I've got to do now is to get the second wrench on the cap end. To do that I need both hands to tighten it up, which means I shall have to let go of the other wrench. Damn and blast. 0731. I'm going to have to take the first wrench off and put it on again so that I can hold it in position with my knee while I put the other one on. 0732. Well here goes. 0737. That's the first one on again. I don't think it can be a trembler or it would have gone then. Now I can hold that one steady with my knee. At least I I could if I (didn't catch it). Hell, it hurts. 0739. Now I'm going to put the second wrench on the cap end. Capt. S.

talking under his breath—can't catch it. 0742. That went on quite nicely. I'm assuming that it unscrews anti-clock-wise. Just a minute. 0744. I'm now going to try to unscrew the cap with the wrench in my right hand, holding it steady with the wrench in my left. Hold everything, chaps. Here we go. Capt. S. talking under his breath—can't catch it. 0745. No go. Either isn't a screw thread or damned tight. Have another go. 0746. Shifted her. Yes. Quite a bit. 0747. I've shifted it a complete half turn. Now I shall have to take the wrench off and put it on again for the next. Sergt. Groves reports Capt. S. shifting his position. 0752. That's two turns. Quite loose now. Try fingers. 0754. I have the cap off. Get this. I'll say it slowly. The cap screws off anti-clockwise on about six brass threads. Clock mechanism is in the cap. Straightforward trembler mechanism in the top of the body. Ah. I see. Wait a minute. 0756. Yes. That's it. Two insulating slips which go in on either side of the trembler so that it can't act. Then the clock mechanism winds them out and leaves the trembler set. Clever these Chinese. (Capt. S. talking, can't get it.) 0758. Before I go any further I'm going to earth this trembler. Hang on. Sergt. Groves reports Capt. S. going to slit trench. Capt. S. going back. 0759. I'm taking one side of this contact to earth. That's very obliging of Jerry to put that there. 0804. Well, unless the electricity they taught me is all wrong, that ought to be hunky-dory. I think I'd better just tremble the trembler to see. Yes. That seems O.K. 0807. Well, boys, unless there's a very small man inside with a lighted match or something, I think that's probably all right. There will be special matinees this week on Wednesdays and Fridays. Just let's have another look. What's this hole? 0809. No. Positively no deception. Bob's your uncle. I don't see why the hell they wanted such a long lead on the insulators—but there. At this point 0810 the explosion occurred, and the transmitter was destroyed. Sergt. Groves who was watching through the glasses reports that at the time Capt. S. was kneeling upright with what appeared to be the cap in his hands."

Strang came in and said, "Ready for a cup of tea? It's in my room." We went through to his room. The tea was real Army gun-fire, but I was glad of it.

Strang said, "Well, what d'you make of it from the notes?"

I thought for a bit and said, "I don't know. It seems pretty clear that one of two things happened. Either he hadn't earthed the trembler properly, or else there's another fuse of some sort that he missed."

"Groves was watching through glasses and he swears that Dick wasn't touching the thing at the time. He was kneeling upright with something in his hand."

"Yes. But he still had the wrench on the body of it. He may have moved it with his knee or something."

"You don't think there can be a charge in the caps itself?"

"I shouldn't think so."

When we had drunk our tea Strang said, "Have you got a programme worked out?"

"More or less. I shall do exactly what Stuart did up to getting the cap off. Except that I shan't use a wrench to hold it. I want both hands free."

"What will you use then?"

"Clamps if I can get them. You know—the sort of things you use in a lab. Then I can work the sand away all round, and get at it better."

"Yes," said Strang a bit doubtfully. "We haven't actually got anything like that. I suppose we can get hold of something."

I said, "Is there a lab. anywhere near? Or even a big school. They'd have some. You know the sort of thing I mean?"

"Oh yes. All I'm wondering is whether they'll hold it firmly enough against the turning. Lab. clamps aren't very strong, you know."

"No," I said. "I may have to hold it with a wrench while I'm actually turning."

Strang said, "Anyhow, I know the sort of thing you mean. I'll see what I can rustle up." He paused and then said, "When d'you want to tackle it?"

"As soon as possible."

"I doubt we can get clamps before the light goes—which means leaving it till to-morrow morning. That all right?"

"Yes."

He said, "All right. Then we'll aim for that."

I went out just as it was getting dusk and walked down to the beach. After about a hundred yards you were out of sight of the bungalows, and it was very solitary. The tide was just turning, but the sea was still like a mill pond.

I stood looking at the gulls for a bit, and tried to think that it might be the last time that I should see it all. But it didn't mean anything. I was still turning over in my mind the last bit of the shorthand notes. It seemed unlikely that a chap like Stuart would have made a mess of earthing the trembler. He wasn't like that. It was far more likely that he'd missed something. That would mean another fuse.

I sat down on a rock and started to go through the shorthand notes in my mind. He had said it was a simple trembler. He had talked about a hole somewhere, and he had said he didn't see why the lead was so long. If the clock withdrew the insulators from the trembler, how could the lead be long? If it was longer than the distance from the clock to the trembler it wouldn't withdraw. But in fact it had withdrawn, because apparently the trembler was set.

I couldn't really see the thing clearly enough, and after a bit I gave it up and sat and watched the gulls. I remembered that they were supposed to be the souls of dead sailors. It was very quiet and peaceful, which felt odd, because I hadn't felt like that for days.

We had a sort of picnic meal at about eight o'clock. I hadn't had any food all day, but I wasn't really hungry. Strang told me he had sent for some clamps, though he didn't know if they'd do. Afterwards Strang said, " Do you play chess ? "

I said, " Yes. Rather badly."

He said, " Then what about a game ? I've got a pocket set. We might have gone up to the pub but it's rather a hell of a way."

We played three games. He was keen, but not very good and you only had to wait for him to beat himself. About ten we packed up and went to bed. I was very sleepy, and though it was a camp bed with just blankets and no sheets I went to sleep almost at once.

XV

I WOKE UP at about five o'clock. It was still dark and I lay for a long time listening to the gulls and the wash of the sea on the beach. There was more wind than there had been the night before. At six one of Strang's people brought me some tea and said that breakfast would be in half an hour.

I got up and dressed. I was very cold and rather depressed, but not at all excited or scared. Over in the other bungalow Strang and Pearson were already having breakfast with two other officers who were in charge of the cordon down on the beach. I didn't usually eat breakfast, but I thought that if I didn't have any they would think I was nervous, so I ate some fried bread and bacon.

Strang said, " I've got some clamps. I don't know if they'll do. They're rather big heavy things, but they'll be firmer than lab. clamps. Now what else do you want ? "

I said, " I don't think there's anything else except just the things that Stuart had."

The cordon officers finished up their tea and went off.

Strang said, " We'd better tell them when we shall be down. What d'you think ? "

I said, " Oh—in an hour's time—if it'll be light enough by then ? "

He said, " I think that'll be all right."

After they'd gone we went out to have a look at the clamps and the other stuff. The clamps were iron, with big broad heavy bases and toothed jaws tightened by a thumb-screw. I don't know what they were really meant for, but I thought they would do well. Two chaps were working on the field telephone, and it occurred to me that it must be a new one because the other had been written off.

Strang said, " Try it on so as to get the harness right for you." There were no earphones, since they weren't going to be sending to me. It was just a transmitter that fitted on your chest so that you could speak into it by bending your head. It was quite comfortable but it struck me that it would be rather a nuisance, particularly with wire trailing about.

They showed me the wrenches and the reaching rods. The reaching rods were just like stiff fishing rods that you jointed together, with weights in the butt ends to balance them when all the joints were in. I thought one joint would do as a walking stick which would be useful if I had my foot off.

Strang said, " Is there anything else you can think of that you'll want ? "

" I don't think so," I said.

" Then how d'you feel about getting the stuff into the car and going down ? "

I was just going to say " All right " when I suddenly remembered that there was nothing on paper about what I was going to do. I told Strang and he said, " Yes. I suppose you ought to do that. Why not go in and do it now ? No hurry. There's buckets of time."

Up until then it had all been all right, but as I went back into the bungalow it went wrong on me. It was having to stop when I had been all ready. My hands began to tremble and made my writing abominable. I wrote after Stuart's last report in his notebook.

" 0800 hrs., 25th. I propose to tackle B in exactly the same sequence as Captain Stuart tackled A, except that I shall try to fix it in iron clamps instead of steadying it with a pipe wrench. If I succeed in removing the cap and neutralising the trembler, I shall assume that there is another fuse which must be located and neutralised at once. I am working on the assumption that after Captain Stuart had earthed the first trembler, he slightly disturbed the body of the bomb, thereby operating the second fuse. There is at present nothing to indicate where this second fuse is situated. But since there must be some way of putting it in, there must be some way of getting it out. Possibly the whole charge lifts out. This I cannot tell without closer inspection."

There didn't seem much more than that to say, so I signed it. When I came to read it through it seemed rather tame as the last thing I might write. There had been something about Stuart's notes that was very characteristic of him, whereas anybody might have written mine. I knew I wanted to put something else, but couldn't get it clear. I put down, " I am scared, but it doesn't really matter fundamentally, as I do not mind much if I am killed." But that wasn't really the point, and it looked damned silly, so I crossed it out very heavily so that no one could read what had been there, and left it at that.

It was only about two miles to the beach where the thing was, but we had to go right up to the top of the cliffs and along and down another hill that was like one side of a house, so it took quite a time. Pearson drove and Strang and I sat in the back. My damned foot was aching, and I hacked my shin good and hard.

Strang said, " Got your notes fixed up ? "

" Yes," I said. " There wasn't much to say."

" You'll go through all the business with the reaching rods again ? Or will you take that part as read ? "

" I think I shall. It's probably a waste of time but there's always the chance that this one might be different."

" Just what I was going to say," said Strang. " I don't think you ought to take anything for granted."

The road led right down on to the beach. There was a knot of people standing together and Pearson took the car across the sand to them. They had a table with the field telephone and glasses on it and a box for the shorthand writer to sit on. They looked at me in an interested way, and I rather wished I'd been wearing different clothes. It seemed out of place to be in a hat and overcoat.

Strang called the sergeant aside and talked to him. Pearson said, " You can see the marker, sir, to show where it's lying. About thirty yards up from the edge of the sea."

I looked along the beach. There was a red marker flag fluttering in the sand about a couple of hundred yards away.

I said, " It looks like a golf hole."

Strang came back and said, " I've sent Groves off to send the cordon chaps away. They're just going to try the line, and then we're all set." He turned to Pearson and said, " Just see they check it over properly, Don."

Pearson went off and they started to pay the wire out. Strang said, " Let's get out of their way."

We walked a little way up the beach. Strang looked at me with his baby blue eyes and said, " Well, old man— how y' feeling ? "

I said, " Oh, quite all right."

He smiled and said, " Good. We'll take it easy and stop for a rest if you feel you're tiring. There's plenty of time." He paused and then said, " I don't know if you're the same, but it always helps me in mucking about with these things to remember that they don't just explode, unless you do the wrong thing to them. So you can always stop and rest or stop and think."

We walked on a bit farther. I said, " I wish I'd got some different clothes."

Strang said, " Oh, I've brought you some shorts and a vest. You can't possibly work with trousers flapping about. It's too bloody dangerous."

I looked round. It was very blue and gold, with a thick band of foam where the surf was breaking. I didn't feel sick, but my legs felt odd and unreliable, as though I'd just come off a ship. I glanced at the flag and thought it was a full brassie shot away against the wind. Strang said, " There's more sea running than there was yesterday. This is a good coast for surfing. Have you ever done any surfing ? "

They seemed to be a hell of a time messing about with the telphone, but at last Pearson came up and said it was O.K. Strang said, " Right. Then we're all set whenever you're ready, Rice." The sergeant and the two men had come back to their table. It suddenly struck me that I was going to have to change in front of all of them.

There was a cave further up, and for a moment I thought of saying I'd go to that, but I should have to come back to get the telephone and the other things anyhow.

Strang said, " Now, have you got everything you want?"

I said, " Have we got anything I can carry the wrenches and the clamps in ? They'll be rather a lot to carry in my hands."

" Oh hell ! " said Strang suddenly. " I can carry them out with you."

I said, " No. It's quite all right. Here's a bag."

I put the things in the bag and started to take my overcoat off. I still didn't like the idea of stripping. Strang seemed to catch that because he said, " You can use the car as a bathing machine if you like." I went behind the car and undressed, remembering Stuart's tip and putting my handkerchief in the bag. As I took my watch off it was five and twenty past eight. It wasn't cold and the air on my skin was rather pleasant. Strang had brought some tennis shoes and I thought they'd be more comfortable on sand than my own, so I put them on. My legs were a bit shaky and I had to sit down to do it. My garters looked damned silly so I took them off. My socks covered the attachment of my foot all right. I collected the stuff, balanced the rods across the basket and came out from behind the car.

Strang said, " All fixed."

I nodded. Strang snapped out, " Telephone ! " The sergeant came up and put the harness on. He said, " You'll find it'll pay out quite easy, sir. Mind you don't get too much slack when you get there or you'll be liable to fall over it. Drop your head when you want to speak."

Pearson said, " Shall I take the bag, sir ? "

" No. I will," said Strang.

Pearson said, " Good luck, sir ! " The men muttered " Good luck ! " after him.

I said, " Thank you." I wanted to say something cheerful but I couldn't think of anything.

We started off. The sand was rather soft in places which made it rather heavy going. I suddenly wondered what salt water and sand would do to my damned contrivance and wished I'd worn my own shoes. Strang didn't say anything.

By the time we were about a hundred yards from the thing I could see it quite plainly, lying in the sand on the land side of the marker flag. I'd forgotten that a part of it was red, because of course the photographs didn't show that.

I said to Strang, " Right. I'll take that now." He hesitated for a moment, and I thought he was going to start fussing. But he just said, " All right." He gave it to me and said, " Can you manage ? "

I said, " Yes. Easy."

He patted me on the arm and said, " Good luck, boy. Good luck," and started back.

When he had gone I suddenly went panicky. As long as he had been there I had just felt generally scared—not scared of anything in particular. I think I'd been worrying more about what I looked like than about the job. But now that Strang was gone and the thing was lying there in the sand, only about 50 yards away, I began to be scared stiff. I made up my mind not to look at it until I got to the trench so I put my head down and ploughed on. There were a lot of gulls wheeling about overhead, and I kept wondering if one of them would swoop down and disturb it.

I got to the trench at last and dropped into it. It was only a scraping in the sand and not very deep. When you were in it the thing was only the width of a room away. I was panting as though I'd been running hard, and sat down in the trench to get my breath. I thought, " If I'm going to make this fuss about just coming within yards of the thing, what will it be like later ? "

I looked along the beach at the base. Strang had got back, and I could see the wire from the telephone lying in a crooked black line on the sand. I thought I'd better see it was working so I said into the transmitter, " I'm just trying the wire. Can you hear me all right ? " It seemed a damned silly question for a moment, as they couldn't speak to me. Then I saw the telephonist wave a handkerchief to show he'd got it.

I looked at the thing and said into the telephone, " The object is about ten yards away, lying almost parallel to the

179

edge of the sea. It's rather deeply embedded in the sand at the cap end, so that I can only see the top half of the cap. The other end is hardly embedded at all. It looks as though there's a pebble under it. I think Stuart said there was. It looks exactly like the photographs of the other one, but I shall try it quickly for metal and shading and warmth just to be sure."

I started to put one of the reaching rods together. They had plastic ferrules instead of metal, and my hands were shaking so that I couldn't get the joints together for a bit. Anyhow the length of the thing made it very awkward to handle in a trench. But as soon as it was together, the weight in the butt made it handle surprisingly easily if you held it about eighteen inches up. There was quite a lot of whip in it, and it struck me that things needed to be fixed on it pretty carefully in case they fell off on top of the bomb. I fixed one of the pipe wrenches in the clip at the end. It seemed quite safe. I said into the telephone, "I am now going to try it for metal."

I pushed the rod out, keeping it well away from the thing until I'd got it fully out. It would just about reach and no more. I couldn't see for a moment how I was going to work the rod without having my head up. Then I realised that Stuart had cut a groove for the rod to lie in so that I could put it against the ground and just tip it up and down to bring the wrench near the thing. Trying on another bit of sand with a pebble, I found that it would go within six inches or so quite easily with my head down.

I was feeling a lot better now, and anyhow it was pretty certain that all this was really a waste of time, so I got through dangling the wrench round it and then trying it with the shade quite easily and quickly. The only difficulty was that the damned telephone got in my way when I wanted to get my head down. After that I thought for a bit about the heat thing. It had always struck me as rather unnecessary, because I wasn't going to be holding the thing in my hands, and it was crude and rather tricky. It meant taking heated pads out of the thermos container, putting them on the rod and putting them *against* the thing, so that you stood quite a chance of shaking it. Stuart had said he nearly did. I thought for a moment of just telling them I was going to cut it out, but I thought Strang might be annoyed, so I decided just to go through the motions. Even with glasses they wouldn't be able to see if I actually put the pad against it or not. I just put the pad on the rod, put it out well away from the thing and reported " No reaction."

It was only when I had pulled the rod in and taken it to pieces that I realised that I had rather burnt my boats. I'd been concentrating hard on not disturbing the thing with the rod, in case it should go up ; but if it had gone up while I was in the trench I should have been all right, and it would have let me out. There wasn't another one to try, and every one would have thought it was just an accident. It was a very queer feeling, this. There was no question of putting the rod together again and deliberately sending the thing up. But I felt that if I'd thought of it before, and could have done it as a half-accident, it would have been all right. I remember being very angry with myself for not having thought of it, and yet being quite glad I hadn't.

When I had finished with the rods I sat in the trench for a minute or two and thought. My hands were sweating and the sand was sticking to them so I got out my handkerchief and wiped them. I found I didn't much mind the idea of getting out and tackling it, but there was the question of what to do about my foot. I'd tried the thing for metal, and anyhow I was going to use metal clamps and wrenches, so there was no real reason for taking it off. But I was going to be working kneeling down, and kneeling down in it was always awkward because it was difficult to get it at a comfortable angle.

It would have been a relief to take it off, because it was still aching a lot, and I thought at first of hopping the ten yards to the thing, using one of the reaching rod joints as a stick. But there was the basket to carry and the telephone wire lying about, so finally I decided to keep it on.

Through thinking about that I got up beside the thing without worrying much. When I found myself right on top of it it reminded me of my vision of it when I was in bed at home just lying quietly on the sand waiting. But I reminded myself of what Strang had said about things not going up unless you did something to them and that helped quite a bit. I checked that it wasn't ticking and then got the clamps and wrenches out of the basket and sat on the sand beside it and thought it over.

My general idea was to get the jaws of the clamps holding it firmly, and then to scrape away the sand so that it was left clear of the ground and I could get at it all round. I reckoned that if there was a second fuse, Stuart might have missed it through not being able to see the underneath part of the bomb as it lay on the ground. I said this into the telephone, got up on my knees, and turned to get the clamps. In doing this, I pulled the telephone wire slightly. It hitched a bit and for one ghastly fraction of a second I thought it had caught round the end of the bomb and yanked it. It hadn't of course. It was just caught in one of the wrenches. But it had turned me cold for a moment, and I thought it was too dangerous to have something that was liable to move about on the ground every time I turned my head. Besides, the darned transmitter thing was in the way. I said into the telephone, " Look, this thing's a damned nuisance. I'm going to take it off and put it on the ground and talk down it whenever I've got anything to say. The first thing I'm doing to do is to try and get the clamps on. I shall put the first one just behind the cap and the other at the other end." Then I took the harness off, put the telephone behind me out of the way and started off on the first clamp.

I suppose it was lack of imagination, but even after reading Stuart's notes I had never had any idea how tricky this part was going to be. It was the sand that was the trouble. It was dry and quite loose, which meant that though it got in your way it never gave you a firm surface. The jaws of the clamps were on short, thick arms, so that I had to put the base practically touching the bomb to get the jaws over it. The base didn't seem very firm, but as soon as I pressed down on it to get it properly dug in, the sand started to fall away from round the bomb and I thought the whole thing was going to come loose and move. Then when I did get the jaws over it behind the cap, I realised that unless it was perfectly centred between them it would be pulled or pushed by one of the jaws when I tightened it up. Anyhow, there was bound to be a lot of sand left between the body and the jaws when they tightened, and that might mean that they would slip. Finally I had to scrape the sand away from the side of the thing where the jaws were going to grip it. I was sweating like a pig, and the sweat kept running into my eyes and smarting like hell, so that I was afraid I shouldn't be able to see properly and should do something silly.

When I'd got the sand cleared away ready for the jaws I sat back and rubbed my eyes with my handkerchief. I wanted to be able to see for certain that they were properly

centred. By getting down and looking along the side of the
thing, and I could see that the clamp wanted to be about
half an inch further over. I went to move it slightly, forget-
ting that the base was right up against the bomb. It didn't
move easily so I pushed harder, and of course the base
pushed the thing and I saw it move quite a bit in the sand.
I jerked away from it in a silly way but nothing happened.
It only moved a fraction of an inch, but it scared me sick.

I tried to go on, but my hands were shaking too much,
so I sat back for a moment and rested. Maybe I was making
a fool of myself, because even a trembler fuse needs more
than that to work it. While resting, I thought of the telephone. I picked it up and said, " I've now got the jaws of the
first clamp over it, and am just going to tighten them up.
I've just hit it a good clout with the base of the clamp and
made it roll about a bit, but nothing happened."

I got down again and looked at the jaws. They were
practically dead right, so I started to tighten them up, still
watching to make sure they would grip at exactly the same
moment. As they came together I could see that the far one
was going to grip just a fraction before the other, which
meant that the thing would be pulled slightly. I didn't see
what to do about it because the clamp wouldn't go any
closer without pushing the bomb again. It was only a
fraction, so I decided that the only thing to do was to
chance it. I went on tightening up very slowly, and finally
when one jaw was touching the side I could just see light
between the side and the other. I took a breath and went
on screwing up, and a moment later they were both gripping.
I didn't see the thing move at all that time.

I was getting a bit worried about shaking so much. It
wasn't only my hands. One of the big muscles in my thigh
had started to do things of its own, and my back was aching.
I told them down the telephone that I had got one on and
that I was going to rest, and sat back for a minute or two.
My eyes were still smarting and the handkerchief was so wet
that it only made them worse. I was a bit worried over the
time everything was taking, because I'd hardly started really.
It was no good starting to feel tired considering how much
there was still to do. I thought that at that rate I should
be all in just when we got to the tricky part. I remember
thinking, " Too much whisky—or not enough," and grinning
to myself.

The second clamp went on a good deal more easily. That

end of the thing wasn't so deeply in the sand, and anyhow I could work more freely now one end was firmly held. Once they were both held I had meant to dig the sand right away so that the thing was held clear of it everywhere in the jaws of the clamps. But I found that if I took too much away, the sand started to trickle away from under the bases of the clamps into the hole and I was afraid they would start getting unsteady. But I got enough away to be able to get at the thing properly.

Like a fool, instead of resting I went straight on with getting the cap off. The clamps were holding quite firmly, but the jaws were only tightened with a thumbscrew, and I decided that I couldn't risk their holding on while I twisted about with a wrench ; otherwise they might give, and the whole thing would spin round. I should have to use two wrenches as Stuart had done—one to hold the body and make sure it didn't turn and the other to turn the cap.

The clamps made it easier for me to get the wrenches on than it had been for Stuart. But I found that I couldn't turn the cap. I heaved with all my might, but it wouldn't shift. I thought perhaps it was a reverse thread and tried the other way, but it was still no good. Finally, I braced the other wrench with my knee as Stuart had done and used both hands. Still I couldn't start it.

That shook me to the wick. I think it was because it had never occurred to me that there would be much difficulty about it. I suddenly realised that if I couldn't get that cap off I should have made a mess of the whole thing, and that it would all have been for nothing. I started to heave again with all my might. I must have shaken the thing quite a lot, though the clamps held it well. The sweat was pouring off me and I could hear myself panting loudly. I had to stop at last, and when I looked up my head was swimming and everything looked a curious green. I put my head down and shut my eyes. I thought, " I shall never shift it now. My arms are going." I knew that gutless feeling of old. When I opened my eyes again, things had gone back to their normal colour. I took hold of the wrench again and gave a terrific heave. Probably it had been started before really, because this time it moved quite easily. It was still rather stiff for a turn or two, but after that I could undo it with my fingers. I took it off and sat back with it in my hand and panted. For a minute or two I was too done to look at it. I just kept my eyes shut and waited

184

to get my breath. After a while it got a bit better and I started to look at the thing. It was just as Stuart had said. The clock mechanism was in the head. There was a lead coming out of it which forked and carried two flat bits of stuff which looked like insulators. In the top of the body there was a simple brass trembler tongue lying between terminals. The movement for contact was about a quarter of an inch either way. I thought, " The first thing to do is to earth those terminals and I can't do it because my hands are too shaky." The muscles of my hands and arms were all to hell with heaving to loosen the cap.

I knew I wasn't thinking very well any longer so I stopped and sat back and tried to go slow. I told them down the telephone where I'd got to and that I was going to rest. My eyes were stinging very badly and I shut them and tried to think slowly and carefully.

After a bit it gradually dawned on me that earthing wasn't really very tricky, because it was the terminals I had to get wires on to, not the trembler ; and the terminals were quite solid. As long as I didn't get a wire across both the terminal and the trembler it would be all right even if my hands did shake.

After a bit I felt better and started to try to get a wire on. It was quite easy really. If I'd been fresh I could have done it in half a minute. As it was it took me a long time, but it was only tedious—not particularly dangerous. Getting them earthed cheered me up a lot. I think that was the first time that I began to feel as though I might beat the thing after all.

This was where it had gone wrong on Stuart. I took a lot of trouble to make sure that the earthing was all right, in case that was what had slipped up. It struck me that it would be very easy to knock the clamps with my knee, so I crawled round to the other side of the thing, and started to look for any signs of another fuse.

I saw two things right away. The hole Stuart had talked about ran down into the body ; and, as he had said, the lead from the clock seemed too long. It was about four inches long, and the distance from the top trembler to the clock must have been very small when the cap was on. I thought that if there'd been another shorter lead for the top trembler, I should have guessed that the longer one ran down into the body through the hole to a second fuse. Then I suddenly saw. I picked the cap up and looked up inside it, and there it was. Of course the shorter lead wound up right

185

into the clock, so that no lead was left showing. I could just see the ends of the insulators and that was all.

I went over to the telephone and said, " I think I've got it. The lead Stuart found is to a second fuse, in the body. The lead to the trembler that he found winds right up into the clock, and he didn't notice it. Judging from the length of the lead to the second fuse it's some way down the body. I'm going to look for a way in on the body. If there isn't one, then the fuse must be put in before the charge, and the charge may lift out."

I went back to the thing and had another look. As far as I could see the body was a straight plastic cylinder, with no sign of any opening. I was just deciding that it would have to be tackled from the top end when I noticed that the surface seemed to have flaked slightly underneath, where it had hit the pebble. Then I realised that it wasn't the plastic that had flaked, but a layer of varnish. The varnish was black, like the plastic, and until it was chipped there was no way of spotting it. I grabbed a knife, and started to scrape the varnish away. As soon as I'd moved a bit of it I could see that there was a junction in the body, and I could guess that it screwed together. I went back to the telephone and said, " There *is* another way in—at least I think so. When you scrape the varnish away about three inches from the non cap end, there is what looks like a joint. What it comes to is that there's a cap on both ends, only one's obvious and the other isn't. I'm now going to try to unscrew the second cap."

The jaws of the clamp were right across the joint, and I started to unscrew the clamp to shift it. Then the nasty bit dawned on me. If the second trembler was in the body, then it would be all right to unscrew the cap. But if the second trembler was *in* the cap, then starting to unscrew it would send the whole thing up. I had to decide whether to hold the body still and unscrew the cap, or hold the cap still and unscrew the body from it.

I must have been getting pretty queer, because I remember hearing myself make a queer moaning noise as I thought of it. I think it was the disappointment of realising that I still wasn't out of the wood, and a silly feeling that it wasn't fair that I should have to deal with this after beating the other end. I sat there for a bit just staring at the thing hopelessly and not doing anything. I knew I *thought* that the second trembler was in the body and that it was the cap that I ought to unscrew, but for a long time I couldn't see

where I'd got the idea. It wasn't until I picked the top cap
up again that I remembered that it was the length of the
lead which gave it to me. I put the cap down beside the
body and stretched the lead along it. The top lead had
wound up about an inch and a half. Assuming that the long
lead had wound up the same distance, it had only been
about seven inches long in the first place, which meant that
it could hardly have reached right down to the bottom cap.
I went to the telephone and explained this. Then I started
to shift the clamp off the joint and wholly on to the body.
It went quite quickly and easily—probably because I wasn't
thinking about it much. I was thinking about unscrewing
that cap. I remember thinking, " If I'm right about that
lead I've done it. If I'm wrong I'm dead." I was still
thinking that as I fixed the wrenches on again and started
to try to loosen the cap.

It stuck, just as the other had done ; and that finished
me. It was the fact that the strain came on exactly the same
places as before. I don't suppose it was as stiff as all that
really, and if I'd been fresh I dare say one big heave would
have done it. But my hand and arm muscles were all to
hell, and instead of giving one big heave I had to keep
giving a series of little heaves, which did no good and just
took what little guts I'd got clean out of me. After the
first few goes I knew I should never shift it. If I'd had
any sense I should have stopped and rested, or thought of
another way of doing it ; but that never occurred to me. I
just went on pulling at the damned wrench, never even
believing it was going to move.

I don't know how long this went on, or why I didn't
shake the thing so much that it went up. I remember
hearing myself sobbing with each pull, and that I kept my
eyes shut because the sweat made them smart so much.
Finally my hand grip just packed up, my hand slipped off
the wrench, and I half fell backwards. I made a sort of half-
hearted effort to get up, and then just lay there sobbing and
panting with my eyes shut. I heard somebody call something and opened my eyes and saw somebody misty about
ten feet away. I blinked my eyes clear. It was Strang. He
was wearing shorts and his chest and arms were naked, and
looking up at him like that made him look enormous.

I got on to my knees and said, " Keep away for Christ's
sake. There's one not done. I can't shift it." My throat
seemed to shut and I began to sob again.

Strang said, " Easy does it, old man. What's wrong ? "

I said, " The cap. There's another fuse. The bloody thing's stuck."

He glanced at the wrench and said, " Well, that's all right. Let me have a go. You want that turned ? "

I looked at him for a moment standing there with his big shoulders and the thick black hair on his chest and I knew I'd lost. I said dully, " It's got to be held steady with the wrench on the right while the cap's unscrewed with the other. Be careful. If you don't hold it steady it'll go up."

Strang nodded. He knelt down in front of the thing. Then he turned to me and said, " Look—if I'm going to put my big feet into this you'd better get into the trench, o'man. You've done your share."

I said, " No. Why the hell should I ? "

Strang hesitated. Then he said, " All right. Then here goes." He caught hold of the wrenches and I saw the big muscles suddenly bunch up. He gave a little grunt and I saw it move.

When it was off he said " Now you tell me what to do, squire. It's your party."

I said, " Come out of the way. I can do it now."

He moved aside. I looked at it. It was just as I thought, except that the second trembler was set transversely.

I said, " Wire." He handed me a piece and I started to try to get it on the terminals.

Strang said, " You're earthing it ? " I nodded. He said, " Manage, or shall I ? "

I said, " I can do it."

I got it on at last. When it was on, I sat back and looked at it.

Strang said, " Now what ? "

" Get your people and steam the charge out."

" And that's that ? "

I said, " That's all."

Strang telephoned back for the steamer.

I was very stiff, and when I tried to get up I couldn't. Strang said, " Half a mo'." He put his hands under my armpits and picked me up on to my feet as though I weighed six ounces. He hesitated for a moment and then said, " Look, why the hell should we carry all this stuff back ? You sit down for a moment and I'll go and get the car."

He started off, running along the beach. He ran beautifully, as though running were one of his things. I went over very slowly and sat down on a sand hill. I looked back at the thing lying there with the caps off and the earthing wires. I thought, "I shall never be able to pay more than that for anything, and even that wasn't enough."

XVI

I GOT a train back to town just after lunch. I was dog-tired, but I had to get away from it quickly and anyhow I knew Susan would be worried. It would have been easier if Strang hadn't been so damned good about it. He'd seen me lying on the sand. And he knew I knew. But he never so much as flickered an eyebrow to show it. I might have been the toughest thing on earth from the way he behaved. He came to the station to see me off. As we shook hands he said : "Well, good-bye old man. Have a sleep in the train. You've earned it if anybody ever did."

The train was coming in. I suddenly realised that I might not see him again, and that I must say something about it. I said :

"I could have shifted it all right if I'd been fresh. It was the first one sticking that did it."

He pretended to look surprised and said, "But of course you could. Damn it, you'd been working like a nigger for an hour and a half. I don't see how the hell you stuck it."

I don't know what I wanted him to say, but that wasn't it. I said desperately, "No. Not that stuff. I really could. My arms and hands are very strong. If I'd had the sense to stop and rest I could probably have done it as it was."

He looked down at me with the baby blue eyes, frowning slightly. Then he grinned and said :

"Get on with you, old man. If anybody ever has any doubts about what you can do with your hands and arms or any other bit of you, you send them along to see me."

I still hesitated, but I knew it was no good. He'd made up his mind what line he was going to take and nothing I could say now would alter it. The train doors were open. I turned away and got in. As the train started to move I looked out at Strang and waved my hand. He waved back, and then pulled himself up and saluted. I thought, "If only I'd messed it up in a different way and killed myself, he could have done that and meant it."

I lay back in the corner and closed my eyes and tried to go to sleep but for a long time I couldn't. I kept on turning over in my mind what I ought to have done—to have made Stuart wait—to have rested and waited for my grip to come back—to have made Strang go away ; or that when he came I ought to have faced it and gone away. Then I had a patch of being very sorry for myself and thinking I'd worked very hard and that it had been bad luck. But it always came back to the same thing in the end. I'd made the fuss and someone else had always done the difficult bits. Stuart had just tackled the thing from cold, when it was really risky. I'd made a hell of a fuss about doing exactly the same thing again. And then when there was something new to do I'd messed it up, and somebody else had had to do it. All I'd done was to realise that there were twelve inches in a foot. The thinking had been all right but when it came to doing anything I'd been gutless as usual. I wondered what it would have felt like if I'd got that bloody cap off and done it, and been going back to London having won. I remembered coming down in the train and thinking about it. It had seemed a simple issue then—either I should be killed or I should do it. What I hadn't reckoned on was making one more mess and being still alive, and having to go on from there. I thought of my note to Susan. It looked pretty silly now.

I went to sleep eventually and didn't wake up until we were nearly into Paddington. I had a vivid dream about Charles and his air-mortar. He was explaining that it had a much longer range now. He showed me some cloth of some sort and said, " It was simply a question of paying more to get decent material."

It was rather a slow train and it didn't get in till nearly seven. Paddington was crowded. Every one seemed to be hurrying off somewhere. I walked slowly down the platform, trying to make up my mind what to do. I knew I ought to get in touch with Susan, but I didn't want to. I told myself that I didn't know where she'd be at that time. She might be at the office or she might have gone home.

I wandered out into Praed Street. A cab came by with its flag up and I suddenly decided to go to the office.

It was half-past seven when I got there. There was no light in Susan's room. I looked in, but it was empty. Waring had got a card on his door saying " Deputy Director. R. B. Waring." All that seemed an awfully long way away.

I went upstairs. Tilly was still there. He was drawing a graph with his long red nose about two inches from the paper. He looked up and said : " How did you get on ? "

" Oh, all right," I said. " We got it fixed."

Tilly said, " Good," and went on drawing his graph.

After a minute I said, " Has any one been after me ? "

" No," said Tilly. " It's been like the grave."

I said, " What are you on with ? " I didn't want to know, and I knew he didn't want to be talked to but it was better than having silence again.

" Your low temperature stuff."

" But we've chucked that up."

" Yes. But I thought it would be nice to have. It's rather pretty. I'm trying to fit a curve to the plot of starting weight against concentration of your stuff."

I said, " You never will. It isn't that sort of relationship."

Tilly just went on drawing without saying anything. I thought, " It's no good. I'm going to have to start thinking soon, whatever I do."

It suddenly struck me that I could ring Susan up.

I said, " This is me, Sue. I thought I'd just tell you that I'm all right."

Susan made a queer noise and said :

" Darling. Really all right ? "

" Yes."

" And the thing ? Did you do it ? "

I said, " More or less. Anyhow, it's done."

" Oh, Sammy . . . ! Look—where are you ? "

" At the office. I thought you might still be there."

" Oh, *damn* it. And I've only this moment got home. Darling, come right away. Get a cab."

I hesitated and said, " In a minute—I've got a thing to do. But I'll be with you within half an hour."

Susan said, " Look—you really *are* all right, are you? Wouldn't like me to come and fetch you ? "

I said, " No. I'm quite all right. See you in a minute."

I put the receiver down and got up. I was glad I'd done that. It gave me half an hour to get it straight. I said, " Good night," to Tilly. He just grunted.

When I came out it was just beginning to get dark. There was a cold wind blowing and I felt very stiff and aching. I put my hands in the pockets of my overcoat and tried to go inside myself out of the cold.

191

I cut through behind Grosvenor House, across Park Lane, and into the Park. I thought, " The trouble is that I'm dead really. I shook the thing trying to get the second cap off, and it blew up and killed me. That's why I'm cold."

The Park was very empty. The wind was bringing the leaves down and blowing them in my face. When I got almost to Kensington Gardens, I realised that I hadn't thought of anything, so I sat down on a bench, and tried to figure it out.

The facts were that Dick was dead, and Stuart was dead, and the Old Man was gone and Waring was Deputy Director and I was just where I had always been. The good chaps went and were killed and the crooks got away with it. But I just stayed put.

I tried to think of something concrete to do—resigning and going to the Old Man or something like that. But it wouldn't fire. I knew it didn't really make any difference where I went or who I worked for. And I was too tired anyhow. I looked at my watch and knew I ought to move. I'd said I would be home in half an hour. But my legs ached, and it was hard to make up my mind to move. The moon was just going down behind a tree. I decided that when it disappeared I'd get up and go. I sat and watched it going and I knew there was no answer. If I'd been a bit sillier, or a bit more intelligent, or had more guts, or less guts, or had two feet or no feet, or been almost anything definite, it would have been easy. But as it was, I didn't like what I was, and couldn't be what I liked, and it would always be like that.

I thought, " I'll go home now and hand over to Susan. She's got it all worked out in the way women always have. They don't worry about anything except being alive or dead. And being dead to them means beginning to smell. It'll be all right with Susan. She'll take it and make it into what she wants, just as Strang did. We shall all know, but I'm the only one who'll mind."

I laughed and said, " I did it, darling. All by myself, except for half a turn with a wrench. What's that among friends ? "

There was still a rim of moon showing. But I was cold and I wanted Susan, so I didn't wait for it.

THE END